The
Silver
Screen

The
Silver
Screen

Maureen Howard

VIKING

VIKING
Published by the Penguin Group
Penguin Group (USA) Inc., 375 Hudson Street, New York, New York 10014, U.S.A.
Penguin Group (Canada), 10 Alcorn Avenue, Toronto, Ontario, Canada M4V 3B2
(a division of Pearson Penguin Canada Inc.)
Penguin Books Ltd, 80 Strand, London WC2R 0RL, England
Penguin Ireland, 25 St. Stephen's Green, Dublin 2, Ireland (a division of Penguin Books Ltd)
Penguin Books Australia Ltd, 250 Camberwell Road, Camberwell, Victoria 3124, Australia
(a division of Pearson Australia Group Pty Ltd)
Penguin Books India Pvt Ltd, 11 Community Centre, Panchsheel Park, New Delhi–110 017, India
Penguin Group (NZ), Cnr Airborne and Rosedale Roads, Albany, Auckland, New Zealand
(a division of Pearson New Zealand Ltd)
Penguin Books (South Africa) (Pty) Ltd, 24 Sturdee Avenue,
Rosebank, Johannesburg 2196, South Africa

Penguin Books Ltd, Registered Offices: 80 Strand, London WC2R 0RL, England

First published in 2004 by Viking Penguin, a member of Penguin Group (USA) Inc.

10   9   8   7   6   5   4   3   2   1

ILLUSTRATION CREDITS
Page 1: Collection of the author. Page 97: "View of Fairhaven from the New Bedford Shore." John W. Barber from *Historical Collections of Every Town in Massachusetts, 1841*. Courtesy of The New Bedford Whaling Museum. Page 145: *Poison Ivy*. George Emerson, *Report on the Trees and Forests of Massachusetts*, volume 2, 1875. Page 159: *Six of Spades: Insurance on Lives*, #66 Schreiber catalogue, The British Museum. Page 195: *Sharecropper's Bed, 1936*, Walker Evans. Library of Congress, Prints and Photographic Division, FSA-OWI Collection. Page 227: *The Workingman's Watch* (altered for this use). Private collection.

PUBLISHER'S NOTE
This is a work of fiction. Names, characters, places, and incidents either are the product of the author's imagination or are used fictitiously, and any resemblance to actual persons, living or dead, business establishments, events, or locales is entirely coincidental.

LIBRARY OF CONGRESS CATALOGING IN PUBLICATION DATA
Howard, Maureen, date.
   The silver screen / Maureen Howard.
      p.   cm.
   ISBN 0-670-03358-8
      1. Motion picture actors and actresses—Fiction. 2. Conflict of generations—Fiction. 3. Parent and adult child—Fiction. 4. Loss (Psychology)—Fiction. 5. Married women—Fiction. 6. Rhode Island—Fiction. I. Title.
   PS3558.O8823S55 2004
   813'.54—dc22   2004047789

This book is printed on acid-free paper. ∞

Printed in the United States of America

To Cleo and George Kearns

Acknowledgments

I am grateful once again to Joanna Scott, James Longenbach, my careful and inspired readers; to Binnie Kirschenbaum, Carol Armstrong, Elizabeth Wyckoff; and for Andrew Weissmann's short course in the Witness Protection Program. My greatest debt is to my cousin, John McCall, once a Jesuit, a great teacher always. Kevin Brownlow and Walter Bernstein have informed my movie world. Philip Pauly came up with the lovely illustration of poison ivy. Ansonia, Connecticut, is somewhat mythical, as is the Murphys' town on the bay in Rhode Island—both projections on the silver screen. Mary Witkowski of the Bridgeport Public Library keeps me in touch with the history of my industrial roots. As I write on in my quartet of the Four Seasons, Paul Slovak, my editor, is a great support. My thanks, always, to Gloria Loomis. Mark Probst is my beloved muse, in foul weather and fair. And special thanks to the Dorothy and Lewis B. Cullman Center for Scholars and Writers at the New York Public Library.

The
Silver
Screen

———

I

The Day of the Dead

Methinks we have largely mistaken this matter of Life and Death. Methinks that what they call my shadow here on earth is my true substance.

—Herman Melville, *Moby-Dick; or, The Whale*

Sea laps the shore. We need not know what shimmering sea, what pure white sand. Girls frolic—ten, twelve of them. A show, a game? Beach balls in the bright air. They catch and throw flip-wristed, and for no reason at all dash to a rickety wooden bleacher set up on the beach. Arranging themselves for a still shot, arms and legs flutter, won't be tamed. Amusing pets, all pretty. Some have ribbons round their bobbed hair. Some wear brimless hats molded close to the head, a flirty curl or two escaping. Their bathing suits, belted or sashed, are striped, a few checkered in harlequin patterns. Silly girls laughing, smiling to beat the band. (The band, set to the side, an upright piano, clarinet, mandolin.)

The Bathing Beauties have been rehearsing. Now they romp to the twanging beat of the music, which drowns out the grind of the camera. Play ball, dash for the bleachers, pose in the jersey bathing suits that cling to their delicious bodies. The soft cotton maillot caresses their breasts and thighs. So concealing we find it, these seventy, eighty

*years later. Look again at the seductive wrapping on the package—
bold stripes on the hip, molding of crotch, bouncing buns. See them—
window dressing, background, chorus—naughty and nice, harmless
girls. They stop, turn suddenly in mid-action. The clarinet bleeps to the
end of a phrase.*

"She's a beaut!"

"Which one?"

"With the curly black hair."

"Jeez, Mack, there's five with curly black hair."

*"The one laughing at us," says the man in the boater, squinting into
the sun. "Girl with the cupcakes, that one."*

*From a crude stab of his cigar in her direction the girl knows she is
that one and crosses her hands on her breasts, a saint in mock supplica-
tion. Then a fellow in a floppy cap reaches for the buckle at her waist,
tugs her out of the crowd of ten or twelve or thirteen pretty girls. He is
wearing a linen jacket, sweat-stained at the armpits. The boss with the
boater, cool in gray Palm Beach suit—vest, watch chain and all. These
men might be lawyers, bankers, Chamber of Commerce—any town,
any bright summer day.*

*"Step down," the boater says to the pretty girl with the black curls.
"Walk. What's the hurry? Turn the head. Give me the eye." She pulls
a sultry pout, sashays slowly through the sand. "Peachy."*

*Then from the fellow sweltering in white linen, "What's your
name?"*

*In the brittle sunlight, her voice rings out mellow and clear, "I am
Isabel Maher."*

*She is given instructions. A palm tree and a cabana are set next to
the bleachers.*

"Take it again, girls."

*Pretty girls romp while the band struts its stuff to their tune. They
make a run for the clattering wooden bleachers, pose for the picture while
the vixen breaks away, away from the fun, and slowly, lips puckered,*

MAUREEN HOWARD

makes her way toward the famous clown who has been lolling all this time under a beach umbrella held aloft by a lackey. He is rumpled, waddling—so accomplished a fat fool in his antics, America laughs till it cries.

Chin up, Isabel Maher gives him the eye.

FATHER JOE IN THE SHADOW BOX

My mother thinks me wise. Let her believe it. Stooped with age, Bel cocks her head like a curious bird to meet my encouraging smile, the professional smile of a priest—hopeful, indulgent. The bold young woman who rents a house down the lane calls her the old lady. Each day I steal out of my boyhood bed, dress at dawn for the morning walk, my sister already fussing in the kitchen. It is Rita's pleasure to re-create the pancakes and muffins of our childhood while I march smartly down the lane with the prop of my worn leather breviary, as though I might read the morning office, supplications and prayers committed to memory a half-century ago.

"Visiting the old lady?" a wisp of a girl in a scrap of bathing suit asked my first day home, still calling it home. She balanced awkwardly on the rim of a deck chair, greasing her thighs and belly to protect her pale flesh from the first rays of the sun. It promised to be a scorcher, the air heavy, humid.

"Visiting." I passed quickly on, but not before a strap fell, disclosing the white hemisphere of her breast with its pole of brown nipple. For a moment I wished that I wore the Roman collar, not to disapprove the flaunting of her body, to scold her with a clerical look. She is not permitted in her cheery, childish voice to call my mother the old lady. Yet how true—Bel's sparse white hair, swollen blue veins, odor of stale rose water—essence of old lady bent to the ground as though to seek out the comforts of the grave. But when would this girl frying in the sun have seen her? My mother is always at home now. If she tends a flower, throws crumbs to the birds, she cannot be spied on behind the tall privet hedge closing our house from the world. A house long guarded by our private ways.

It is my illusion that, set in our roles, my mother and her children will go on as we have forever. My visits to this hillock of New England which looks out to Narragansett Bay are the occasion for stories of the past repeated so often they might be told by the faded wallpaper or deadwood of kitchen table. Was it the hurricane of '38 or tidal wave of '54 swept our picket fence into the sea? The Irish setter or blind terrier wrestled the Christmas turkey off its platter? The hard winter of measles or mumps? Adrift in uncertainty, we prattle each day of my visit as though silence is forbidden us. We are sure of one thing. Our stories begin in this house—Bel in labor, clutching the bedpost while my father, who sold insurance against death and disaster, changed a flat tire on the Ford. The past had no preface to the blistering summer day on which, with the help of a neighbor, I was born to Isabel Murphy while her husband stood by with a spanner wrench in his good hand—his left arm, wounded in the Great War, hanging limp at his side.

. . .

But I must take the giant step forward. I came round the hedge on this, the third day of my visit, tripped on the crumbling cement path. My sister was at the open door, still and speechless.

"What?" I asked. The flesh around Rita's eyes pale and soft, the defenseless look of the shortsighted without glasses. "What is it?"

The bulk of her blocked my way, though I saw past her to the stairs—to the mirror reflecting the empty hall above and a ray of sun with dust motes churning to no purpose. Finally, she stood aside, my little sister grown bottom-heavy as a giant pear. I knew that I must run upstairs, see myself for a fleeting moment—a gray-headed man with the high forehead that once defined me as brilliant. I must steal down the hall past the tidy room they keep as a shrine for my visits, past my sister's virginal room with its stuffed panda propped on the bed, souvenir of some festive night in her youth, past the gleaming bathroom scoured clean of our bodily functions, past the hall window that frames our view of the sea, the sun on the water blinding this Summer day, flags rippling on the promenade. My desperate journey to the room where Bel lay, mouth in a slack smile, gaze strangely bright—looking at last upon her Maker.

The body still warm. With faint hope, I turned to Rita, who looked on from the hall, then came to the bed lightly with the tip-toe steps of a heavy woman defying gravity. We found no words for this dreaded occasion. I turned to my sister, knowing she often attended to the dead. With a sweep of her hand Rita drew our mother's eyelids shut, then presented me with one of the mysteries of our childhood, the black leather box, the death kit of last rites that lived in a cupboard behind the sheets and towels of daily life. I made a stab at my priestly duties, turning down the coverlet to anoint the extremities of the body, the eyes and the mouth with holy oil, mumbling prayers half remembered. My mother lay straight in death, no longer bowed by the weight of years.

As I pulled the window shade, my eyes smarted at the glittering day, an unlikely setting for sorrow. Stunned, our silence heavy, prolonged. "A blessing," I said at last, "to leave us in her sleep." Rather too quickly, Rita surveyed our mother's closet, pulling out a Sunday dress and dainty shoes for the body's presentation. I had not forgotten that as a physical therapist my sister went from house to house of the infirm and aged, the dying, though I had never seen her at her efficient work.

"She went peacefully," I said. "Bel left us in the night."

"Not at all. She called your name, but you were off on your morning stroll."

"Called my name?"

"Jo-ee! Jo-ee!"

Rita attempting our mother's two-noted bleat, her sweet clarion call reining me in when I wandered as a child. When my sister speaks up for herself—it is not often—her eyes blink behind thick glasses, her neck mottles with red splotches. "You didn't wonder why she wasn't up and about?"

For years I had not wondered at anything in that house. True, each day, as I headed out on my morning walk, I saw our mother perched on her kitchen stool already awaiting my return, when she presented her withered cheek for my kiss, eager for my every word.

"Now, then," Rita said, "the arrangements."

The arrangements were to carry us through the next days. Casket, flowers, mass, burial. Our mother was well over ninety, the date of her birth uncertain. Not a friend left to mourn her, but she was always a woman alone. More than a privet hedge grown beyond clipping set Bel apart from this town. At the wake, two women from the agency who assigned my sister the rounds of her practical mercy were in attendance, and a parade of ghosts from the past—the aged boys and girls we had gone to school with. All now strangers to me. Father, they say as I listen to tales of their children and grandchildren, their divorces and ailments. I can't bear their deference. They are not curious about my work, the daily grind of a schoolteacher. These shuffling men I'd run bases with, coy housewives I'd kissed in the back seat of my father's car had their scripted response to my black suit and the legend they will not give up on—that I had left them behind for the higher calling—though we sweated as one beast in the close living room with the television pushed out of the way for the casket.

Bel lay prettified in her white velvet nest. When my father died, she wrote to me. *I buried Murph from the house. We do not rent a commercial parlor.*

A sturdy woman with sleek black hair, many rings, bracelets, a costume all fringes and gauze, detached herself from the hushed sippers of Rita's iced tea. "Just think," she said, "your mother was toddling about before the First World War." Boldly sipping a glass of whiskey, she held out a hand with scarlet nails, "Gemma Riccardi. You took me to the prom."

"Gemma!" I was about to say something foolish, tell her she was lovely as ever, when the first noisy crackle preceded the shrieking trajectory of a rocket. Fireworks on the promenade. With our many arrangements, we'd lost track of the day. Night had descended on the Fourth of July.

"What a send-off." Gemma's laugh rumbled across the silent room. "Bel would have loved it."

"*The bombs bursting in air,*" I sang.

We sang, Gemma and Joe: "*O'er the la-aand of the free . . .*"

And that is how Father Joseph Murphy, S.J., disgraced himself at his mother's wake. But let me tell you, we had all turned to the open windows. Bottles of wine and the Irish were brought forth from the sideboard, plastic glasses handed round. Some of the old school chums were already out the door. The lane that runs by our house has always been the best vantage point from which to view the patriotic display, the burst of colors across the heavens in a spectacle of lights. Somehow I was to blame for this pleasure, had given my blessing to the breathless wonder of the mourners. The women from Rita's agency of good works climbed up on the high hood of their recreational vehicle, but I noticed that my sister was not with us. I ran to the house thinking she kept solitary vigil with the dead.

My mother lay alone in the parlor with abandoned sandwiches and crumpled napkins, at peace in her repose. All the embalmer's art could not mar the beauty of ivory brow, strong sweep of jaw,

9

defiant tilt of her delicate chin. *Gone, gone away,* recalling the times when she stood apart, dreamy and distant—even in sunlight—the laundry basket held aloft as if our socks and underwear flattened by the mangle were bounty she presented to her gods; or she might walk from us to touch the bark of a tree, kneel to a powdery anthill, caress a shard of beach glass, a rubbery frond of seaweed. *Come back*—I wanted to cry in those moments of childish despair— *back to me.* She never heard. When she turned with a blink of her agate eyes, turned to us—her children, her husband—it seemed she must remember to step through the frame, breathe in our everyday air. *Carapace of old lady, where did you go?* Mysterious in her coffin as the iridescent shell of a dung beetle in a museum case, scarab of the redemptive afterlife. That's the embroidery of memory. I am only certain that I stood alone mopping my brow in the dreadful heat, punishing myself with the final distance of her death, when the phone rang.

The phone rang in the kitchen. A great pity I picked up. Rita chatting with a man.

"They'll soon be gone," she said.

"Not soon enough."

Vulgar endearments—pet names, wet kisses.

"Sitting on your bed?" the man asked, and in the husky whisper of seduction began an intimate scan of the washstand, marble-top bureau, the looming wardrobe and collection of girlish trifles which adorn my sister's room. The stuffed panda not excluded from his prurient tour.

Apocalyptic finale to the fireworks. Burst upon burst of hosannas. It was then Rita told this fellow of the unlikely scene. His guttural laugh. Well, who would believe it?

"And the holy father?"

"He's out there with the rest."

"Don't call me," he said. "You have the instructions."

"It's you shouldn't call me."

Ever so softly I lay the receiver in its cradle and returned to the casket, head bowed as if in prayer. *Well,* I said, *here are your precious children—a fraud and a sneak. God knows it's not your fault.* For a moment I wanted to laugh at Rita's kisses, as we laughed gently at her failed projects—baking, knitting—but the bitter scrape of her words was a harsh note never heard. The mourners, shuffling with shame, turned to the house, looking to say a last word to the bereaved, and there was Rita hustling downstairs, out the front door to receive their final condolences. In the distance a band played a Sousa march, the one we sang when we were kids—*Be kind to your web-footed friends. For a duck may be somebody's mother.*

Only Gemma Riccardi poked her head in the door, bracelets jangling, to say in a sodden slur, "Schorry, so schorry."

My lips were sealed. I said nothing to my sister as we tidied the parlor, nothing of the treachery I'd overheard.

Rita said, "Wasn't it awful about the fireworks? And you with that Gemma Riccardi?"

Meaning awful of me to make light upon this solemn occasion.

"Bel would have . . ." I did not finish the thought that our mother delighted in theatrical hoopla, and cut back to the days when my sister and I had something on each other, might tattle, or not tattle, in a childish power play. And so we moved about the rooms in silence, discarding the rubbish, Rita devouring the sandwiches, crusts curling in the heat. Speaking of my sister, my mother often said, *You must befriend her.* Knowing her daughter was destined to be unloved, she had used that cool word. Befriend this simple soul.

We parted with a swift kiss at the bottom of the stairs, and as I turned back it seemed our mother smiled on us with a tweak of her lips, pretend animation, like the trick moves of a flip book. As I settled to the night watch, my thoughts were not of the past with

THE SILVER SCREEN

its safe fragments of memory, but of my sister's betrayal. We had counted on Rita being simple. The verbal dalliance I had spied on clotted in my throat, foreign matter I could neither swallow nor expel. I'd not said a word, thinking that this night was Bel's show—no calling my sister back to exact a confession. And what might I say, my fury cloaked in pastoral indulgence? That I feared her moving beyond the emotions of a dutiful daughter and the narrow routines of her life. Our mother gone away this time for good, yet I felt that she might speak, Bel's gentle commands directing us still, that her children must be as she ordained us—priest and spinster. *We are that, Bel, your spoiled fruit.*

Not long into the night watch, a dread came over me. I was to officiate at the Mass of the Dead. Deserting my post, I went up to my room to prep with a tattered missal left on the shelf with my *Boy Scout Handbook, Caesar's Gallic Wars* and *The Sultan of Swat*, a life of George Herman Ruth written when the Babe first slammed sixty. And Ovid. How I loved the cheap edition given to me by my Latin teacher, an old Yankee who drilled us in declensions, who saw in me the one student who might go on with the dead language he was killing off. Delaying my sorrowful duty, I turned through the flaking pages. There they all were, gods and goddesses disporting themselves in stiff translation, tricking each other, exacting revenge. As an earthbound boy, I understood the creation of their world from lumpy matter and discordant atoms to be fantastic, no more than comic-book tales. This room with its white iron bed was a wet dream of innocence. Oh, I'd been such a good son—the mere recall of my mother's expectations shamed me, that I would please her—training for the higher life. Lightly said, dead serious—the higher life, that phrase of her invention when I was about to leave home for the seminary. I believe she convinced my father somewhere back in time, the time of my baseball triumphs, of spelling-bee victories and grammar school orations, that I was not meant for this world. Or back in kindergarten, when Bel's hand caressed my head, a gesture of sanctified selection drawing me apart in the playground from the play of ordinary boys, Madonna and Child of the Crosswalk at Pleasant and Elm. Little sister trailing behind. A miracle I was not mocked as Mamma's boy. Her grace, her authority was my protection. *Or I was the miracle, wasn't that the ticket, Bel?* The love child conceived in virtue, nothing off base about it, just to say that, growing up, I was always in training. In your comforting marriage to Tim Murphy, we were a team.

When I was first a young Jesuit portioned out to a parish when the regulars, as we called them, were on vacation, men and women spilled every sinful thought and deed to a green priest concealed in the confessional. How many times, I would ask, did you steal, lie, perjure, sodomize, pleasure yourself and, probing for the old reliable, how often *commit* adultery? As though I had knowledge of lust, I advised against the occasions for sin. I absolved foolish pranks of children, spiteful thoughts of old women, knowing they could not see my faint smile behind the net screen; still, as clerk of the court, I demanded an accounting. Often, I barely mumbled the formula for forgiveness, the first hint that I was unfit for the job. My job for many years: not listening in the shadow box of the confessional, but solving simple algebraic problems in the humming fluorescent light of a schoolroom.

But in the morning, I must assume my pastoral role. Flipping the gilt-edged pages of my missal, I came upon "Sequence to be said in all Requiem Masses":

> *Day of Wrath, O Day of mourning,*
> *Lo, the world in ashes burning—*
> *Seer and Sybil gave the warning. . . .*

Wondering who to blame for such doggerel. *Seer and Sybil?* Hangover from Greek mythology, embellishment of some prelate schooled as I was in the classics, out of touch with common speech of the faithful departed. My old black book was outdated. I must choose each word to memorialize Isabel Maher Murphy, whose life was—well—remarkable, though uneventful as I knew it. My last pastoral role, sharing the daily life of peasants in Salvador, so if I tripped up on the liturgy of Lesson and Tract, I trusted my mistakes would be taken for grief.

. . .

Rita wore the prescribed black as they carried our mother out the front path to the hearse, though I saw that she had set out holiday clothes on her bed, the proverbial riot of color in splashy yellow and red costumes, a pair of enormous checkered pants and the straw hat of a coolie. I hovered at the door of her room while she stuffed diaphanous scarves and silver sandals into a tote bag with the legend *Ambrosia—the Heavenly Spring Water*.

Rita with the new rough edge to her words, "I've paid my dues, Joe."

True enough. It was then, while the undertaker's men waited for the grieving family, that she told me of the Portuguese fisherman who was to spirit her off to retirement in everlasting sun, of his children glad to be rid of him, of a bright future by the pool, their cruises and card games so long delayed, all told with a belligerent sniff. They were to be off on their adventure before the flowers wilted on our mother's grave. A truly practical nurse, my sister had tied up with the husband of a woman who did not survive her efficient care. And Rita knew that I knew, the way we knew each other's scams when we were children, that every word was a lie, her neck now blotched vermilion.

"The car is waiting." I escorted her briskly downstairs. In the limousine, my sister's heaving sobs did not alarm the driver, who turned to us professionally with a box of Kleenex.

"Paid with my life, Joe. You know it."

"Save it," I said, believing she cried for herself, not wanting, as we followed slowly behind the hearse, to hear her inappropriate story. If this is my confession, then let me say it was a sin not to hear her out, to award this last day to Bel untainted by our needs, Bel, who paid with her life—whatever that means—in giving herself to us. The comfort of our hired car that came with the arrangements was no comfort at all. I took Rita's hand in mine, feeling it my duty, and discovered the gold ring on her finger. It looked a gaudy affair. "You will have to wait by the coffin till I'm vested."

"Getting into your livery, Father Joe?"

We had laughed at that one with Bel. Irreverence fell flat in the cool of the limo. My sister now placed a black veil on her scrambled gray curls, turned to me with the shadowed face of celebrated widows costumed for public mourning.

"Rita!" I spoke her name sharply, my reprimand a mix of pity and anger at her costumed grief. She did not get my meaning.

My little sister is sixty-eight. I am seventy-one—blood pressure controlled by medication, heart off-beat in a rambunctious rhythm of its own. I pee maybe four, five times in the night. My father, the insurance salesman, would not issue a policy on my life. It's all a risky business—he died on a Sunday afternoon watching the Red Sox wallop the Yankees, therefore died happy, but that was our solace in the midst of bereavement. *Their* bereavement, Rita's and my mother's. I was in a tropical country sweating the booze out of my body each day while the poor, discovering their dignity, learned to tell their stories. At times I taught the children old-style to add and subtract, scratch the alphabet in sun-baked earth, never to pray.

Rita and I knew little of each other, only the tangle of old yarns—Dad shooting squirrels in the attic, Mom winning the

Buick in the Holy Name lottery. Hidden behind a scrim of anecdotes, we discounted the present. When I returned to the States and resumed my visits, we played our simple parts. I now believe our mutual deception was cynical. Muffins, pancakes, bloody steaks I loved, the glass of non-alcoholic wine, Rita's fat-girl laughter at my mildly profane jokes. And my mother, who had been such a stunner driving about town in her big-assed Buick, ready for any diversion, had slowly, slowly retreated to life behind the barricade of our hedge grown thick and tall. Bel awaited my school holidays when I took the train from Grand Central, the bus from Providence, and walked home from town. There were times when I thought to turn back, that in honesty I could not go another block through the neighborhood streets, head into our lane with the houses I once knew so well—the Dunns' sloping breezeway, the Pinchots' carport with its artistic display of hub caps, the Mangiones' cast-cement lions guarding their patch of lawn. But as always, I found my way to the door which my mother left unlatched. There she waited, dressed in her finest, hair pinned back from her face radiant with her belief in me. Lord, as the fella said, help my disbelief.

Why turn back to Rita's desperate laughter or, for that matter, her sobs in the comfort of the air-conditioned limousine? No turning back to my father, Tim Murphy, watching the Yaz field a line drive for the Red Sox in a near-perfect game. I never knew if he knew the score or passed away at the seventh-inning stretch with the bottle of Bud held firm in his good hand. Both of our parents, departing this life without the pain of departure, as though they had recited the Prayer for a Happy Death, were beckoned at the fateful moment, and simply obeyed. Oh, my mother called out my name, but I was gone more than the quarter mile down the lane, long gone. Joey, Joe Murphy, will not come again to her weathered house by the sea.

Day of the funeral there was no one—that is, no one but Gemma Riccardi in her dress-up and a young woman I could not place who sat in the back of the church, perhaps a stray. I had managed the Mass of the Dead with the help of a young parish priest confused by my bumbling with the sacred apparatus of chalice and paten. I blessed the mahogany coffin for a very old lady, its waterproof lining chosen some months ago by her daughter, who had long awaited this day. I had prepared a few words beyond the liturgy, pieties about Bel as mother and wife, true enough, and truly felt, yet insufficient. Then I spoke to my sister and Gemma, the girl my mother took under her wing when we were children, now a strange woman with coal-black hair, her large body hung with exotic silks and bangles. Just the three of us, I said, to remember Isabel Maher of silent movies which we seldom spoke of. (During the night I'd done my homework, discarded *Sybil and Seer* for Ecclesiastes, a line to recall that closed book of my mother's life.) *Better a handful of silence than a handful of toil and a striving after the wind.* She left the glitter and bright lights, came home, I said in the heavy candle-wax air, to marry Tim Murphy, and so we must feel we were chosen. Bel's role was to be our star. (Rita's response to my words hidden by the black veil.) What comes to mind this morning, more than her love and endurance, more than all she witnessed in the length of her years, is Bel's excursions. (Gemma mopping her eyes.) Just the three of us kids in the Buick. The year, if I remember correctly, was 1943. Excursions, that was her name for the pleasure trips she fashioned to places of note. She drew a circle on the map and marked what grand sights we might see and still get home in time for supper.

Then I recalled our transgression, that we skipped school for the day, named the Arcade in Providence and the Narragansett Pier as our destinations, that we crossed to alien territory in Massachusetts and Connecticut. What did she hope for us? That she might impart her spirit of adventure. Perhaps I'd come upon the excursions to escape the mystery of our parents' marriage or the hard truth of my mother's domestic confinement. As I stood over the expensive box that held her body, I figured for the first time that in these outings with three kids, sharing our treats of frankforts and soda pop, Bel was the truant. I did not say it. *Better a handful of silence.* I let my eulogy lapse into a prescribed prayer. In the heavy atmosphere of the church my vestments clung to my body. Unaccustomed to all but classroom speaking, my heart beat its tattoo. My daily audience is schoolchildren. I go by the book. If I elaborate, make some small story of an algebraic problem, they do not listen to my every word.

"Just the three of us on Bel's excursions." I turned to the stranger, a weeping girl. The skinny girl down the lane. I had not recognized her with clothes on. I called her forth to include her in my blessing. Stumbling through *In nomine Patris et Filius* to the wordless end.

CAMERA OBSCURA

The day of the funeral, I took a gentleman's kimono out of the closet—ancient gray silk bought in Kyoto, a swank shop for the tourist trade. The saleswoman, into the aesthetics of wrapping my package, remarked upon the kimono's age, then, with not an ounce of disapproval, "It is forbidden to wear the clothes of the dead. Forbidden to us." Her politeness perfected—culturally, commercially. She didn't say the kimono fit my broad back as it would the girth of an honored man. Under the kimono I wore a Tahitian pareo and a tunic of sequins glittering like the iridescent scales of an exotic creature washed up from the sea. I dressed for the dead woman. When I was a girl I worshiped Bel Murphy, fashioned myself to please her. I thought to please her now. When I returned

18

to this place a few weeks back, she delighted in my colorful garments—Indian silks, African batiks—that proved I'd been somewhere.

"Is that Gemma?" she'd ask, as though my costumes concealed me.

"It's me, Bel." We settled to our talk as though I'd never been away, though we talked of my travels.

Our simple routine of discovery began when I was twelve. Twelve—breastless, my privates smooth as white marble, those sexless museum maidens of Canova.

Hot the morning of her funeral, moist summer air of this Southern New England with its pretense of a temperate climate. The flowered pareo flapped against my ankles, the better to display my feet squeezed into satin slides. The sleeves of my kimono caught at my fish scales. Waiting for Bel to arrive trussed up in her closed casket, I recalled the cool smile of the Japanese saleswoman, her indulgence as I took the exquisite package and crushed it into my knapsack with my work clothes—dirty T-shirts, torn jeans.

No one to see Bel out of this world but her children and a young woman with sun-bleached hair. And yes, the hired pallbearers weary of their task. The revelers at Bel's house were nosy, had paid their respects. I took up my post dead center in the church I'd known so well, each crudely stenciled emblem of fish, palm, dove and the plaster stations of the cross. Front row, Rita Murphy, round and black as a beetle, scrabbling down on her knees, black purse whacking the pew. The pews sticky in this heat, and I recalled once describing Holy Name as Shellac Gothic, a dinner party in Chelsea where guests confessed to the architectural horrors of childhood— city halls, grammar schools, synagogues. When the service began, I no longer knew when to kneel, when to stand. A robotic young priest assisted Joe who looked grand in purple moiré. His eulogy was an odd affair, made quick work of Isabel Maher of the silents and Bel's long run as wife and mother. Joe dredged up the excursions. How could I forget playing hooky, tooling down back roads and highways in Bel's Buick past the golden dome of the state capitol in Hartford, or to the Seamen's Bethel in New Bedford? Those giddy day trips, the beginning of all my journeys. Joe switched to *the dearly departed*, looked to the girl with the sun-streaked hair, called her to join us. He handed us each a rose from the stiff basket which stood by the coffin, a ritual of recent invention, more likely his idea that the three women would stand eye to eye above Bel while he made a quick exit to shed the purple drag. Well, I'd seen him disrobe, seen him buck naked, a strong boy's body, when we skinny dipped with our classmates, flaunting our innocent flesh in the cold waves weeks before the summer sun warmed our bay.

Three grieving women with the stiff red roses standing over the remains of Isabel Maher. The sun-scorched girl rents down the lane from the Murphys, a troubled young thing, that much I knew from Bel, that she stole round the hedge and sat with an old lady.

"For comfort," Bel said, "never my strong suit."

"What troubles her?"

"Lost love, the old story."

It was good of that girl to come stand with us smartly turned out in white linen, blue eyes tearing as she placed her rose. Sweet face, bronzed by the sun, forgettable features of young actresses or models who come and go. Crying for lost love, not Bel. Take that thought back—the girl down the lane may have been enchanted as I was by an old lady's adventures, the theatrical lilt that came into her voice when she was about to tell no one but me of her working days in the movies. Rita another matter entirely, dry-eyed in her beetle black, she would not give up her rose. We waited in silence. My memories of the dead woman at odds with her daughter's. I stole Bel from her when we were kids, or Bel found a likely prospect in me. *Get the hell out of here*, she once said to a restless girl, *the world awaits.* I thought she meant something as grand as moving pictures or never to settle for Tim Murphy and a house on the bay. But what of Rita? Dumpy, middle-aged before we were out of high school. I was surely a thorn in her side, but it was the thorn on the hothouse rose pricked her finger as we stood over Bel. She did not cry out, a twitch of her lips, a last smile perhaps at the indignities long suffered being the improbable daughter of the beautiful Isabel Maher. Perhaps, I tend to select a scene, fit the frame to my story.

Joe came from the sacristy in a shabby seersucker suit, led his sister away. Rita turned, her first words to me since I came back to this place: "Only family going to the cemetery. Family, that's how she wanted it."

I stood on the church steps with the wistful girl from down the lane. "He's still handsome," she said, "with the gray hair. Mrs. Murphy spoke of him often."

"I imagine she did."

"Quite often. How he'd been to the war in Cuba."

"Salvador."

"How he'd been there like a soldier, but he was made for higher things."

"What's higher?"

The child looked flustered despite the authority of designer linen and this year's Italian sandals.

"What's higher," I said, "is to figure whatever they think about these days in the thin air of theology. Ethics, I suppose, how many monkey genes on the head of a pin. That was Mrs. Murphy's belief, that Joe would live in the clouds. She never gave up on that one."

The girl—twenty-five, thirty—girl to me, looked puzzled, then ran to her car, a red Alfa convertible with the hood down. "Need a lift?"

"No thanks." I wanted to see the last of the woman who schooled me. I wanted a shot of the hearse that would spirit Bel away, its black gleam devouring sunlight. Her little funeral procession idled at the stoplight and drove off to the graveyard, a dismal flatland across the state highway. I walked the few blocks to the two-family house I grew up in, making a show of myself in sequins and ancient silk. When I retreated to this middling-sad town, housewives of Cotrell Street spied me from behind their curtains. The children had their frights and whispers at my fancy dress. Three weeks of exposure and I'm old news, absorbed into the dailiness of the neighborhood with the three-legged cat, the Vietnam vet in the wheelchair, the poet who teaches at the community college, the doll woman who stations her replica of Shirley Temple—dimpled, life-size—in a front window to greet her neighbors each day. We are seen yet unseen, background. A dreary professor of film might read our coming and going as static, atmospheric disturbance.

I thought of Bel, who was always visible. The dark hair piled high, Celtic tilt to her speckled eyes and the slight inward smile of detachment. Not Celtic, a Chekhov beauty, one of his lost ladies living in exile. She was never one of us. Her delight in the ordinary goods in shopwindows—dish towels, a length of flannel, an aluminum cooking pot—the spring to her step in the butcher shop. Mrs. Murphy looking up to a true blue sky above our grammar school was confirmation of the day.

. . .

On a Saturday when I was a girl, I'd leave the house early with my allowance, a quarter—you better believe it—that would take me to the matinee, but first to loiter at Brandle's, a dim old pharmacy, dark wood cabinets, white marble countertops. A bell tinkles over the door as I enter. Mr. Brandle looks up from his chemist's lair in

MAUREEN HOWARD

the back of the store—his face gray as a tombstone, gray as his pharmacist's jacket and threads of hair. His trembling hands dish out a scoop of white powder into a brass scale with graduated weights. Oh, it is only the Riccardi girl in a faded summer dress. She will hide behind the magazine stand, never buy one, flip through styles and stars, then sit up at the soda fountain and tap her quarter on the counter for service as though she had the wherewithal to order a banana split, a fresh kid with a false maturity, said to be Frank Riccardi's girl, good for a small cherry Coke. She lingers over the magazines. Today she takes one, saunters to a stool at the counter. Brandle continues his calibrations. He has no one to help him in the store this Saturday. It's 1942 and they are hiring again at the naval boatyard and at the woolen mill, which has the promise of government contracts. His boy has quit, and Brandle will have to ply the spigots and taps of the soda fountain. Riccardi's girl is studying every word of the movie magazine, the one with Garbo on the cover. Brandle can pick out the headshot of an unyielding Garbo with his eagle eye trained over many years to see the Hershey Bar slipped into a pocket, the Wrigley's Spearmint palmed. He has unpacked the newspapers and magazines, set them in place himself, a menial task. The girl swings on her stool in a dither, taps her quarter. Brandle hears but ignores her cry, a high screech of discovery. She is flapping the fan magazine, punishing the pages she will not pay for.

Tinkle of the brass bell announces a woman with a smart straw hat tilted on her head, a dark curl stuck to her ivory forehead. She's something rare, the forward thrust of her chin acknowledging her beauty: So what? What do you make of it, when I make nothing of it at all? Mrs. Murphy waits at the counter with Brandle's scant supply of cosmetics and cologne. Frills, he calls them, an invasion of his authorized alchemy, his healing compounds and tonics. The third offense of the morning, yet even old Brandle will take pleasure in waiting on Mrs. Murphy, noting her idle amusement of buying a lipstick this Saturday morning while her gifted son plays baseball, her plump daughter lumbers her way through Dan Quilty's tap-dancing class. A warm day, he turns on an electric fan, a new device which flutters her skirt.

I believe it was the beginning for me, the magic moment when I looked up from *The Silver Screen* to discover the mother of the Murphy kids buying a lipstick at Brandle's. The establishing shot in which she called to me:

"Which shade do you like?"

She came to the soda fountain, swung up on a stool, drew two lines on the back of her hand—a scarlet, a magenta.

I touched the purplish red.

"Right." Mrs. Murphy pleased. I'd made the clever choice. And then, "You're in Joey's class. You're Gemma!"

I did not answer, boldly flipped open the movie magazine to display "Sweethearts of Yesteryear." *Where have they gone?* The Bessies and Mays, Louise Brooks, Viola Dana, Isabel Maher— pretty girls—then turned to the page with Mrs. Murphy distant and rare as a queen in a silver gown, a gleaming helmet of black hair. A promising heartbreaker lost to the business, Mrs. Murphy with a dark shadow of herself cast on the wall behind. Joe's mother on a white lounge, pearls falling on the graceful rise of her breast.

"Yes?" Taking the magazine from me, "A publicity shot. That couch was a punishment."

"Will that be all?" Brandle fussing with the dusting powders and toilet water, glasses down on his nose the better to look in the dim light of his emporium at the curve of Mrs. Murphy's hips under a cotton wash dress, on any other woman in town matronly.

"And this, I'll take this." Bel, as I would learn to call her, tucking *The Silver Screen* into her purse.

My star brought down to earth, poor angry girl, the puzzle twisting my face.

Her question no more than a breath, a whisper, "What is it, Gemma, what do you want to know?"

I couldn't come up with an answer, which was yet another question, till years later, when I was about to quit college before they dismissed me. Impudent, seeking attention with my questions in the Louis Quinze classroom of a Newport mansion. Dante torments lovers when all he knew of lust, puh-leeze, his crush on a little girl? Wordsworth's *Prelude*—prelude to boredom? Why the H-bomb? We've got one that works. I was a nettle in the fallow fields of my long-suffering teachers mired in their lesson plans, pressing my glib questions beyond the strict borders of inquiry. Tired of my small notoriety, I packed up to leave Salve Regina and this place called home, but not before I asked Bel Murphy what I wanted to know.

"Why quit when you were—famous?" And, wanting to sound smart, "Ahead of the game?"

I expected she would laugh. "What game? Count all of us famous, the girls who came off buses and trains to find work in the movies. You might not be called out of the pack."

Before I left town, I recalled our recognition scene in Brandle's. "The silver gown? The pearls?"

"Wardrobe. I no longer believed in their costumes. Make-believe scenes they set me to play. I wasn't much of an actress. All in how they directed me, vamp down a flight of stairs, kiss the old man who kept me. Snub the famous clown with his music hall tricks. Don't fuss about it, Gemma." And then Bel said, I will never forget how deliberately she delivered the line, "It wasn't my life."

I was being dismissed. "That's all for today," she'd say when I was a kid and helped with her garden. "That's all," when we heard the squeal of tires. Then I'd run under the willow tree, slip through a hole in the hedge, turn back to see Rita Murphy lumbering round the house with her bike, overalls split at the knee, her mother coming down from the porch, the languorous descent of a social belle in a romantic comedy, descending to the skirmish of comforting her daughter. Rita searching her mother's face for something not there, because she had given it all to me.

Had it not been for Bel Murphy, I'd have lived in a shabby house, wrong side of town, all my life. I blamed her for sending me into the world with nothing more than a desire to make my name, to prove that she was wrong choosing exile. Her very grandeur, picking her kids up from school, gracing the bleachers at the dusty ball field, buying lipstick at Brandle's, was absurd, but she carried it off. I knew, even at that age when everything was black and white, the textbook authority of my fledgling Catholic college, the se-ductions of New York or Boston within grasp of Gemma Ric-cardi, I knew that she lied, that she was in fact a brilliant actress and that we—the whole town, her neighbors on that narrow lane hov-ering above the bay, Tim Murphy, the man who came home in time for supper, her children, blessed and blighted—we all believed Isabel Maher welcomed her celluloid grave.

"The world is full of disappearances," Bel told me.

I knew about disappearance. Gemma Riccardi, at times cited as Riccardi. I liked to think my father was a made man in a lineup with a big brimmed felt hat and long overcoat, well tailored the way Mafiosi dressed like gentlemen, at least in the movies. Not just a man who tired of his wife and child, walked off from family life. Took a powder. I liked that language, imagined he was rubbed out or in the slammer. But he was just a guy who disappeared. I thought I might spot him in a newsreel, one humiliated man in the long breadlines of the Great Depression, stunned men holding out their hands for a crust, a cup of soup. Or living in a tent courtesy of the CCC, some lowly job meted out to him. All let's pretend on my part, pretense my strong suit. Were my parents married? The neighbors thought not. I heard their disapproval in the twist put on "*Mrs.* Riccardi." Little to go on, not even a photo, all mementos destroyed, yet I could call up a tall, dark man with a crooked smile, a tooth set in gold from some time when he'd been flush. Crinkly black hair receding, the shine of his high forehead. The scratch of his two-day beard. Later still, I imagined I'd find him in a brutal story—realismo of Rosselini or De Sica—a long take of an American GI seducing a wistful Sicilian girl. Then I gave him up, gave up the romance with my father.

What did I want to know? Why the boarder in the back bedroom, Mr. Dunphy who kept the books at the mill. We were that bad off with only the rent from upstairs and needed his few dollars paid weekly, folded in a small brown envelope discreetly laid on the telephone table. His shy coming and going to the diner where he took his meals. On Sunday he brought us a pint of Borden's ice cream, always the Neapolitan brick—chocolate, strawberry, vanilla—a treat for all three of us. Spoon at his pursed lips, blink of his rabbit-pink eyes as he looked from me to my mother. She called him Phil upon these homey occasions. They spoke of the weather and their work, for my mother had been trained as a bookkeeper. Now, defense contracts coming in at the mill, she at last had a job. They spoke with some relish of payments due and their terror of receipts not entered while I let my ice cream puddle, and then one day Dunphy began to eat breakfast at our kitchen table—his toast dipped in egg yolk, his coffee sweetened with condensed milk—and when he had gulped the last, my mother dusted the crumbs from his lapels, smoothed the errant strands of his ginger hair. Next it was dinner and what, my mother asked, did I want to know?

"More greenbacks in the brown envelope?"

"Gemma!"

But when I saw my mother, always so determinedly drab, with a perm, clear polish on her nails, well, what was I to think of the spring in her step as she walked to Dunphy's car, slingback pumps, open toes? And off they went to the mill, to their orders and receipts, to their clerkly gossip of a duplicitous foreman, devil of a union boss and the rectitude of the heroic mill owner and his condescending wife, who my mother, subservient as a maid in the movies, addressed as "ma'am" at the Christmas party, a skimpy fête with dime-store presents for the kids. I thought it all a shame, more than a shame when she married Dunphy with a gaggle of redheaded Dunphys never to be seen again. Dunphys come from factory towns, Worcester and Lowell. Dunphys in their stiff Sunday best toasting happiness, a life sentence. I wished hard Frank Riccardi would come in the front door of the house he left heavily mortgaged, then their glasses would slop the pink champagne and those Dunphys with freckles and watery eyes would skedaddle. I would run to the arms of my father, our two long Italian faces on display, the green tint of our skin, almond eyes, downward slope of our Giottoesque noses, though I knew nothing of Giotto, being thirteen, but played the scene over and over, this rescue by my father. Sometimes I cut the Dunphys to his old mother dabbing at her wet lips with a hankie and one reptilian sister with no lashes, just the witless moist blink of her eyes brimming with sentiment at this preposterous union. Can I have been that hurt? That heartless? No wonder I fell head over heels for Bel Murphy.

Forty years later, I thought of my mother's wedding as an assistant set up the tripod, held a light meter to the face of a Park Avenue matron. A shoot for a shelter magazine, paying the piper for my peppers—the era of my curvaceous chilis, sensuous studies of vegetables, apples I'd shot in homage to Cézanne, all to rival the famed edibles by Weston, Cunningham, O'Keeffe. But the problem at the Park Avenue moment: how to light the perfect beige wife, give depth to the woman in the wing chair, which was really the whole point, wasn't it, the ancient brocade chair set beside a witty modern table? Daddy Warbucks looking on, both of them sanded smooth. When they turned to each other, old man and young wife, I saw their corporate deal. The itemized accounts of her chill good looks, his cultivated taste in the furnishings of their life, all their books balanced. More than a marriage of convenience, they were courtly with each other, displayed a tidy pleasure in their triumph against the odds. An upscale show, but so like my mother's regard for Dunphy with his ice cream treat, dusting the crumbs off his shoulders; so like Dunphy holding the car door open for the lady, his compliments for the poached egg, his gratitude for laundered socks and underwear neatly folded. In the artificial light of Park Avenue, I shot four rolls of a woman who had settled herself in an extravagant chair. And I wondered if her husband slept apart from his prize, for while I lived at home Phil Dunphy never left the back bedroom.

It was my mother's husband gave me the secondhand Brownie, loaded it with film in an attempt to include me in the wedding party. I fiddled with the knobs, but did not want to record that wicked event. When the tiered cake was brought forth, I stole past the wedding guests, ran all the way to Bel's garden. When I arrived at the Murphys', she was digging in manure. A Saturday afternoon. Joe at his baseball. I could see Rita at the window of her room, closeted on this sunny day.

"Aren't you the pretty thing?" Bel cried.

I was dressed for the wedding, but would not speak of it. The camera. I had run off with the black box, held it up to take her picture. She threw down her spade, came toward me, put her hand over the lens. "Come, come along, Gemma, we'll see the end of Joe's game."

We drove right by the ball field. The sour smell of cow clung to her apron. "Tell me," she said, "where are we heading?"

"Cotrell," I said, the name of my street. The door of our house was thrown open for whatever breeze. We heard a phonograph churning out a fox-trot and in the shadows my mother and her husband were dancing, just the two of them shuffling about the worn carpet. Bel watched till I was swallowed into the heat and half-light of the dying party. I took pictures of the Dunphys smiling and the wreckage of the cake, of my mother in a pale blue suit with a wilting corsage. That night I shut the door to my room, pried open the black box and exposed the film to the glare of the overhead light.

· · ·

The week before she died, I rocked with Bel on the Murphys' back porch under a canopy, an old bedsheet stretched over metal pipes that once supported an awning. Two old ladies now, surveying the devastation of the garden, in full bloom when I was a kid.

"You were not fair to your mother," she said. "Children never are."

"Your children think the world of you."

"Rita doesn't think much of the world. She counts the days till she'll be rid of me."

Bel's words seemed a lamentation for her daughter, "Well rid of me." A cruel thought, but Joe was coming for his visit. How swiftly she brightened. Since I'd come back to this place with its threadbare memories, more than once I heard heroic tales of his ministry in Salvador, and, as ever, his great draw to theology.

"His thoughts are way beyond us, Gemma."

I placed Salvador as twenty years ago, and how to figure Joe's teaching high school involved the heady abstractions of theology. Bel must see he would never be shipped to Rome to set the big guys right on weighty matters. A very old woman, she was entitled to her dreams. It wasn't dementia, not with Bel. Bright as always; the chirp of her laughter when I said I'd clear out before Rita came home. Was the hole still in the hedge?

"The hedge is overgrown. No one to clip it after Tim died."

She seldom spoke of her husband—clean-cut with even features, bland as the model for American Dad in an ad for a Ford V8—that's all I remember of Mr. Murphy who sold insurance. A full head of gray hair, gray suits and, yes, the black Ford sedan. Dunphy, who had a policy on his life, spoke of Tim as a pal. Murphy would pay up in the eventuality. . . . Impossible to think of this mild fellow with a ready smile as Isabel Maher's prince, the lover who lured her away from wardrobe and script. Her boy she loved beyond reason. I knew that when I helped her in the garden, when I fled the sight of the wedding cake with its sugar roses, when I quit school believing that in a city of my prodigal dreams there would be answers to my impossible questions. I was the charity case. Joe the prize. The prize she gave to God in a crazy payback, a hope that her darling, the best looking boy in town, that his devotion would make amends for what failure of Bel's I could not know.

There was an urgent note the day of our last meeting. Bel held me with questions about my work. I let her look at me through the lens of my camera. Look at me, Gemma, in the ethnic garments I affect! Then I took the very old lady's picture. She did not flinch or hold out her frail hands against the flash, but preened a little in the rocking chair, head tilted coyly, a parody of the publicity shot in *The Silver Screen*. A froth of white hair, brittle bones poking the cotton dress she might have worn that day in Brandle's, its pattern of simple polka dots blown by his feeble electric fan against her full breasts and thighs.

Bel pushed herself up from the low rocker, toddled across the burnt-out lawn to a patch of weeds, all that was left of her garden. She swayed slightly. I ran to steady her.

"Now, Gemma, it won't be long. I mean to hang on till Joe comes for his visit."

Stooped over a few flowers, she clipped with a scissors hidden in her pocket. "Cosmos, self-seeders. For your mother." For a moment I thought I'd caught her out, the muddled old mind, but she raised her head. "It was cosmos I sent home with you to your mother. Hardy and plain."

When we were settled again, I asked, "The sound barrier?" She gave me no answer. I pressed on. She must tell, now or never. "Was it sound?"

She knew at once what I was after. Impossible for her to cross over to talkies, to leave behind the gestures and grimaces of silent film?

"Yes, that was it." She laughed. "I emoted."

I didn't believe her. "Your voice?"

No answer, and why would she answer? Her voice thrilling in its range, its timbre . . . From our first encounter I was taken with her laughter, throaty and rich, no one's mother laughed with such abandon. On our excursions Bel's words rang with teacherly command—*profundo*, the terrible storm that carried off the whalers, or *diminuendo*, softening at the wonder of Mark Twain's folly of a extravagant house. On the beach at Newport she did a quick turn with a song, naughty but nice—*By the sea, by the sea*—in a churchy soprano—*Oh, how happy we'll be!* When I settled in New York for a season, I watched the few movies salvaged from Bel's brief career, curiosities, classroom stuff, which displayed the expert camerawork of the late Twenties, just before sound came in, great lighting, subtle shadings of black and white. In a room at the Museum of Modern Art, not much bigger than a telephone booth, I set the brittle celluloid spinning to watch Isabel Maher, who did not emote, not even in the one-reeler where she humiliated a clown on a Hollywood beach. She played it—the vixen. In *My Darling Daughter,* Bel is at first enchanting, simple delight. Society girl loves poor guy, is betrothed to richy-rich fool. Heartbreaking, her defeated smile as she leaves her lover, the flip of her wrist at the cruel snobbery of country-club class. Her every move elevated the stale plot, which involved the heroine's father, who the rich fellow would bail out of some scandal. 1928, Bel on the brink of sound. I have been told that actors in silents rehearsed, did not babble nonsense. They learned their lines, went through the emotional paces. Frame by frame, Bel's mouth without voice spilled forth desire, mockery, grief. The soundtrack, falsely gay and moody music, was splendid, better than it would be for years to come in the talkies. She was good as they get, almost a great actress.

I believe it was Bel's commanding silence, on screen and off, her refusal to answer, that set me to photography, my life's work. A photographic image is in need of no words. Light, shadow, selection read with the lens, the only sound the soft whisper of the shutter. With the camera I am in a state of silent reception. No questions asked. But I natter on, as I did often enough to the shrinks who abandoned me to my *forgotten material,* when the swagger that masked my fears was perfectly simple, but I could never say to the best of them, an old man of the old school— listening to the trivia of a love affair, the incestuous reincarnation of Frank Riccardi, the easy substitute of Bel for my mother—why I mistrusted words while I talked and talked, reversing my image in a long exposure with the pinhole camera. Why my questions contain their answers. Why I so desperately needed the silence of my pictures to cut off my punishing words.

. . .

As though I knew it would be our last visit, I brought the book with me, the selected edition of my works and days. I thought Bel owed me a hearing, a look-see at a travelogue illustrated by the author, in fact a book of photographs which render my subjects harmless, whether indigenous people in joyous celebration or cityscapes of desolation. Skill failed me, even the Pulitzer photo— girl in a tattered First Communion dress running toward my lens (1977) while the body of her mother bleeds into the dirt road— too perfectly composed, white flash of dress distracting the eye from the bundle flung out of the mother's arms, pitiful possessions strewn in the dust under the bright sun still, still as death. No one to claim this ordinary killing on an ordinary day. The isolation of mother and daughter, their tragedy singled out. I had used the old Leica for the shot of the kid running toward me, toward a woman who jumped out of a jeep while the soldiers ran into the conceal- ing pampas which muffled the peppering of shots. The screaming of the child silenced. The photo born deaf with the click of my shutter. Riccardi, a serious tag-along photojournalist, making her picture story, which would register for a day or a week, end up be- tween covers, an expensive item to place on a glass table with handsome art books. The Argentine photos of the dirty war still mildly disturbing, but flip to the early studies of our bleak family house on Cotrell (1958), to sexual declivities of the chili peppers (1983), the simpatico studies of Native Americans (1992) in the confusion of neon tepees promoting casinos and the trailer-park reservation with the women in Gap sweatshirts weaving ancient designs into their baskets—to get the full range of my recycling, my mechanical art. *Riccardi echoes great art photography of the past, embraces repetition* . . . and so forth. I took it as praise. What else can I do other than submit to words airy as cheesecloth? Flattery of the worst sort, like praise of a plain woman's eyes, and I fell for it. I became their Riccardi, acclaimed as a mimic, not the woman who wanted to shoot reality—political or poetic. I was like a student staked out in a museum, painting my Rembrandts and Van Goghs, a copyist—take it or leave it. Leave it.

Gemma sang a popular song from her childhood, "Little Sir Echo."
Sir, an odd gender switch, singing it to the last of her lovers, a curator at
a university with a football team that mattered and a museum tucked
away with one blowsy Renoir, two minor Grant Woods and an overload
of Remingtons, gift of a trustee. The curator, a faded academic trying to
catch up, thus Riccardi. She was glad he was out there in the Midwest,
that he read all the current double-talk in the art journals that brought
her round again, her lookalikes reinvented by the kids who believed ap-
propriation made outright theft admirable, more than OK.

"You're hot," he said, the sweet man who brought her flowers when
he came into New York. He had recently lost his wife to an insignificant
mole on her cheek grown angry, invasive, and Gemma was touched by
this courting thing, the flowers and dinner at a bistro he'd researched
online. Five years her junior, at least. He didn't mind that she was a
head taller, flashy in her flashy garments, a figure in a world he'd once
yearned for, standing the endless hours as a uniformed guard at the Art
Institute, earning his way through a doctorate. And she seemed not to
mind that it was mostly impossible in bed what with his manners, call it
manners. When it didn't work out, they talked for a while—her dark-
room adventures, his classes—and slept. So there was to be this show, as
well as the Riccardi retrospective in Barcelona, which would travel to
Paris and Geneva. Gemma traipsed after, dishing out interviews in
which she said the most awful stuff about iconic reproduction and fak-
ing the fake. When she was done with all that, she headed out to the
Midwest, where the sweet professor waited, her prints waiting too—
cabbages and pimps, drag queens, redwoods, desert sand, camouflaged
guerrillas, famous poets and tramps—uncrated, waiting to be hung.
Lined up like so many clay ducks in a shooting gallery, or in the boxy
white rooms given over to Riccardi. When they were sorted out by early
and late, by portraits and politics; when the helpful graduate student
went back with the curator to some business in the office, she was alone
with her work, her retrospective, as the flier said. And, looking back, she

could assign each photo its Leica or Rolex, coated lens, seconds of exposure. Perhaps it was that very nice man with his friar's rim of pale hair, his spiffy black T-shirt, trying to look New York, or his regard for her as he popped a bottle of champagne for their private viewing, that started her song. "Little Sir Echo, how do you do? Hello! (Hello!) Hello!"

"What's that?"

"An old song." But when she went back to his neat house on a leafed-out street near the campus, Spring having finished off the lilacs and laurel in his front yard, she said she must be leaving. "Sorry, an assignment." Which he knew was untrue. Riccardi no longer worked on assignment, so they drank tea in the living room with his wife's chintz chairs and botanical prints in gold frames on the walls hung next to a Warhol multiple of Liz which she knew must be his.

"Thanks for coming out to the boondocks." They spoke of insurance for the run of the show, of the lighting, which seemed a touch harsh. Then he drove her to the local airport, and Gemma ran across the tarmac with her backpack and camera bag to a little prop plane, as she had many times when on assignment.

Echo—her story is sad. No matter we are charmed by her repeats, she can never begin, must always follow. Her crime was chatter. Chattering, she drove the nymphs away so Juno could not spy on her husband, who desired them for his pleasure. Or so the goddess thought, her jealousy thriving on suspicion. Echo's punishment was ingenious, without mercy. Silenced, she can only repeat the words given her. Not all the words, the last phrase. Denied originality, what voice she has is a trick of nature. Thoreau was enchanted by her voice in the woods, but he had to speak first, didn't he? Feed her the line.

Gemma is no nymph. Big-boned, rangy, she figures she is the image of her father, that Riccardi was a lean Italian from the north, articulated limbs of a Giacometti, ropy arms and legs, strong limbs, elegant for a man, a burden for Gemma until recently. Now what does she care if she looks like a leathery tennis champ on the senior circuit? Ethnic costumes *engulf her, echoing Oriental garments draped on models—the Studio Apartments, Tenth Street before her time—or flaunted by long-gone Bohemia, the daring women at soirees of the Photo-Secessionists. She is a throwback to the carefully calculated time of time exposures, and to the expedient reportage of photojournalism in a world in which back is now forward, her work honored for some ironic intention never intended. Click: see what the old girl can do when her mission is mimicry.*

One day, after her flight from the admiring professor's retrospective, just weeks before she returned to this town, hometown, Gemma Riccardi, shuffling through old prints, discovered a photo of a photo taken on the outskirts of Mexico City—a crumbling cement wall with an advertisement of aching hand-painted teeth, bleeding gums.

SERVICIO DENTAL SIN DOLOR

A beautiful girl with thick black braids stood in front of the crudely drawn mouth. The child, holding flowers for some occasion, did not pose, just stood under the decaying teeth waiting for the day to happen. That little parable might have been shot by any number of photographers in the shutterbug hall of fame. Gemma shot her printed photo of the girl again and again, thinking to beat the imagers of the image at their game. If you can't beat them join them: devalue the original. The Mexican girl in her many copies had not traveled the museum circuit in Europe. Riccardi had thrown the prints aside in her New York studio, which did not make up for her copycat shame. She was worse than that good man in the Midwest trying to get with Riccardi retrospectively in the cramped museum a few students might wander into at the end of Spring term. Or the alums coming back for reunion, wanting to visit the Remington cowboys and Indians of their halcyon days. Trashing her photos of photos, painful teeth and innocent child cut to ribbons of surface gloss, she hummed, "Little Sir Echo, how do you do? / Hello! (Hello!) Hello! (Hello!) You're a dear little fellow, I know by your voice, / But you're always so far away (away)." Echo fell in love with

Narcissus. Her body dwindling to stone, she didn't have a chance re-
duced to sound, to air trapped in tunnels, in caves. Her myth is one of
the cruelest, unless we consider that she always has the last word. Word.

. . .

I brought the book with me to show Bel, not knowing it would be
our final day, turned to the picture of a Nambé woman beating a
message on the earth to ward off a storm. A reservation north of
Santa Fe, and the woman wrapped in a blanket wouldn't stop for
the camera, so the print, see here, shows the frenzy of her hands
and the rapture of her face, praying to whichever god might come
through with fine weather for the Day of the Dead. My fingers
stiff with cold, unable to load the next roll.

"Got the metallic sky, don't you think?"

No answer from Bel, who studies the Nambé pleading against
the inevitable.

"Mostly they pray for rain." The woman's daughter pointed out
the black clouds not seen in her mother's trance. "Then she took
me to her trailer to view the family display of candy skulls, stacks
of paper skeletons to sell to the tourists. I bought one the next day,
when the sky was clear and bright, the old woman's prayers answered."

Turning the pages, I showed Bel a luminous print: the boneyard,
an elaborate confection of spun sugar surrounded by cornmeal
coffins, jolly in their way, only to our eyes grotesque.

"For the tourists?"

"And for their people, to honor the dead." I turned to the
photo of a man by a grave with his children, the family stationed
on kitchen chairs the livelong day. The tombstone decorated with
paper flowers, favorite dishes laid out for the departed wife and
mother. "If I'd used a tape recorder, a video camera, you would
hear them speak with the dead, ask questions. They believe the
dead answer. A great comfort."

"Will I have the pleasure of food when I'm dead? I'd like crumb cake."

"It's bound to bring the ants."

I turned the pages slowly. Bel was too frail to hold the big book with *Riccardi* stamped in gold on the fine linen cover. All my adventures tracking violence and hunger, political documentation once current, seemed no more to me than a passing slide show. *Life, Look*, the magazines that sent me on assignment, hustled out of business by noisy moving images of TV. My studies of fruits and vegetables were overripe period pieces showing off what the silver-based process might attain to. Prints to hang on museum walls.

"Lovely, just lovely!" Bel said the wrong thing, scooted on, giving my big book a pat, Riccardi's bound and glossy child. "How far you traveled, Gemma."

She was right about lovely. I'd displayed my accomplishments like a good report card, wanting praise for work I no longer valued. Over the years I sent Bel postcards, made holiday calls begging the connection, keeping the worn threads alive. I developed a personal myth, the win–win option of success over failure, which had at its center the example of a vanished star. Yes, I traveled far, made a vow etched in stone now riddled with fault lines, never to settle for day trips, mere excursions.

We rocked in our rockers. She seemed to drift off, then called me to attention. "Gemma, plant a garden! It will keep you in one place for a season. It will keep you with me."

$\cdot$ $\cdot$ $\cdot$

I closed the book that day, took off in my rented car, rentals a fixture in my meandering life. I drove to a highway nursery, bought packets of seeds, then tilled the spent earth in my backyard with a shovel found in the coal bin. At the nursery the woman advised manure, black and odorless when I cut open the sack, churned it into the soil. Perhaps too late at the end of June; still, Bel had set my course once again. I placed four frail tomato plants in a row, then opened the packets of seeds—lettuce, thyme, Genovese basil, *extra large leaves, excellent for pesto*. Ancho peppers, *deep green to red on bushy plants*. Surely a foolish gesture in the course of my fruitless life, no more foolish than my aesthetic veggies—the fluid surfaces of my chili peppers, the crags and humps of my cauliflower. I turned to the house, the house where my mother and her husband died checking the daily entries and withdrawals of their days. Why did I not sell up? I let an agent handle the rentals, a property noted on tax forms as I moved from post to post, man to man. Now the house seemed to me blank-eyed, slack-mouthed. Little Miss Echo, her cave to hide in. Out of habit, I set up my condenser, enlarger, my emulsions and magic papers—though I swore I'd shot my last roll of film. The neighbors, when they speak to me at all, call me Dunphy. I do not correct them.

When I rose from my patch of dirt, my knees were swollen and spongy. Kneading them with muddy hands, I made a bargain that Bel would live till I brought her my harvest—ripe tomatoes, peppers—the real thing, not the two dimensions of my accomplishment. I bargained like the woman beating the earth in New Mexico, that Bel would live till she answered the hard questions.

Joe's visit, when it came, was no more than a few days. I did not go near the house that looks out on the bay. Let her have her son, all she cared for, let her believe he's destined for the life of the mind, by which she meant soul. Destined like the bright boy leading the high school debate team to victory. At what age are we no longer destined? You did not wait for the basil, *exceptionally sweet*. You had a few good lines, Bel. Controlled by your silence, I chatter to empty air. No agent, lover, curator can find me. In all documents I have listed my place of birth as unknown, my parent as A. Riccardi. A for Ansel, my little joke. In the Sixties I assisted

Ansel Adams in the redwoods, a position much sought after. For a season I toted his equipment, took notes on the camera and lens, the developer, grade of paper. Taking notes did not lend me the great photographer's eye for the spectacle—light and shadow of a leaf, bright foreground, dense background of forest. *Redwoods, Bull Creek Flat:* he created that shaft of sun in the darkroom, scored the bark with theatrical exposure. I learned only the mechanics. You did not wait for my questions? Should I burn my book as worthless? Will I disappear in pale imitation of Isabel Maher?

. . .

Your boy took me to the prom. Joe fooled with girls in his father's car, girls in the popular set who wrote endearments in his yearbook, knowing he was off limits. So few of us were going on. Most hoped for jobs in the Cotrell plant or one of the mills. It was never questioned—Joe Murphy had signed on for the seminary. So the prom with all its coupling and show of grown-up glamour was not in the cards for either of us, Riccardi being a loner. Bel made the match so we would not miss this rite of passage. We danced to the bleat of *Mona Lisa, Mona Lisa.* Proving we were regular kids, we attempted to make out in the back seat of Mr. Murphy's car, scattering the brochures for fire and theft insurance. It was no go from the first flick of our tongues, the zipper of his rented tux caught on the scrambled net of my petticoat, and we gave it up as a bad job. We had been together too often in Bel's Buick, scooting the back roads of Rhode Island, not close as brother and sister, just pals, so we laced our Cokes with rum, drank out of the bottle and ran down to the sandy shore, shed our finery, raced naked into the waves. The lovers on the beach, our classmates, stripped and joined us for the few moments we could bear the chill water. A spring ritual, a purification. We drove to my house in our clammy clothes and parked for a silent minute.

"Thanks for the ride." I used the awkward words said at the end of each excursion, not knowing how to thank Bel for our release from the tight space we lived in, for my discovery that there were vistas within range of my own backyard, broad as if seen through a view camera—the castles of Newport, the gentrified dream of Twain, magic arcades and pavilions. I must have seen Joe at graduation or when I helped Bel in the garden, but I only recall that naked boy shivering in faint moonlight, an object of beauty, not lust, my hometown David, strong, well hung, distant as marble, pure as the stars. With my untrained eye, I filed that image away and it came back to me—a print or a self-selecting slide, wretchedly inappropriate—at Bel's wake. *You took me to the prom.* Tux and taffeta, dressed to kill for our flight from innocence. He wears clergy black, his waxen face well preserved, eyes empty as the blank orbs of a statue. Desperate, I flaunt my exuberant rags. *Mona Lisa, Mona Lisa, men have named you*—let me rest my weary head on your shoulder. Perhaps we are a good match after all.

Picture this: I enter the darkroom (my mother's kitchen), turn on the safelights, enlarge the negative, douse the paper in my witch's solutions. Slowly an apparition emerges, a halo of white hair, chin up for the camera. For the effect of faint resolution I draw the print out of its bath early, fix Isabel Maher as ghostly. She is a shadow, a shade, sweetheart of the silents.

Bel, you didn't wait for my question.

Was it worth your life to be Mrs. Murphy?

Possible to be a Miss Dunphy? To develop a fine print from the negative of years?

THE MULE CHOSE THE WAY

The day after the burial, a morning of heavy silence as Rita packed her sporty clothes. Curtains hung still at the window over the sink, oppressive heat settling in. My heart fluttered, a familiar tremor passing quickly. Rita came down to the kitchen in the clownish checkered pants, a T-shirt, buttercup yellow, spread over the twin suns of her breasts. From birth she amused us with her rosy comic-strip innocence. Today her flat round face wore a sly crack of a smile, the cartoonist moving on to a darker adventure. I was not aware as we sat with our breakfast crumbs that I cradled my mother's Belleek teapot in my hands.

"Take whatever you please," Rita said, knowing I live without possessions. "Manny's not much for antiques."

That's Manuel ———, her ardent amigo. I envision a scene from the jerky old silents of my mother's Hollywood days, a slick Lothario climbing a ladder to Rita's room; my sister, a fluttering fatty with kewpie-bow lips mouthing squeals of delight. Silent, because I presume they were silent in their assignations, creeping upstairs when the old lady was fast asleep. Or did their groans and sighs enter her dreams?

"What would I do with antiques?"

"You might find some use for them at the school where you live. Manny likes everything new, up to date."

My sister's offer of worldly goods was kindly. I allowed that being up to date seemed hopeful, then got down to business. I feared for her life with this Manny who liked everything new and withheld my blessing. "You're leaving it all. Not tables and chairs, Rita, all of your life. It seems a risky business."

"Not that word!" Rita's howl of delight recalling how we laughed when Dad touted his product—*guaranteed coverage, protection from risk.*

At that moment I understood my sister's determination to tie up with this man, her last hope. I drew back to Father Joe, his paternal role. "Chance, then. You're taking a hell of a chance. And what will you live on?"

43

"Never you mind." Rita tufted her hair coyly. Have I noted she was cropped, a lamb after sheering? Thin steely gray ringlets exposed the blanched flesh of her scalp. Never you mind, Manny was in the money. Once a fisherman, he had come up in the world. A union boss. Which did not explain why their courtship, call their shenanigans courtship, why it was clandestine, why her lover of some years—*years!*—had not comforted my sister in these days of mournful arrangements. It seemed a fish story, overly complex like the fabrications of my students, their convenient influenzas and multiplying grandparents who died when projects were due.

"Manny has already moved away." Chin up in a poor imitation of our mother.

"Where might that be? Where are you off to?"

"Can't say."

"What can you possibly mean?"

Rita plucking her curls, "Can't say. It's the law."

"What law it that?"

"Not law, the investigation." Then my little sister adjusted her tortoise rim glasses the better to see my despair and told what she was permitted to say, not what I presume Manuel ——— had testified to the prosecutors, double dealing on the waterfront, New York to Boston, going back through the years, documenting corruption and greed. Rita's story was of her innocent lover squealing to save his skin. I pictured this man under interrogation, his features electronically blurred—TV True Crime. Manny, hands trembling, slick of hair, his gruff gangster voice halting as he answered the prosecutor's questions. But then, I never saw him at all, this stool pigeon, rat of a low budget *Godfather*, third-rate rip-offs Father Flynn and I watched shamelessly in the common room of Loyola on a Saturday night when Flynn could no longer bear my meandering game of chess. Our pretense: dipping into the culture of violence held some thin pedagogical benefit, a connection to our students, wise city kids.

"I am not good," Rita said, "not a good person." The red stain on her neck now the port wine of a birthmark. "They have hidden him. They will hide me, Joey, change my name."

"Rita Murphy, do you know what this man"—this low-life, I believe I said—"has been involved in? Give it up."

"Give him up?"

"This isn't your life." As though I was the stoolie, I spilled forth the unspeakable crimes imagined in my sister's drama. Extortion, perjury, fraud. Murder. I took her plump hand in mine. The gold ring on her finger was designed as two hands entwined, as I had been told to clasp Rita's each morning when she was still in my charge as we went down the lane, turned into Pleasant Street on our way to school. "I'll arrange to come on my visits more often. It will be lonely without Bel. Consider your work, your profession."

"Consider? The way you talk, Father Joe." Rita had found her tongue: "Like a book since you went off to the seminary. Pray, you mean pray. For what end? To grow old with her sideboard and dining room chairs? I thought you believed in a second chance. Isn't that what your prayer is all about? A second chance?"

I could not counter that with faith or reason.

As for the dining room chairs, the offer was merely polite. Isabel Murphy's worldly goods were assigned to her daughter years back. I remember the day my mother—Bel, as she wanted her children to call her—Bel led me out to the willow tree. We sat hidden in its weeping branches. My mother's hair still dark with its fly-away tendrils, though her boy had gone early gray. Just back from missionary duty in Salvador. I had witnessed much hunger, much bloodshed, and was punished with the reward of an easy assignment—teacher of math, though it was not my subject. Evening under the willow tree, Summer, as it is now. Bel drew her knees up to her chin like a girl. The sky darkened.

"If we were out in the lane," she said, "we could watch the storm come in from the sea. Lately, I like to be sheltered."

"We're not sheltered."

"Don't, Joey, don't be sensible like your sister. This old tree is rotten to the core. I suppose we're in danger."

"Taking our chances?"

"Your father," Bel said, "truly believed in unforeseen eventualities. The week before he died he spoke of risk management. He'd been at a pep rally in Hartford, prompted to speak the new terms, *sell the product.*"

How often she made light of that phrase. "Tim," she'd say, "you don't need to sell us the product." And that dear man laughed with her, knowing we were safe in his care, most particularly his wife with scatty ways, as the song goes—*her ups, her downs.* Our dad was no Professor Higgins. Bel chose her transformation, her life with us—the assurance of husband, children, the quaint house safely positioned on a cliff above the sea.

The willow brushed our faces while the first fat raindrops fell, and my mother told me that the house with the furnishings she dusted, waxed, dutifully cared for, would all go to Rita as well as whatever was left of the generous payoff from Tim Murphy's insurance on his life.

"She will be *comfortable.*" Bel laughed at yet another of Dad's words proposing ease in the future, skirting grief. "What do you want with dollars, Joey? With things? What do you want with *comfort?*"

Not the first time I heard dismissal in Bel's voice when she spoke my father's professional lingo, but the sharp note was directed at me. I was home from the War of the Gospel, as we called it doing liberation theology. My mother placed me in the edited version of death squads and massacres that appeared on the evening news, not the day-by-day life shared with the poor. I did not correct her with the bare facts of my story: I had made love to a girl now long dead. In the wake of love I'd had my bout with the bottle. I had never confessed, not counting the pleasure we took in our bodies a sin, writing our own doctrine at Anima Mundi, a Catholic ashram of sorts. Costumed in saffron robes to please Fiona O'Connor, who I bedded or who bedded me, scrambling Loyola and Aquinas in Bengal nights, the path of joy and the path of pleasure meeting in our exercise of love. Bel wished the life of a hero upon me, of a celibate, counting that heroic. I was not ignorant of her motive. She wanted me untouched by the everyday traffic of the flesh, offering the higher life, defying the weight of our humanity in a levitation granted to the saints and angels painted on celestial domes, creatures bodiless or discreetly draped.

Ours was a drama pitched high as the gods I once loved in Ovid, doomed son and mother, but we played it as melodrama. Mother and priest. I did not understand that worn plot until Fiona O'Connor abandoned me to excessive heartbreak, the self-pitying sort that should have cut me up as a boy. It was then I elected celibacy, a self-punishing act of adolescent revenge, and gave in to Bel's belief that I'd sail from the safe shore of faith to deeper waters, contemplate such matters as error in the exercise of freedom. Or the death of Adam, if that's where our mortality was launched? Seer and Sybil questions, no longer up for discussion, but how would I know, liberation in Salvador assigned to history as I dealt with the daily equations of the schoolroom. For over twenty years I came on my visits. After my morning walk, when I might or might not say my matins, I graded student papers at her kitchen table, slow and deliberate in my corrections, so that she might see numbers don't lie. Still, she believed her boy lived adventures of the mind. In the chance it might be true.

The sky grew dark that day under the rotting willow, a clap of thunder and the three magic seconds till lightning struck but did not discover us. We ran for the house, our clothes drenched. Bel's elation as she toweled me off. It was a moment for me to come clean, but I remember my misdirection, the route I take often. I told my mother why the lightning channel is forked, the electrical discharge seeking out the path of least resistance through the intervening air.

"Ah, Joey!" she said, full of admiration for my schoolboy brights. No more was said of my sister's inheritance. Nothing ever said of the lost girl, Fiona. That summer the old willow was uprooted in a storm. Bel's efforts with birdbath and lilies never paid off. The backyard looked naked, disclosed.

. . .

The day after we laid our mother in the ground, I recalled Rita's good fortune: "You'll want for nothing. You'll be comfortable."

Rita scraped her chair from the kitchen table. The red splotch on her neck violent in the heat. She pulled at the yellow T-shirt stuck to her breasts. "They always said this house caught the breeze off the bay. I never found it to be true. Manny prefers climate control, central A/C. That Gemma," she said, changing the subject, "coming to Bel's funeral dressed like a Gypsy."

My sister flapping about the kitchen in her checkered pants. Have I mentioned the silver sandals with glittering roses stuck between her puffed arthritic toes?

"We're not speaking of that Gemma."

"Bel made a pet of her when we were kids. I call her a nuisance." She drew a firm line through a week on the Prudential calendar. "And I can't imagine why you brought up the excursions. They were daffy. Tooling about in the Buick when we should have been in school. I'll take my own trip, thank you, see the country."

I thought it best to clear my head before I resumed my heated persuasion, my winning argument with Rita. Somewhere over the years I'd lost the care of my sister, as though caring was a book I'd

48

laid aside when the lesson was hard, or written in a language I could not translate. My breviary's rote prayers were no solution. Rita's life seemed a Classic Comix version of an ancient tale in which the daughter is offered to the gods, then rescued as an unthreatening plush beast. A miserable few minutes down our lane, no breeze from the bay, I turned back at once to run home, *our home*, all that our mother made of this place.

As a priest I must counsel my sister. Years since I dealt wisdom from my meager store with the peasants in Salvador. I never counseled them to accept their tribulations, that God in His unspeakable mercy . . . In my fractured Castilian, I urged women who would never see their sons and husbands again, men marked for death by the Nacionales, to save themselves by any deception. I still counsel, a double-talk to the anxious parents of my students, soothing the wound of their children's failure. To the kids themselves, dim or simply distracted by the exponential entertainments of the world, I offer the rewards of hard work, faith in themselves, not the Lord.

So—what to say to Rita. No common language between us yet, as I rounded the hedge, I found myself running up the cement path with over-the-counter advice, ready for whatever confrontation. She was silhouetted in the hot yellow light from the hall window above. Hefting two enormous suitcases, she began a torturous thump, thump, thump down the stairs.

"You are not going today," I cried out as an order.

"What would I be waiting for?"

"Your house, your things . . ."

"Don't take me for a fool, Joe. It's all been arranged." She clamped the coolie hat on her head and marched out into the unforgiving heat of the day. Then, like a good brother who must befriend his sister, or like the coward Bel never wanted for a son, I wrestled the bags from her, carried them to the car. In the back seat the paraphernalia of the career she was abandoning—canes, a discarded crutch. She handed them to me, and in the triumphant grin on her girlish face, I saw how determined her departure, how literal her trip to a new life. Meeting up with Manny ———, who had been granted witness protection, a form of legal absolution, my sister-no-longer would assume a new identity. I could not know her destination.

I held Rita by the plump arm I twisted when we were kids. "Squeal, squeal," I'd say to get some worthless secret from her. Now I simply asked in defeat, "What's arranged?"

"Check the kitchen table with your teapot, Father Joe."

Sealed in her car, she turned the key in the ignition, fiddled at the dashboard for the comfort of A/C, and with a screech of tires she was off on her mysterious journey. I ran after her to the end of our lane, waving the crutch and canes in the infernal air, calling her back, "Rita! Rita!" Perhaps my sister's transformation was immediate. She no longer answered to that name.

I walked back to the house, past the Mangiones, the Dunns. Bel laughed at the come-latelies who named their cottages. "*Done Roamin', Safe Haven!* What shall we call it, Tim? *Trail's End.*"

My father did not get the joke, if joke it was.

· · ·

The day of my sister's departure was tropical, no relief in the humid air. I went directly to the kitchen table. Rita had not cleared our breakfast plates. An envelope bulging with legal arrangements was set against Bel's teapot. My mother and sister had been living in *our home* for months on what is termed a lease-back. Rita was in the money. I imagine her figuring the probability of Bel's death from one of Dad's actuarial tables. The quaint cottage by the sea was now the property of Damien Forché, by profession a fashion photographer. The Reverend Joseph Murphy,

S.J., was allotted reasonable time to remove his personal possessions, to sell or distribute whatever household furnishings. . . .

The arrangements: for a week marked on the calendar, the house is mine to live in. Then where will I go? Back to Loyola, to chess with Paul Flynn, who detects despair in my thoughtless moves—*Look to your knight,* game after game, *cover your ass, Joe.* I suspect he let me win on occasion, but Paul will be hiking, working off pounds of the winter's indulgence, his red beard unkempt. Each Summer the Trail until he is counted a Thru Hiker, his journey complete, Georgia to Maine, each lap of the Appalachians with its story. There is the prospect of retreat, a military term, the prescribed refreshment for the soul in which I may dwell on the past with little forgiveness, imagine the future without hope. That's far too romantic.

Or I can settle myself in a room bare of identity, an old priest on a narrow bed with a white cotton coverlet. Plastic chair and battered desk, items discarded when computers were installed in the common room. Crucifix on the wall. Lumpy reading chair worn at the arms to its dry rubber stuffing. One window, the shade drawn against the disturbance of a city street. Theological works scribbled with my queries and emendations are stashed on a top shelf above my black garments and civvies, works abandoned for questions concerning the landless people in Aguileres, *an option for the poor.* The poets are stacked behind math books used for instruction. My poets of contemplation, can I still name them? Herbert and Donne—*love's mysteries in soules do grow*—Sidney and Southwell—*I wage no warre, though peace I none enjoy*—muddling their lines, though I am quite clear about their attraction. They were to step up to the plate for me, replace my faltering faith with cadence, rhyme, a change of heart—*and yet the body is our booke.* Better the teacher's manual with the algebraic answers, figuring Father Joe might not figure. The room plain, ugly, a spare cell, yet I would say I am quite comfortable. On the desk, photos I no longer see, though I can describe in detail my mother's hair streaked with silver, her gardening pants worn at the knee, my father sporting a golf cap, left hand hiding in his suit pocket, Rita smiling *cheese, cheese* in cap and gown with the certificate of her profession in hand. My few companions, those left in the Society, allow themselves radios, cell phones, thrillers, small-screen TVs. All but Flynn regard me as scraped to the bone of my priesthood.

• • •

When Joseph Murphy came fresh to the seminary, the first rousing retreat set him to reading the Spiritual Exercises *of St. Ignatius who founded the order. He was eager to embrace obedience, to work at the progress of his soul from clever boy to . . . He could not say to what spiritual state he aspired. To be good, then better, humble. His mother wanted him to be the best. Joe sensed that, perhaps before he could speak, just reply with a smile to her expectation. It did not occur to her Joey until he was in the novitiate that she named him after the carpenter who fathered no one. Obvious as the delicate nose on her face. Isabel Murphy placed him as nobody's lover, though he was aware that in the family romance he was hers. That seemed home free for a priest, safe as houses. As the shingle house in Rhode Island. St. Ignatius' instructions, which he studied in earnest, were clear about celibacy. His body belonged to Christ.*

Though once his body was given to a girl beautiful as his mother. A student who gave herself to him with abandon and he took. He was teaching rhetoric at Fordham, plugging away at a dissertation on the poetry of contemplation when, in the summer recess, he yearned for a pastoral post. Is that the real story or what he would tell his superiors or what he told himself in seeking out spiritual adventures at Anima Mundi. Jesuits protesting that undeclared war were in prison while he was scanning The shepherds sing; and shall I silent be? *Not silent, a* self-appointed overseer for a commune of Catholics who stationed themselves in an abandoned school, free spirits of the Sixties, only it was the Seventies. Folk song and ecumenical prayer. The bombing of Hanoi again: the many meetings and manifestos not silent yet not heard. Clever quotes of the educated: The weak in courage are strong in cunning. That really got to the crooks in the White House. Mundi politics—simply reinventing the world: the project was wearing thin. His long subway ride downtown, neglecting his duty to students and his poets. A grown man with the open face of a boy—still unused to the traffic of life in general, in particular to bodies, the thigh pressing his on the F train, the grope, the eyes of a woman traveling his broad forehead, tight lips, returning with a smile to the noose of white collar. Then the change of costume, T-shirt and jeans for the next act. Then Murphy went missing, the sleepovers at Mundi, like kids up past bedtime with their endless talk, his encounter with the girl named Fiona, his thoughts of her immediate as the odor of a rose. The girl's freckled cheek was alive, as present as his mother's was necessarily distant, her wild hair the color of garnet, a stone Bel wore in a ring, and her eyes violet blue, the color of the dress his mother wore to his ordination. Foolish, dragging his mother into his thoughts of Fiona, into his love confused by lust.

"Suppose," he once said to the girl, "we were Fiona O'Connor and Joe Murphy, a couple of ordinary micks. Then what would we do?"

They were well past supposing. For some weeks they were blessed with the book of their bodies. He turned her like a prize in their single bed, lifting himself above her to see what must be a miracle, their legs and arms entangled in the light of a street lamp cast through a dirty schoolhouse window. Then she was gone. At the Mundi they said, We are pilgrims, Father Joe, free to come and go. He did not want to hear about pilgrims quoted from their spiritual agenda. Press me not to take more pleasure/In this world of sugared lies—The girl gone. In her place a weight of days followed by inquisition. He did not count their love as sin. They, his superiors, who knew nothing about the swell of her hips, the silken texture of her throat, the lower eye tooth that overlapped slightly, the mole placed like a gem on her right breast, knew nothing of her will to divest, the current word, divest herself of privilege—"As you have," she once said. Absurd, for at that moment he possessed her as the privilege, the angry girl who took her chance on Joe Murphy.

When Fiona disappeared, he could not find her. He could not find her mother, a good soul who came to help the commune with money and untainted kindness. But the Society found him out. He was disciplined for love. Within days of discovering his lapse or his misfortune, they had him on a plane. Salvador—BIENVENIDO! Now there were politics, the real thing. The punishment was just, for Ignatius tells of his rewards in teaching the poor and the prostitutes as Joseph Murphy, S.J., would do in Aguileres. Well, not teaching so much as living in shantytowns with the people in harmony, traveling their dirt roads, eating their bread, witnessing the truth of their oppression. So he would not pronounce upon the contemplative poets in a great university.

When he was a young soldier, Ignatius' leg was wounded in battle and repaired. Still, a bone protruded just under the knee. Vain, he did not want his lady love to see him mangled and asked that his leg be reset. He was crippled ever after, but walked with such dignity his injury was concealed. Slowly he mended his ways, the wild ways of a courtier and lover, got himself educated in Barcelona and Paris. With a band of students he founded a society to teach the way of the Lord. Back story: the Berkshires. When Father Joe goes on retreat, he turns the pages of the Spiritual Exercises, accounting for each day, each hour in which he must balance his spiritual books. He fails to get beyond the world of sense perception, sees the cracked nails of his hands, which hold the book against the black stuff of his trousers. A raised stone in the pavement, the flutter of dandelion seeds, tweet of a sparrow distract him like so many devils. He can't travel beyond here and now to some high road of contemplation. He can never imagine seeing the spot, as

Ignatius instructed, the corporeal world where Christ lived, the desert landscape, humble house with wood shavings, primitive cooking utensils of the sacred place.

He is in a seminary in the Berkshire Hills, Shadowbrook, looking out on Lake Macinac, and can only manage the vision of a small town in Rhode Island—Galilee. During the war he'd gone there with his father, the town transformed to a military installation, nothing like the little fishing village in the Bible. An ensign let him look through a telescope while his father attended to insurance business at a factory. He saw ripples in the channel where nets hung to snag German submarines. As he paced the paths of contemplation in the Berkshires, that day with his father came to mind, not Jesus wandering among fishermen mending their nets. Through a sharp lens of memory, he pictured heavy artillery under camouflage and the crew in training, little sailors scampering like ants on the USS Constellation. On the way home, he told his father he was signing up for the navy, but he was only thirteen. Tim Murphy flipped his good hand off the wheel, a swift and dangerous maneuver, to give his boy a poke of approval, then spoke of insurance against bombardment, his business that day with the factory, which manufactured heavy canvas to be made into duffels and bedrolls for the military.

"For the army," he said, "not navy. Strange how contracts work out."

Trapped in memory that may have its inventions but is always self-referential, Joe, the novice, on retreat. He turns from the Exercises to one story in the Saint's autobiography that a scholar titles A Pilgrim's Journey. Now a lover of Christ, Ignatius, riding a mule, wore sackcloth on his way to the monastery at Montserrat. The monastery's tower, high above on a hill, pierced the heavens. On the low road he met a Moor who laughed at Mary, laughed heartily at the idea of the Virgin birth. When the Moor rode off, Ignatius wanted to follow the infidel, to kill him with his dagger, but just then the road forked. Ignatius stopped.

The mule was God's creature. Let the mule choose the way, that was his thought. The mule began to climb uphill to the tower of prayer and repentance. For years he's stopped counting, Father Joe has lived without will. He reads the story as his, a fable of his passivity. Not the Saint's meaning, and perhaps not a word of it is true, only a work of the imagination.

· · ·

So—I kept the vow named poverty. My personal possessions are the clothes on my back, this day tattered khakis and a shirt from the thrift shop operated by the mothers at Loyola. I read on about my sister's further arrangements with the fashion photographer, then cannot read at all, through tears more blinding than the blindfold of the Nacionales, though then, as now, I see clearly. Ignatius' eyes are often described as misted. I cannot claim his gift of tears. What I have been wanting to say in bookish words picked up at the seminary, attempting to say through this tale of my mother's death told swiftly, and the anecdote of the bright boy outwitted by his dull sister—to confess in this unholy meditation, to say the heart is less bitter than the tongue, my rickety heart more than off-beat: it is a lesion, a festering sore. Or to say, more accurately, that if death is counted at the moment when the spirit leaves the body, I have been at death's door for thirty years.

I never knew them—mother and sister. I dropped in on their lives, a visitor to these women I loved improperly or not at all. How many times, Joe Murphy, did you con them, never reveal your mistrust in the higher life? And if you could call them back from death and departure, would you have the nerve to say it? To say there may be no higher life. Muffins of childhood, a withered cheek tilted up for the kiss, Gypsy costume of Gemma Riccardi, the rewards of a sound insurance policy must suffice. Our music of the spheres is a Sousa march.

MOVIETONE

Wind flaps a dark curl escaped from her aviator's helmet. Fear battles determination in her big, beauteous eyes. In a long shot we see her little biplane, a one-seater, heading into STORM. Angry surf, palms bent to a tropical shore. The plane banks in a dramatic maneuver, the little man-made toy valiant in its flight against the might of nature. We see the control dials wavering, hear the engine sputter, and down she goes, down in a breathtaking spin, crashes in exotic vegetation. This could be the end, but we are not far into the script, which has been largely rewritten. The calm before the storm has been shot in sequence: Dinky AIRFIELD, war-hero Dad, spunky daughter learns to fly. Small-timers bucking for the big government contract. Dad hires a manly fellow—handsome daredevil—who will make the long flight, prove the little airline is up for the job. Should the girl's loyalty to her father overcome her spitfire love for the arrogant pilot who risks everything to beat out the corrupt corporation, make it big-time?

The plane crashing, smoke and mirrors in JUNGLE. A crane working the scene here, swooping down on a fractured wing. Isabel Maher, in an aviatrix costume, snaps off her goggles, climbs out of the smoldering wreckage, smudge on her cheek, rips at the flaps of her helmet, stomps through the undergrowth, bewildered by her turbulent emotions.

. . .

I remember the Mexican children, the girl's sticky hand held out for a coin. A brother and sister, I suppose, urchins who stole past the porters, the doorman, the imperial desk with its uniformed lackeys. The big brother, seven or eight, opened a cardboard box to show us his wares—sugar skulls and tin skeletons, an open pack of Lucky Strikes, a length of red ribbon, a near-empty spool of thread. We were in Santa Barbara, at the Biltmore. We had driven up from L.A.—the honeymoon before the marriage my father might call it, though he knew nothing of my affair with Bill Banks, my man at the moment, as well as the director on my last film. He had taken a chance, dealt me the lead in *My Darling Daughter*, the only role of any weight I ever played. Banks believed he was riding high at MGM, said we'd both cross over. I knew he was scared of talkies. He had never directed for the stage, was all camerawork, lingering close-ups for depth of emotion, superimposed shots—the past haunting the present. These tricks, and he knew it, would not hold off the day when his actors must answer to his direction with voice. Sound was, love it or leave it, happening. Banks was projecting my future at the studio when the Mex kids came along. He shooed them away.

"You got the goods," he said. "We'll have no problem."

As though we had a contractual arrangement, picture to picture.

"Your voice . . ."

"It's my mother's voice," I said, "minus the brogue."

"It'll serve."

The Biltmore was lush, no doubt still is, curried California—Spanish revival—patios, fountains, bougainvillea. The little sister, with braids and a silver hoop in one ear, was barefoot. She could not take her eyes off our plates. Huevos rancheros. We had eaten the eggs and left the thick slabs of steak. An excess of tortillas and toast, a pitcher of orange juice Bill laced with gin from a silver flask—ten o'clock in the morning. I took a tin skeleton out of the cardboard box. The skeleton's limbs dangled. He danced on the edge of my plate.

"*Los Días de los Muertos*," Bill said, "Halloween."

I noted his displeasure when the girl held out her hand. We had come down from our suite without a dime. The boy grabbed a tortilla, then one for his sister. Our waiter—costumed south-of-the-border like a chorus boy in a musical of the Thirties, but it was 1928, we had not arrived at Hollywood's desperate cheer—he came down hard on the children, whacked the cardboard box. Skeletons and sugar skulls, Luckies skidded across the tiles.

"Stop, you must stop," I cried. Until this moment there had

been something charming about the scene, the little peddlers working the room, smiles of the elegant extras enjoying their rich breakfast fare. The punishment of the children did not stop. They were carted off to the kitchen like plaster props, toys. I recall the boy's face blank with acceptance, or I say that to piece this together for Gemma Riccardi. My memory of many years ago adjusted to a story. The adventures of Isabel Maher, not fit for my son or daughter.

The skeleton lay next to my plate. The children had not been paid for this gruesome trinket. I left the table, left Bill Banks, who I'd interrupted well into the rewrites of our current picture, an aeronautical drama, just left without a word and found my way through a swinging door obscured by a screen draped with a Spanish shawl. In the kitchen I walked by fiery burners, by the sweltering staff in their starched white uniforms, by the witch's cauldrons that might consume children. The lady was not to come into this secret place, but they did not dare stop me when I asked for the Mexican kids. One mustachioed man with a fierce chopper in hand, a Chicano, shrugged in the direction of yet another padded door. I ran through a trail of halls and storage rooms that finally opened to sunlight. The children, eating the last of their tortillas, were squatting by a fountain in a blazing patio with birds-of-paradise all around. I took off my dainty gold watch, an expensive token from Banks at the outset of our alliance. The watch was all case, cheap works. It kept rotten time. The girl wondered at this gift, but the boy, that elderly child, accepted whatever token or penalty came with the day. His simple *Gracias*. Our understanding was complete. I found my way around the gardens and paths of the Biltmore and came back to our table as though I'd been off to powder my nose. The children's wares cleared off the set.

Bill Banks had gone up to our room, was throwing his silk shirts and pajamas into a suitcase. His tennis racket, buckled in its leather case, lay on the bed.

I had made a scene.

"Little Merry Sunshine." Banks was good at exasperation. I could not deliver my outrage again, improve my performance. My director was lean and tan, yet his face was heavy, full cheeks, an important nose, which he now sniffed at me in disdain.

We drove back to Los Angeles in silence. From on high, the stunning view of the Pacific along the coast, scrubby wildflowers tumbling down to neat orange groves, pickers hunched over row upon row in truck farms. I did not love this seasonless place, did not love this man who would leave me off at the bungalow I rented with another pretty girl, Lotte Grauber, a hopeful, no talent, never got a break. Bill kept his eye on the road, now and then honoring my wrist with a glance, its faint white circle, the ghost of a gold band.

"Sorry about the watch."

"Screw the watch. You think you did those kids a favor? When they pick them up, you think they'll believe some cockamamie story? Mary Pickford gave them the watch."

So it was not my touching gesture that set Banks against me, but his late discovery that I was naïve, not up to his game. We parted at the curb. I felt exposed, naked to my neighbors on a golden end of day, stranded with my suitcase on the narrow walk leading to the bungalow, as though I had just arrived in this city of childish dreams. I thought my director might deliver his usual line: "When you going to move out of this dump?"

But he called out to me, all business, "See you, Isabel, at five."

. . .

Lotte Grauber was writing a letter in her scrolling German hand. She was dressed in checked gingham, frilled apron, bows. We'd met up at the Miramar, single occupancy only, a fleabag full of hopeful musicians, actors, writers. I wish I could say Lotte knocked on my door to borrow a buck or silk stockings. It was stamps she wanted, however many to send a letter home. Tears in her eyes, *Danke*. I understood enough of her English. She'd been a dancer, music hall Munich, but the gelt was here. The tears were for back home and for the language she could not speak. Lotte paid good money to a fraudulent voice coach, Professor of Diction and Elocution. When that didn't work out, she consulted a Gypsy, who predicted she would cross over, possessed of a silver tongue. If Lotte crossed over it would be walking on water.

"I must *sprechen*, Izzy."

Lotte was not an attentive pupil.

She did not need words to dance, to parade her diminutive body, a Gretel doll with a mop of blond curls. Lotte was on the town, nightclubs, parties with a chorus of chorus boys in attendance. She worked enough to get by, and when I struck gelt, more than a serial, more than one-reelers, when I was Isabel Maher with an agent, my name in the credits, I rented a furnished bungalow, a pretty little place in a row of bungalows, a street with tricycles and kids, with fathers who drove off to work, mothers who called their children home from play. I asked Lotte Grauber to come along. The rent was cheap.

When she had an audience Lotte was a confection, delicious and naughty. At home she was sorrowful, "Oh, Izzy!" Oh, if she had English words. It wasn't the words she needed. It was talent. Lotte was raw ambition. The old burning desire—to see her name in lights. We were an odd pair. Lotte on the town, I stayed home with my scripts, thin stuff I grazed before turning to my books. I gobbled up novels, finding the men and women on the page more substantial than the characters in my working life, losing myself in the story, any story—the soppy romance of *Lorna Doone*, tough talk of Hemingway—but when I looked up there was no kindly old man in Connecticut who let me read well past bedtime, my father with a loupe in his eye plotting the marvels of his work-man's watch. So quiet in the bungalow I could hear the dust jacket tucking in to keep my place. Then I would wash up, not looking at my scrubbed face. Oh, I'd seen it often enough, blurred with doubt. I had my measure of talent, insufficient ambition. Back home, I was a rank amateur, hadn't a notion of how to play, really play to a live audience, which now worked to my advantage. Easy before the camera, the lens was my audience, capturing every stud-ied emotion. We were intimate, the ground glass eye and Isabel Maher. I liked the work, had a flair. A natural, they said, the men who directed me, but I didn't like watching the rushes. Always—I gather you know this, Riccardi—there's always room for improve-ment. But that's not it—I disliked myself magnified, turned away from my enormous eyes, the grotesque mouth of a close-up.

. . .

At first she wanted to love herself up there, all shadow and light, the il-lusion she's really someone, Isabel Maher, but her career had more to do with leaving than arriving, leaving the Brass City, arriving at a destina-tion which fades like a mirage. The screen is a fun house mirror. Our Bel, our Izzy, is not self-enchanted. When the beautiful boy Narcissus falls for the beautiful boy in the pond, he's overcome with desire. Noth-ing will do but the wet kiss of self-consumption. No mirrors in the woods where Narcissus ran free, sloughing off lovers, until his fatal self-reflection in the pond's glass surface. Isabel Maher is well acquainted with mirrors. When she was a girl, the crazed mirror in her bedroom told her she was a beaut, the one with the cupcakes. At Sal's Beauty Box the mirror displayed a hometown beauty. On the set, she watches the mask-ing of her face as they paint her for the camera. Though she speaks out of season, she knows the Day of the Dead and is delighted that Banks got it wrong. It's the day after—All Souls', not Halloween. No cos-tumes, just the graveyard sweets and toys, lively music. Bel hung the ex-pensive tin skeleton on her dressing table in the bungalow, seeing her passing pretty face and his sly grimace in one frame. Pretty enough child, *her mother said,* but we set little store by that. Your nose is a muffin, not grand enough to sniff at the world. *She pulled the child's wild black curls into a braid.* Plain will do us. *But Maeve Maher was never to see her daughter's nose come into its graceful arch, or the plump chin slim to a delicate point. Bel's mother no longer went to the clockmaker's grand house to order the servants about. Maeve moved with caution about the kitchen and pantry preparing for her absence, tidied the closets, pressed Pat's Sunday shirt.* Belle, that's "beautiful" in French, don't you mind it. We speak a simpler language. *The girl knew her mother intended to set her straight if she died bearing the child she carried, a risk at her age. When she scrubs herself clean of rouge and lipstick, she sees a woman of twenty-six with a waning desire to be someone, or be other than Maeve and Pat Maher made her.* Plain will do us.

Without the glacial beauty of Garbo or the kiss-me-cute class of the Gish sisters, Bel traded on her looks in her brief movie nights and days. Isabel Maher, with the flecked amber eyes set a bit too deep, turned on the charm in an instant, as easily withdrew it. She was a girl you wanted to look at. Long after the plot of the movie, you remembered her tilted smile, its wry withholding. Not taken with her face or her body on film, yet over the years she will think what they made of her in makeup as she buys a lipstick, fusses with her hair still unruly and for a moment thinks what she made of herself, the contractual value put on her looks. A thought worth a half-second in Brandle's drugstore or the rearview mirror of her Buick. No way through the looking glass, her reflection is simply herself.

· · ·

Banks had a shooting schedule of four weeks. I'd see him at five the next morning to get the early light. We were to shoot the first scenes on a studio lot set up as an airfield, little planes and a rinky-dink hangar. As I stood on the front walk, the bungalow did look like a dump, its coat of thin plaster crumbling. My director drove off to his house in Brentwood, to his wife, who expected him for cocktails, to his children, disguised for Halloween.

"Vhy *haben* this pout?" Lotte stood at the foot of my bed in gingham and bows. She saw something had gone awry with Banks. She lived off the heartbreak and triumphs of studio girls. "Come on, Izzy, voonderful parrty." Always a party. Now more than ever, parties to distract from the voiceless fear. I heard them honking for her. Then they invaded our little storybook house—a flabby Ben Hur and a Baron with a dueling scar, perfect escorts for the milkmaid with a comic German accent. Halloween seemed unnecessary in this town. We were like children every working day, costumed, begging for handouts.

That night, before I turned to my reading, I studied the script, mouthed the lines I would speak, though no one in the audience would hear me console my father, who flew over Château Thierry to stake out the Huns' position. No Escadrille Lafayette. That story would be cut. No angels with engines. No one would get my sharp tongue as I sassed the handsome pilot. My heroic flight seemed unlikely, one step up from the bread-and-butter serials I'd been assigned to. Banks had been dealt a bum picture. I had a swell contract. At four-thirty in the morning they combed me, dressed me. A photographer from *Movie Star News* shot me waving from the cockpit before he was thrown off the set. My director was bloated, red-eyed. I presumed he'd had a night, the wife's trick-or-treat, a night after our nights at the Biltmore. The script trembled in his hand.

"Leaden," Banks said to the writer. "Give them a couple of laughs!"

The writer stood up to his scolding bravely. Meyer Wolf, a kid out of college just into this trade. A few jobs as a title writer, this was his first script, another hopeful. We were losing the soft light of sunrise. I thought, They should have duked this out before production began, before the dollars spun off like a strip of film flapping out of control. We waited, stars and crew. The writer said people could laugh at the shorts, his script had social purpose, which sent our director into foul-mouthed fury. They powdered me down, spritzed my hair again with sticky brilliantine. Banks won, as I knew he would. The writer was through.

That night, Meyer Wolf called.

"I have no pull with the director." I felt it might be true, though Banks slipped back to intimacy, just a touch in the small of my back, a tilt of my head for a shot with a hand that lingered.

Meyer Wolf said: "It's not the fuckin' picture. Sorry, Isabel."

"That's OK."

He asked if he could come round. Lotte was entertaining a German director, a man recently arrived in California who didn't know Lotte Grauber was no one in particular. I didn't want Meyer to see her attempt at American flapper, so I sat on the front porch of the bungalow with this tightly wound young man, his eyes blinking behind thick glasses, blinking as though he did not believe the swift pace of the studio, the smart talk, the money calling us all to the big parade. He was scrawny, I thought underfed, but I would learn Meyer ate heavy Jewish food as though he would never eat again.

He asked, "So what did you do before you got into this racket?"

"Teacher. Eighth grade. Public school."

"Gosh, Isabelle Maher!"

"No gosh, just what I did nine months of the year."

"You are working-class!"

I laughed, couldn't help it, my father assuming I had come up in the world with my education, my advancement to the coveted eighth-grade position in the Maplewood School. In a rags-to-riches interview in *Photoplay*, I was the daughter of poor working folks. Not quite true, and true is the way I must tell it. Gemma, all dodging, dissembling canceled in the afterlife. When I was a child, I believed there was a sort of celestial library where a big book had my name on the cover, much like the book with *Riccardi* stamped in gold. Isabel Maher: all the sins and good works of my days set down. There would be a reckoning, hell or heaven meted out, perhaps a mild sentence in purgatory. Well, it's simply lonely and damp in this place, like our house after Tim died. I am speaking out of turn. No one has come to my grave with flowers and crumb cake. I am consumed by their silence.

In fact my father worked in a foundry. . . . Ansonia, Connecticut. The Brass Capital of the world. He cast parts for clocks, elegant little gears and escapements that ticked away time. Some molds were of his invention. So you see, Patrick Maher was not poor. He was not in his first youth when he married a woman from Ireland who kept house for the old gentleman who owned the clock company. My parents were successful in their way. Maeve was my mother's name. When she died I was seven, a little girl, yet I sounded so like her, as though her voice had been recorded and played on a miniature Victrola set in my tender throat. When my father came home from work, I'd call out to him or sing a little tune. "Maeve!" he'd cry, as though she was still with us. Our own Nellie Melba, they said when she sang in church, though there was little singing then—the carols at Christmas; at the end of High Mass, Schubert's "Ave Maria." Not her unwavering high C, or her everyday voice with the pure note of her passing kindness or hush of correction, it was my mother reading at bedtime that branded my heart.

Though she was tired from the day's housekeeping for the strict lady of the clock company, from cooking and washing up after our supper, our reading was sacred. My after-school hours were spent with a daffy neighbor who crocheted endlessly, dealt herself solitaire and fiddled with the ivory needle of her phonograph to coax a popular tune. I believe my mother ached to be home with me, but her position directing the maids, cook, gardener of the Victorian mansion with a view of the Pequonnock River, had a distinction about it. I knew this as a child and was pleased with her honor in our small industrial city. After supper I had her all to myself, so there was no question of balking at bedtime. I sat at attention propped up in my bed, its iron curlicues stuck with brass balls at the end like golden jawbreakers. My mother took her place in the rocker, book in hand. *There was an old woman who lived in a shoe.* The rhymes I liked better than stories. Though they were for very young children, I'd beg them from her. Then her voice came to me as song, with stops and starts that were thrilling. "Belief" is the worn word that comes to mind. I believed *There was a little girl*, you know that girl with a *curl / Right in the middle of her forehead*. I believed *Hickory, dickory, dock* and *Bobby Shaftoe's gone to sea, / With silver buckles on his knee.* Now that there is no going back, Gemma, I might say that I believed in Maeve Maher's performance, if that's not too fancy-pants—for her voice was never that. It was as strange a gift or blessing as perfect pitch, and all she did with it was sing from the loft stuck at the back of our church and read her girl rhymes and stories all true to me. When she was gone from us, attempting to bear another child, to have a family, you see, I held on to my belief *the clock struck one, and down he come* and *Pretty Bobby Shaftoe he'll come back and marry me.*

At home I took up my mother's duties, the care of the house and the man who grieved with never a word assembling brass parts at the kitchen table. He had contempt for the electric clocks they were now turning out at the factory. So—Pat Maher began building his workman's watch, accurate to the tenth of a second, one that would adjust automatically to the Greenwich Mean Time no matter where you might be in what season of the year, a wonderful watch. "Mean time?" He explained as best he could, or as best I could comprehend, about a magic site in England, until, tired of my questions, he stuck a loupe in his eye, the better to see the tiny works. Each evening when I finished washing up, I sat with him and read, careful not to disturb the gears and tiny screws that lay about. Counting myself grown, I did not read the old rhymes. I read a set of *Chatterbox* books put out for children at Christmas, full of games and stories illustrated with lovely pictures. Well, I did not know they were long out of fashion, thought them grand, the lithographs of wild animals and sailing ships, of boys and girls in the midst of their moral adventures. I gave myself wholly to my reading, to stories more real than lessons at school, the children on the page drifting in and out of my head.

My father was a large man with a strong head of white hair and white beard like St. Nick on the cover of a *Chatterbox*, portly, too, but not jolly. Absorbed in his invention, he lost track of time. When I looked up from the page, there was the pocket watch without hands, the numbers circling the white face of no hour at all. Way past bedtime he discovered me: "Isabel, put your book away. Tomorrow is another day."

Tomorrow might hold some hope beyond the continuation of our sorrow. Each night he sat in my mother's rocker by my bed and told me about his watch, how it might be strapped to the wrist and wind itself with the movement of an arm, how he might devise it to chime accurate to the second. He would write away to the Patent Office in Washington. It was an odd bedtime story with diamond chips and emeralds so tiny you could not see them with the naked eye. *Gemma, what is it you want to know?* That my mother turned me into a bookish girl, that I grew beyond my father's mechanical dreams and *The Chatterbox,* that Patrick Maher sat by my bed no more. I would leave him after supper to the action of his coiled springs, or he would leave me to go down to the cellar, where he set up a small shop to draw detailed plans of his watch, the case yet to be fabricated, a workingman's case of brass or base metal. It would outsell the Ingersoll Dollar Watch.

. . .

Until, one day in school, I was made to recite a poem. *I was a child and she was a child, / In this kingdom by the sea, / But we loved with a love that was more than a love—/I and my Annabel Lee.* Then I heard the eerie likeness that startled my father, the cadences of my mother's voice pulsing in my throat, spilling out of my mouth. My classmates, ready to snicker at any pretension, were silent. In the hushed classroom, a nub of respect, even awe. I thought, Well, that's done it, set me apart, better to be the class clown than the speechifying sort called upon for all trumped-up occasions from grammar school through normal school, where I was taught to teach what was being taught in those days. Miss Isabel Maher will now read a passage from *Evangeline*, will sing (never a voice lesson to my name) Victor Herbert's "Sweethearts," lead us in the Pledge of Allegiance, the Lord's Prayer. *Speak, Monkey. Speak.* My theatrics intoned from every platform and podium in town, so, when I was awarded the honor of teaching the eighth grade, don't you know I directed the variety show. Magic tricks, recitations. One year selections from *The Mikado,* next *Trial by Jury.*

I was courted by Tim Murphy, older by some years. He'd been down the road to Yale for a term, then off to the war, a hero wounded in France. Tim with so many feints and dodges you'd never know the left arm hung dead at his side. Love? You must have wondered about my love for this man you found ordinary, not the only one who wondered. Love, wasn't that one of your questions, Gemma? One of the answers you were after, silent star and insurance agent—how does that come about? And I wondered too—oh, not when you dare not ask me, when I was settled with Tim and our children in the shingle house on the bay. I wondered back in clock time, why I cared for him when we went out with our crowd to the movies, the dance halls, canoed down the river, Tim punting with the good arm. And I did care, believe it, while I

69

thought, This year it's *He's going to marry Yum-Yum* and next *I love him—I love him—with fervor unceasing: / I worship and madly adore,* and after church Tim will drive me home and go all the way round the car to open the door for the lady and come in and listen to my father talk his watch talk, though the old Sessions clock on the wall said Pat had missed Mass again.

Idling at the starting line. No one blew the whistle. Primed for the performance. The curtain never went up. Which is to say, I felt as you did, Gemma, when you came to me in my garden, that there was another Riccardi, another Isabel Maher. Someplace else a miraculous mean time set the hours of my life truly, and that watch without hands was the frozen white pond of my life. It would take years to see myself as one of the never ending procession of green girls and boys who set out from the farm, the cottage, the hamlet too small to contain them as in a *Chatterbox* story.

This is how I remember leaving the familiar faces and comforts of home. I am at Sal's Beauty Box, my hair being shingled into the sharp edge of a Twenties bob. It's a Saturday, no school. My music folder with the score of *The Mikado* sits on Sal's dresser with the apparatus of her trade—curling irons, metal instruments to effect rigid marcels, scissors in a tumbler of murky water. Sal a peroxide blonde with a plump, dimpled doll-face, eyebrows drawn on in permanent amazement, rouge aplenty to advertise her Beauty Box. Two women who once knew my mother have smiled sadly upon me, still cherishing my loss. Their tearful memories of Maeve at last silenced under steel hair dryers. So it's me and Sally Donafrio, a chum from high school days, a woman with a boyfriend known to be trouble—drinking, philandering (Sal choosing that word now that I'm a teacher)—a bad egg all around.

"Always the handout, as though I'm in clover." Sal snips at my nape. "And how's your Murph?"

My Murph. "Swell." I suppose it's not even the talk of the town, just when we'll tie the knot—a slip knot, as I've begun to see it.

One old girl pops out of her dryer. "I'm cooked!"

Sal sticks her back under the steel helmet with a *Woman's Home Companion*, returns to my unruly hair with a bottle of brilliantine.

"Just leave it."

"No shine?"

Then Sally Donafrio hands me a mirror to admire the severe cut of my hair, exposing a pale neck. "Gee, Isabel, you're a stunner. What I wouldn't give."

I poke up my chin, make a fish mouth, face to face with what's taken for beauty in the here-and-now of the Brass City. I set no value on this beauty at all.

"I'm fried!"

"Lord, don't you wish she was boiled in oil?" Sal, running to rescue both old ladies from the torture of the Beauty Box. I pay up and I'm off.

Off to the Bijou, which I am granted use of for my variety show, a walk-through on the narrow stage to see how I'll position my kids in their derbies and canes for the skits, their home-sewn kimonos for *The Mikado*. Saturday matinee letting out, the audience blinks into the last of the Spring sun, speechless, under the spell of a ruined life—*Stella Dallas*. In the lobby, this poster:

Tonite!!!

THE MERRY MERCHANTS

The Toast of Broadway!!!

Comedy. Song and Dance.

Starring The Prince of Piccadilly, Alec McBride

Queenie Dundee, Songbird of London and Paris

The Varsity Girls, Dipsomaniac Dogs AND

Baby Rose with the Voice of an Angel!!!

Not the first cut. At least we were on the Keith Circuit, two-a-day vaudeville along with the movie. A tearjerker wasn't enough for your money. Alec McBride, the headliner, with scraggly whiskers, high-stepping in a battered top hat and gentleman's tails. Queenie, full-bosomed, sniffing an admirer's rose.

The empty Bijou filled me with awe, the candy box gilt of the mezzanine, the blue sky of its dome with doves and angels forever approaching the crystal chandelier, velvet draperies pinned back for murals of maybe Versailles or Rome. I had the theater to my-self, lights up, no blink-eyed audience in the aisles after the show. Still, I had always preferred the flickering dark, in which I lost my-self like most girls eager for the terror, poised for the kiss of a happy end. I will tell you, even now a shameful confession, Gemma Riccardi, though embarrassment was never in my bag of tricks, I will tell you that I saw myself up there, that I mouthed the words of the titles as though practicing in front of a mirror, though only when I went to the movies alone. I can't blame my girlish dream on recitations of Poe or Longfellow, the Gettysburg Address or my mother reading *Hey, diddle, diddle, / The cat and the fiddle.* Seeking cover in the dark, I felt chosen, that I should be up there, my smile, my head thrown back in silent laughter, make-believe in which I would one day be discovered and which I out-grew, left behind in the toy store of the imagination.

The stage in the Bijou is bare, the screen snapped up. I begin my blocking, what *A Concise Manual for Drama in Our Schools* tells me is blocking. At the Maplewood School, I hustle my students from the grand sweep of history and geography to the bread and butter of long division and adverbial clauses. Drama is holiday fare, the prize in the heavy pudding of final tests at the end of the year. I'm humming in the empty theater, *Three little girls from school are we,* the *how-de-do* of Gilbert and Sullivan's mocking Oriental splendor, the might of empire playing well in the giddy years after the Great

War. I am prancing the mincing steps of a Japanese maiden as my voice enlarges into song.

> *Here's a how-de-do!*
> *If I marry you,*
> *When your time has come to perish,*
> *Then the maiden whom you cherish*
> *Must be slaughter'd, too!*
> *Here's a how-de-do!*

Someone accompanies me. Down in the pit, someone dims the house lights, someone plays Sullivan's tune on the untuned piano, which rumbles the low key of gloom, tinkles the happy resolution of the weekly serial. Someone with a plummy actor's voice suggests, "A bit of a stretch, dear girl. Take it down."

He strikes a chord. I take my pitch, comfortable in this register, and when I chirp the last *how-de-do*, my pianist reels off *The sun, whose rays*, the opening bars of Yum-Yum's solo, which I've not given to any girl in my class, keeping it to myself—the sweet simplicity, the soft modulations of the bride-to-be that break my heart. I look to the yellow moon just above the dusty chandelier in the Bijou.

> *The sun, whose rays*
> *Are all ablaze*
> *With ever-living glory,*
> *Does not deny*
> *His majesty—*

All the way to Yum-Yum's shameless end—

> *Ah, pray make no mistake,*
> *We are not shy;*
> *We're very wide awake,*
> *The moon and I!*

Applause. One man clapping. The Prince of Piccadilly comes up on stage. He is clean-shaven, ruddy, with the bumpy nose of a stage drunk, the masking odor of peppermint pastilles. It is June, but he's dapper in a heavy woolen suit of a jagged check we call houndstooth. Hot in the Bijou, I figure he's accustomed to the footlights.

"McBride. Formerly of D'Oyly Carte."

"Isabel Maher."

"Are you buried in this backwater, dear girl?"

I tell him we are in the Brass City. The backwater is the Pequonnack, an Indian name. A little maid from school am I, blushing with civic pride. "We make clocks here, and guns."

"An inspired combination."

McBride corrects my prim Oriental walk, tucks my arms together as though concealed in a kimono.

"So when you flip your fan thus—a small surprise for the audience."

But there is no fan. We play to an empty house.

"A silver voice. When, may I ask, do you open?"

I can't say eighth grade, that I prompt my children who won't learn their lines, only snippets of *The Mikado,* the rest of the program is, well, card tricks, a comic recitation by our fat boy, banjo solo, bold Ginny Shea in a tap routine, sing-along "Down by the Old Mill Stream." Gilbert and Sullivan will be a mess, my high-minded attempt to bring them all on stage for a chorus.

"No performance, just practicing." I thank Alec McBride for his instruction and I never forget how gently he turns my face up to the lights. He will recommend me to Flo Ziegfeld, but at the moment doesn't have a card.

Never forget the vaudevillian's sly wink, his cockney twang attempting an American accent, "Sweethaat, you oughtta be in pitchas."

74

Never forget that I'm about to confess to this stranger with an unconvincing wig the idle moments when I still dream myself onto the screen, but then the troupe troops in, on parade up the creaking steps to the stage, making their way back to their dressing rooms, the stuffy backstage cubicles of the Bijou. Baby Rose in a pout, her ringlets in need of the curling iron. The Varsity Girls, six of them, long out of school. Queenie, songbirds stuck on her hat, too grand for the circuit, gives me the once-over. I am dismissed, an intruder. I sneak down the aisle out into the dusk of Main Street, where the Dipsomaniac Dogs sit at sober attention.

That night—a Saturday, when we usually dance or play cards with our crowd, which has dwindled, our crowd married, tending babies—I am at home with my father and the Murph, as Sal calls him. Tim is helping my father write a letter to be directed to the U.S. Patent Office. The watch, grown more and more elaborate, will sport dials within dials, record the day, the month. I set my music portfolio on the upright piano, open to Yum-Yum's aria.

Tim says, "Give us a tune, Bel."

I can't sing a note. My father is describing the accuracy of his workingman's watch to the half-second. I reckon the years of his timeless dream to be eighteen. They are drinking beer that our neighbor Otto Sauer brews in his cellar. It's nine o'clock. I swivel off the piano stool and steal past them to my room. I take down the old valise that may have come with my mother from Ireland. It is our only traveling bag. We do not travel. At nine-thirty, I kiss Tim out the door. I endure Sunday till Monday. When I should be on recess duty, I run to the bank and take out all my savings, not knowing what I was saving for other than a wedding dress. I write a note, which I will leave for my father with the springs and dial where he can't miss it.

The next morning I take the train to New Haven, from New Haven to New York, in New York not recommending myself to

Flo Ziegfeld, sitting up overnight to Chicago. In Chicago I write a letter to Tim Murphy, the envelope splotched with tears. I see him opening it with the good right hand, the quick movement of his fingers as he flips the folded page with the empty assurance of my love, the excuses for which there is no excuse.

I once told you Hollywood stories, censored for a curious girl, bootleg booze and cut-rate jazz, the beaded blue chiffon for the *Photoplay* interview, satin for *The Silver Screen* to play against the curved Art Deco walls favored by MGM, the Production Code that ordered movie husbands and wives to sleep in separate beds while it was custom to bed down in Tinseltown—production to production, but gosh, I'm working-class if it pleases Meyer Wolf, who follows me to my room in the bungalow when Lotte goes off to a party with her German director. I had not unpacked my suitcase with silk pajamas and tennis whites, costumes for my gambol with Banks in Santa Barbara.

"So—before you got into the game?"

"I told you, eighth grade." I threw the soiled clothes in a hamper to be dealt with by the Negro maid who looks after Miss Maher. Meyer picked up a silk evening shoe with a glittering cut-steel buckle, held it at arm's length, a dreadful object. I told him, as I've told you, Gemma, of the dreamy watchmaker employed at the foundry and the housekeeper to the Captain of Industry, such a plain story. As I hung a peach georgette gown in the closet, a few of its gold spangles fell to the floor. Meyer chased them, held them out to me as an indictment. Then wasn't I lectured on *the odious instability of fashion.*

I laughed. "The beads dropping off?"

No laughing matter, those beads had been sewn on by hand. *By hand* made medieval peasants of the people. *By hand* was the obsolete canon of taste, limited editions with thier *pecuniary distinction to the consumer.*

Meyer found Maeve and Pat Maher thrilling types in his bible, Veblen's *Theory of the Leisure Class*. My father's aim at *ideal precision attained only by the machine* was admirable, a challenge to the *canon of conspicuous waste*. My mother's apron and cap of a domestic only emphasized the ornamental idleness of the lady she served. The lady in question was pure Yankee, who exhausted herself with good works, not a frill in her closet, but the guest lounging on my bed was well into *the scheme of pecuniary culture*. Oh, what can be said of Meyer Wolf, who idolized Thorstein Veblen, who wore the same cheap suit and soiled shirt every night, those nights when he came to the bungalow threadbare, patched, buttons dangling— costumed as a radical, one of the rabble or a tenement kid in Griffith's *Child of the Ghetto*.

"Isabel"—stars in his eyes—"you're privileged. Your people are working-class."

Seduction may come in the oddest of forms. I had been praised for my beauty, my acting, my song, for my way with fractions and transitive verbs, but never for being the foundry man's daughter, the housekeeper's lass.

"Take off your glasses," I said, "they're tinted to soften the picture."

He said that in his dreams my clothes fell away.

"Then dream."

It seemed fitting that I was in charge, directing the writer. *Do this. Do that.* A schoolyard game. *Hands on hips. Touch your toes. Your nose.* It soon became apparent that Meyer was passionate, blindly feeling his way, and I was moved by this poor boy down at heel, holes in his socks. I entered his dream of the socially responsible movie, perhaps even the dream of Isabel Maher born again— working-class. The little airline of his script with its old barn for a hangar would triumph over the slick corporate boss. In the morning Meyer groped for his glasses and watched me dress. I left him when the big black car from the studio drew up next to his jalopy. When he came by in the evening, he asked, "What's Banks doing to my script?" No need to answer, he knew what my director was up to, making it light and airy. He'd hired an old-timer who once wrote skits for Sennett's Bathing Beauties, a rewrite man who inserted aeronautical mishaps and a loose-jointed comic to play against the lockjawed hero. Give them a few laughs.

In time that escapes my father's accuracy in Ansonia, I am tracking less than three weeks with Meyer. The doctored picture moving ahead of schedule, Banks getting it out before words were about to spew from actors' mouths in a chattering Tower of Babel. We worked late. We worked Saturdays. My face ashen, eyes bruised with exhaustion, heavy duty for makeup. Now, when I was driven back to the bungalow, Meyer talked with Fritz, Lotte's German. In German. She dressed for the parties—classier, I noted, but we were set aside as pretty girls.

"What are they on about?"

Lotte pouted, "Important Jews in Hollyvood, gelt, *politisch.*" Then she brightened to tell me Fritz had "Vork *mit* Lubitch."

Which may not have been true. Poor Lotte, Fritz's successful compatriots in Beverly Hills were restrained. Lots of *sprechen,* no dancing.

When they left Meyer to me, he'd ask about his script. I could say nothing to please him.

"Garbage," he called the rewrites, "stinks to high heaven," mourning his ruined plot, the downfall of the corrupt giants of rampant industry, the danger of outmoded government regulations. Banks a predator, the male lead a weak matinee idol. A gentle rube was Meyer's idea, a shy, shuffling Lindy, and how could I betray the watchmaker in the foundry, the girl from Ireland stoking the rich man's furnace at dawn? The grand house in Ansonia was equipped with a modern oil burner, but the writer cherished his stories, and after yet another summary of his abandoned plot—the little plane flew into the blue, having secured the coveted contract in the face of adversity—we drove out to a hole in the wall. I watched Meyer eat potato pancakes, herring and boiled beef as prelude to . . . call it lovemaking, which absolved me from my betrayal of the working class. And in the morning I went back to work for Banks.

My last nights and days in the movies, I thrilled to this balancing act, as though I was writing a script of my own with no resolution. Thrilled? As far as feelings go, in the grave memory is a touch dramatic, not diluted like the milk tea I served my children. Still, I had once been an actress, and hope, if that's allowed with its assumption of a future . . . hope what? With my old fashioned recitation, to stir the emotions of Gemma Riccardi, a woman hardened off by her travels, a girl still seeking my answers. You may see my performance as a program of dramatic monologues which aging actresses of note once indulged in between engagements—a bit of Juliet, Desdemona, Hedda, then a comic turn in which the swells take their lumps, finish off with a sentimental reading from Mrs. Browning. Even in our small industrial city such refined entertainments played at the Guild Hall, at the Bijou. And so I began to feel, if I can re-create feeling, that I was trapped in a movie I had already made, the silent that transformed Isabel Maher from starlet to star teetering on the edge of notoriety. *My Darling Daughter,* running the scenes over and over, the girl torn between a brash young lover and the cynical fellow who will save her family's financial honor. Gemma, with your snapshots carefully selected, you may think I ran from an intolerable situation like the pretty girl in that film, which is surely lost, celluloid cracked on the reel.

I knew there would be no honor in Banks' next movie—a passing dollop of fame, but that's not the story. Pressing ahead with two-men-and-a-girl when I was called off the set by Mr. Mayer—not the big cheese himself, a secretary from his office who spoke officiously of the Sound Stage. We knew what this was about,

79

Banks pleased though it interrupted CRASH: *She climbs into a biplane resolute in her purpose, a wave to movie Dad, propeller spinning.* I was called away to be tested. "Look that over." The secretary handed me a page or two of dialogue. An aging bit player—weak chin, hair dyed Valentino black—came into the big blank room, where a camera and a microphone on a metal post awaited our performance. We went over our lines. Then a man from production working with Banks on our fly-by-night drama gave us instructions. We were not to move beyond a circle he paced out on the floor. We must not turn away from the lens of the camera. And so we began, the Movietone standing sentinel, first a test to get the register of our voices. Of my voice. The pitch of the bit payer's fluty words sent a squeal through the mike. We began the scene again. I remember nothing of our dialogue, but when the words were spoken the assistant to the assistant producer called out, "Miss Maher!"

The poor actor pasted down his sideburns, cleared his throat. Dismissed before he read a line. I was given a tattered script of *Major Barbara* marked with Barbara's cues, stage positions.

"Impromptu, no acting."

I wore high boots and canvas pants, the confining costume of the aviatrix, and asked if the test could wait for another day. I had seen Shaw's play in New Haven at the Shubert, taken the bus down with a teacher friend from school, a girls' outing. The actress who played Barbara was grand altogether. I could not face the humiliation of mauling her lines. I would intone, elocute like a back number between engagements. I flipped through the script to find Barbara militant, but a paper clip marked a page toward the end.

"Just read." Movietone dictated the moment.

That's why I have no class, Dolly. I come straight out of the heart of the whole people. If I were middle-class I should turn my back on my father's business. . . . I read on right through the stage directions. *I have got through with the bribe of bread. I have got through with the bribe of heaven.* All of Barbara's impassioned farewell to her ill-spent life of good works. And when I went back to the set, to Banks checking the time lost, to the propeller about to be spun by my war-hero Dad, I still had *Major Barbara* in my hand. Perhaps they did not need it for testing another silent actress—fit or unfit for sound. I took the script back to the bungalow that evening, thinking that Meyer would be amused by Shaw's *middle-class . . .* , but he did not love the upper-crusty language.

"A parlor socialist. So what does it prove? There's a lot of overeducated writers in the business, could have you reading Lady Macbeth, the telephone book. Your voice, Isabel, is the product."

And Meyer didn't fancy the price of theater tickets at the Shubert any more than the hash Banks was making of his script.

I said: "Move on, Meyer. New idea, new story." And then, rather cruelly, "In a few days we'll be shooting the jungle scene."

"Where the hell did he get a jungle?"

"From a serial we made."

"*We made.* Isabel, he owns you. You are an adornment."

"A working girl." But I was tired of being scolded, and that night I sent Meyer home to his family's house in Bel Air, to the velvet lawn and pool, to the indolence and conspicuous consumption that sent him to Stanford to study Veblen.

. . .

He was right. The next day Banks had a proprietary air. "You did swell, kid."

On the set, a press agent and a photographer from a fan magazine took up valuable time, but who cared. When the workday was over, Banks said, "Suppose we have a look-see." Not a suppose, a command. He dismissed the studio car, and I did suppose we were back on more than friendly terms. He took me to a swank office with a screen. Now, this is the scene, not the sordid fisticuffs back at the bungalow that played out that night between Meyer and Banks, Lotte in lacy step-ins, Fritz *in flagrante* chasing my lovers with a fry pan.

This is the scene: palatial office at MGM. Sophisticated set, white on white on white. Publicity shots of leading actors under contract, men and women under the spell of their glamour and gloss. Banks, cock o' the walk, puffed with excitement, hand at the small of my back. I'm his chick introduced all around, Isabel Maher. These men have seen me, seldom in the flesh. We sit in big leather chairs. The room darkens. The flickering movietime light and shadows appear, a bit of blank footage, a mechanical scratching. I face the camera smiling, read my lines to the bit player, who paces in the little circle as instructed. Banks lights a cigarette, squeezes my hand. The scene being played out is rotten, so what. The important men whispering to each other, a murmur of praise for their cranky apparatus, their film synchronized to the sound of my voice. We cut to Barbara, *Major Barbara*. I hear the words of George Bernard Shaw as my mother speaks them, at first with a lilt of amusement, a touch of the brogue. *That is why I have no class, Dolly. I come straight out of the heart.* I am an impostor in my canvas getup, the military jacket of the Great War, but when I close my eyes I hear my mother swoop down to a husky contralto, impassioned, rich with purpose. *I have got rid of the bribe of heaven. Let God's work be done for its own sake; the work he had to create us to do, because it cannot be done except by living men and women.* The creak of her rocking chair by my bed as she trips over a stage direction before gliding into an aria of happiness. My belief in Maeve's words, no longer the words of stage or movie, ends in Shaw's triumphant *Hallelujah!* My mother speaks through me, a ventriloquism more miraculous than their scratchy Movietone. Then I hear Maeve's voice free of me, free of the clever arguments of George Bernard

Shaw: *When she was good, / She was very very good / But when she was bad she was horrid. Now, isn't that the silly jingle, no reason to it at all. Bel, I expect you will never be horrid.*

Silence. Then the film flapping free of its sprockets, talk of important men.

"Cat's got her tongue." Bank's little joke as he pulls me out of the deep leather chair.

"Miss Maher!" Big studio guy, awed by the performance.

I could not come back, Gemma, back to the blank screen, cigar smoke and their stars framed and hung on white walls.

"A regular Bernhardt. She played with a stump, right? Half a gam."

Banks pressing on to my future at the studio. "You're right up there, kiddo."

"Can she dance?"

"We'll teach her to dance."

I found nothing to say. Garbo, Lillian Gish, Norma Shearer looked down from the white walls, larger than any life I imagined as a starstruck girl mouthing lines at the Bijou. When at last I spoke, I aimed to please, even to dazzle with my modesty: "It's been a long day." A technician wheeled out the Movietone projector, another test, another screening room, another hopeful, but it was strict business with Miss Maher. I was no longer—perhaps had never been—just a pretty girl.

I have spliced scenes out of sequence. The much ado at the bungalow came in real time, end of day after my talkie success. My lovers, Lotte and Fritz did their slapstick turns at the little house— round-about chasing and pratfalls. Meyer punched Banks in the nose. All that was missing was the frantic music to accompany a silent run at top speed. A sober moment when it was over. We were like children, ashamed, not up to our passions, if our comic affairs were passions, not movie amours.

Left to myself in the bungalow, I went over the scene in the jungle, always the studious girl, fully prepared before Meyer came calling those steamy nights. We'd shot STORM with the instruments conking out, but I had not yet climbed into the open cockpit, a frail plane of wood and cloth, a remnant of the war, the only real thing left in the movie. My war-hero Dad had not twirled the propeller, stepped back in its brutal gust to bid me farewell, worry in his misted eyes, FAREWELL. The JUNGLE lay ahead on Lot 9.

I was to tramp through the gigantic foliage, fronds and vines slapping my face. I would then meet the trained monkey—

"Monkey?" Meyer brought to the brink of tears. "Isabel, who will believe such crap?"

Believe it, the monkey full of show-biz charm was to be my guide to the hut of sticks and twigs in which I DISCOVER the wounded pilot brought down by a sputtering engine and pride. Love story to bloom. I threw down the script, bored with Banks' entertainment.

In the closet of my bedroom, I found the old valise I'd traveled with cross-country. I set it beside the sleek leather case bought at Bullock's with fittings of silver bottles and crystal jars worthy of the Santa Barbara Hilton. Three weeks since I'd come back from that excursion. Just after nine on the traveling clock, a parting gift from my father, though he never thought a day would come when I'd take the train from Ansonia to New Haven, New Haven to New York, passing up Ziegfeld's Follies, New York overnight, sitting up to Chicago, and on to sunny California. Looking at my battered valise, I had no clear idea of when I would leave, where I might go. It was, as Patrick Maher would say, the shank of the evening, at least in Hollywood. Lotte and Fritz had tripped off to a party with gossip of my wounded suitors. There had been that scene at the bungalow. I imagined Banks nursing his bloody nose, a bruise on his cheek. Meyer at his typewriter with a gem of a socially responsible plot. Isabel Maher curled snail-tight in her bed, protecting her body. But that's like the titles run off with silents, Gemma, titles to direct the story. I slept on and off, in both waking and dream states heard my mother's voice . . . never cross, though not soothing, as it had been when she tucked me in bed with a prayer. I did not believe in ghosts, yet I was haunted. I barely believed in the cloak of belief, the saints and heavenly rest accepted whole cloth by my parents, still my mother's words reached me from the afterlife. Day of the Dead, Gemma. I was three thousand miles from her grave and had nothing to offer Maeve Maher, not a seed cake or tortilla or flower, yet she spoke to me. *Bel, you will never be horrid.* Then I took the tin skeleton bought from the enterprising children I did not save, threw it in my valise and slept for no more than an hour, yet I was not courageous, not ready to call it quits.

At five I made small talk with my driver, at five-thirty with my dresser at the studio. Banks wore a small plaster on his cheek, as though he'd cut himself shaving, his eyes bloodshot, lips rubbery and swollen, liquor on his breath six in the morning. "You look like hell," he said and sent me back to makeup.

We shot FAREWELL. We trooped to JUNGLE Lot 9, leading to DISCOVER hut of sticks and twigs. The director directed me without mercy in each silent gasp of fear, every show of bravery, repeatedly calling me Miss Maher, *our star*. Like him, getting personal on the set. There was no question of his power. The tension not relieved when the monkey arrived with his trainer, a woman with colossal buttocks and breasts. She wore a vest with many pockets, which the monkey clawed at for seeds and nuts. They spoke to each other, a complicated sign language, punctuated by clicks and clucks. The monkey was let loose in the tangle of limbs and vines. Not loose, for he followed his trainer's commands, the snap of her fingers, the clap of her hands. Much amusement. As Banks would have it in his rewrite, the script indicated a cloying scene, a twinge of mutual fright followed by curiosity, then trust blossoming between monkey and battered star. I was twenty-six years old, still playing the innocent. That was surely amusing, though not indicated on the page. My invasion of the tropical growth, the monkey's home after all. At the end of each take he leapt into the arms of his trainer, balanced on her breast to receive his reward of nibbles.

The sun had climbed the sky, the jungle shadowed by a huge stretch of canvas overhead. Banks was ruddy under a planter's hat. At the sharp flip of his hand, I took my place. Once again I parted the vines that slapped at my face. I did not please. My fear unconvincing. The smudge on my cheek retouched. My joy when I entered the clearing was incomplete.

"Chrissake, you've been saved!"

I came into the clearing, lifted my face to the sky. The monkey's cue. He jumped, swung, screeched. His performance was perfect.

Banks rose from his canvas chair, came to the edge of the jungle, turned me to the cruel lens of his eyes. "It's a miracle you're alive."

A true thing finally said, but the miracle had nothing to do with the last of my director's silents. I tore off my aviator's cap and threw it to my fellow actor, who caught it and scampered away. I heard his trainer laugh at this trick along with the crew, as I walked off the set. A display of temperament so unlikely for our star, no one followed. What did they figure? She'll come round. Shoot the talented simian. He's a pro. In my dressing room, I grabbed my crocheted purse trimmed with beads, the fashion that season. A practical working-class woman, I checked for dollars and cents, walked out of the studio, took the trolley. Booted and buckled into a heroine's gear, no passenger gave me much notice. This was the city of dreams, dreams that would soon be heard by an audience living on dreams in 1928, as '29 drew near with MOVIES THAT TALK LIKE REAL PEOPLE. It was one-thirty-two as we passed Grauman's Chinese Theatre, the new tribute to Hollywood's gods. Banks, in his fury, had not broken for lunch. Only the monkey gobbled off camera. At the bungalow, I called my agent, left a message to forward all money, if money was due on a broken contract, then I packed the old valise, left the swank one for Lotte.

I took the train. In Phoenix I blamed the two men in my bungalow life, Banks' touch cold as though the blood could not travel to his thick manicured fingers, chill on my naked back, grasping at my waist. His directing me, twisting me with superior knowledge—who makes it, who fails. And Meyer, dreamy boy, writing me into his blind pursuit of a shabby proletarian script. Leave it. Leave them. In Chicago I believed it was the monkey, his scrabbling brown fingers clinging to my breast like a child I'd never have. Leave that mangled plot. Sitting up all night to Grand Central, I knew it was Maeve—*when she was horrid*—my mother's voice called me back. I chose the miracle, Gemma, that story. A miracle that had nothing to do with the movies. *I come straight out of the heart. Now, isn't that a silly jingle?* I had crossed over, communed with the dead.

For three years, I'd been in a world always Summer. Now I traveled back east without a coat or warm hat. It was cold changing trains, cold in Grand Central as I waited on the platform for the last leg of my journey huddled into a tennis sweater and a velvet evening wrap. In New Haven I was a curiosity, perhaps crazy. When I finally arrived in the Brass City, I called my father. Midnight. Not knowing if the Model T was in running order, did I dare say it, "Come get me. I'm home." Pat was bundled in the old pea coat he wore each day to the factory. He placed it round my shoulders. I was warm for the first time in days.

"A foolish girl! What were you thinking?"

Chiding me as a vagabond, or no coat in cold weather, but he could not be cross. The car sprang forward, balked at every turn like the boxy black cars that chased faster than real life down empty streets and back lots in hilarious one-reelers. My father still lost in time. Though I wrote to him, called each week, first from the Miramar of ever-hopefuls, then from the bungalow, and though he'd paid the price to see me at the Bijou as Bathing Beauty and blooming star, he looked up from his springs and gears my first night home, stuck a loupe in his eye as though I'd never left. "It's accuracy itself, Bel. True time for days without winding. I've applied for the patent."

The next week the banns were published from the pulpit of St. Bridget's, and in quick time I married Tim Murphy. I believed in our vows and our blessing. He never asked why I'd come back from *out there*. Out there in the sunshine. Out there with eucalyptus and date palms. Out there with wardrobe and production, with the pretty girls and the moneymen with their lure of studio contracts, cut-and-paste scripts, their mangled stories. Tim never asked and he was not a fool. He knew my answer would undo us.

We lived with my father, believing it was temporary. Tim sold insurance. Before it all came down, people still fancied protection against fire and theft, insured their lives with a weekly premium, though in '29 many defaulted. We went to church, played cards, frequented the Bijou on a Saturday night. In the shops, no one knew how to address me. I had failed them as Isabel Maher. Women I'd gone to school with, mothers of children I'd taught could not get their tattling tongues around "Mrs. Murphy." In Skydell's, I bought a drab winter coat and lace-up Enajetics, scrubbed my face for their approval; still I was not one of them. Where were my bright lips, penciled eyebrows, pearls and the clinging silk gowns?

I welcomed the snow. When my chores were done in the

morning, I walked down to the river. Ice formed at its shore, cold to the touch, and the bare branches above were not painted backdrop. I looked upriver to the factories along the shore—their billowing smokestacks were the life of my city—and one day I walked up to what was left of a town square. In the library I searched out the sinful books written by wild men, so we were told by the parish priests, who never read much, surely not the books I held in my hand—Veblen and Shaw. Call it a lapse or a relapse to the nights with Meyer, not to our steamy kisses, not to the edge in his voice denouncing *Major Barbara* or his poor eyes blinking in wonder at Isabel Maher, working-class girl. I left those books unread on the library table. Now that, if you want an answer, was foolish, believing that limited to my normal-school education, I had never understood the harangue of Meyer's lectures. I did not open those books, fearing their arguments would slur the clear voice of my mother. I held to the miracle. When I left the library, I took the streetcar home and could not help thinking of Meyer, who praised me for taking the trolleys, the fair ride of the people, when every starlet scooted Los Angeles in a little runabout. I believe my not learning to drive was my Brass City resistance to Hollywood. As I climbed the street to our house, I was warm and pleasantly tired, blamed it on the first breeze of April, feather leaves of maples sprouting. I did not yet know I carried the first weight of a child.

A neighbor stopped me, a woman whose husband worked in the clock factory with my father. "Will you be going back, then?" she asked. "Back to teach school?"

I was an oddity, a trouble to her. Like the rest, she had seen me magnified, the swelling pools of my tears, the enormous mouth of my laughter. I'd shrunk to life size. They wanted proof of my failure, that Tim Murphy was what I settled for, second rank on the Keith Circuit. Only my father and Sal let me be Isabel, daughter and school chum. At the Beauty Box, Sal asked, "How's the

Murph? How's the hubby?" Sal's boyfriend still on the take, always the hand out. "Gee, your hair is swell. You'll never need a perm."

My father spent his nights with his dials and jewels when the table was cleared after supper. Once he looked up—"Past your bedtime, Bel"—as though Tim was not in the next room reading the *Sentinel*. One night we came home from the movies to find Pat Maher in a rage. He crushed a watch face with the hours circling, swept his hand across the table, and all the little screws and brass works skittled across the floor. He'd been reading *The Watchmaker*, a trade journal.

"Bel, it's all been a waste."

There was the notice: a clock had been invented—the article was beyond me—a clock with an oscillator, accurate to one-tenth of a second each month. Quartz, not the dread electric timepiece, did my father in, though it would be years before the miraculous discovery was manufactured. In the days that followed, he dwindled, his hearty Santa Claus self disappeared and in his place an old man leafed through the binding agreements of his patents. When he died, before Summer set in, the men who he'd brought along with his skill, workingmen, and their wives came to the funeral. The ancient owner of the Clock Works stood by his grave with his wife who tacked the Protestant ending onto the Lord's Prayer, *for Thine is the kingdom, and the power, and the glory*. So he was not forgotten, while I was surely forgotten by Meyer and Mayer getting on with their talkies. I had not thought of the death knell of Pat's synchronous clock, same year as the silents, until my daughter came home one day with a thick steel chain on her wrist fit for a prisoner, a hideous thing with flashy red numbers. Rita said it was accurate to a tenth of a second in a calendar year.

· · ·

Day of the Dead, Gemma, I am speaking out of turn, out of season, but it's all in the timing. I learned that from a famous fatty when I was a pretty girl—the hesitation step, the double-take—and I was instructed by Alec McBride, formerly of D'Oyly Carte or so I believed—the quick flip of a fan, eyes searching out the still point of the moon. My husband's timing was perfect. He moved us away to begin life with our proper names, the Murphys living down the lane from the Dunns and Mangiones. The one thing saved from my days in the movies was money, enough for a little house, for our comfort. Tim settled me in to await our child. He was licensed in the little state of Rhode Island to insure the mills against fire and flood. The banker who had been his officer in France gave him this plum, though he never went begging, not even when the mills were empty, barely worth the premium. In the lean years, he checked dented bumpers, the char of kitchen fires, small disasters, small claims. Tim plotted our safety. The biggest risk he ever took was on me. Now, I ask you, who was the hero? The man with the wounded wing, who saved us from whispered stories of who we once were, hero and star fallen to plain folks, or Meyer of film flam, who wrote the political endings before the first words of his script were played out, or Banks, with his box-office calculations? I ask, not needing your answer. Salvation—my life after death in the movies. Tim never speaking of my injury to him.

We lay on our bed in late Summer, the window open. On a clear night the voices of revelers on the beach below rose to meet the murmur of delight in our bodies. What is it you were eager to know? How Mr. Murphy could please me after the Hollywood romp which you presumed from stale gossip in *The Silver Screen*. Not from Banks' use of me. Not from Meyer laying a working-class girl. Summer nights in our new house, once a fisherman's cottage, the bay was still as a pond. Tim's heavy hand, the dead, senseless weight exploring my breasts and belly nine months swollen.

"I can feel our child," he said, as though love cured all.

"Not possible."

"It's true, Bel."

The only lie he ever told me. I turned from him, very wide awake, the moon and I.

That first year in our house, I stuck geraniums in the ground. My mother had valued red geraniums. I believed her advice: "Give them a shot of manure tea. Don't overwater." We seemed to be one voice, one in our household duties as the Summer days went by. When the nights turned cold, I cried. The frost killing off my geraniums seemed a personal affront, but I never wanted to live in all that damn sunshine, did I? This was where I belonged, with Autumn tides rising and I planted a hedge to cut the wind that swept down the lane. Privet for privacy, still fearing that first year that someone might spot me, Isabel Maher.

One night, before Joe was born, we went to the movies. I've no notion what we saw, something cheery, and Tim asked, "Bel, do you miss it?"

"Not at all." The only lie I ever told him.

This is where I belonged, with my boy, the spitting image of his father.

· · ·

Packets of mail were forwarded from the old address in the Brass City with sharp words from Meyer, and once a letter from Lotte, who had married her German, so she would never have to speak the slithery American words in any picture. *I vas turn to lovk mit Fritz I haben.* Love or Luck? I could not guess. Either word was one up for Lotte.

Duet for one voice, Gemma. Your questions to my answer. Not a word for my children, who never asked about my round trip to a seasonless dream. They came on the set of the shingle house on the lane when the past was stowed away. The shrapnel in Tim's arm was a War Story. I had only the skeleton in the closet. Well, in

a box with the model of my father's watch—patented, never manufactured, never made a dime. If Joe comes to my grave on the
Day of the Dead—not Rita; Rita has surely traipsed off after the
only love of her life; I can no longer presume my daughter's comfort or well-being—but if my son comes with prayers, his questions will be different entirely. Questions of the afterlife once
brought to mind by his study of theology, or perhaps he will simply ask about our excursions. Way off the mark in his eulogy. I
didn't take flight in my flighty way, abandon the duties of cooking
and cleaning or the rewards of my garden. I wanted to show my
children more than a tangle of blue roads on the map. I chose each
destination and drove my big Buick to places the world might take
them—my son, my daughter, Gemma with your impertinent
questions. And yes, we mostly came home in time for supper, the
return seeming part of the day's adventure. Tired and hungry, as
though sitting up at night Chicago to New York, New York to
New Haven, New Haven to my Brass City.

What you wanted to know may be different than what you
should know. A short history of film: In 1936 Marie Pinchot sat
with the children and off we went, a night out at the movies.
Chaplin in *Modern Times*, Charlie bollixing the conveyor belts, performing all the old pantomime tricks, lost like Pat Maher in the
mechanized world of cogs and wheels, undercranking the camera
for inhuman speed, lots of titles in case we got lost in the plotless
plot. An almost silent movie, so much for talkies. A gibberish song,
Chaplin's only concession to sound. "Like an extra arm," Tim
said, "he didn't need it." 1941—with my children at a matinee,
Major Barbara. Wendy Hiller in her Salvation Army uniform, perfect as Barbara, cheeky, resilient, though in the end what is it she
wants? *A house in the village to live in.* I was no one in Hiller's
shimmering world of art, never had been, just middle-class, the
kids on either side of me, Rita appeased by popcorn, Joe straining

to figure Shaw's anti-war bombast. Silent tears, I had got rid of the bribe of talent. In 1952 Tim and I went one night to the movies. Joe safe in the seminary. Rita an aide in the hospital. Tim parked in the lot they'd paved behind the old theater in town, same vintage as the Bijou. He said the parking, paved by the mayor's brother, was money thrown away. No one went downtown at night to the movies. The show was a hit, but the musty theater was half empty. We watched *Singin' in the Rain*. It was all about my time, the crossover when sound was coming in. Gene Kelly was great. That doesn't say it, a small miracle his dancing and singing in the rain. The silent movie star with the screeching voice was a hoot. I would have played the talented girl—sweet, undiscovered—but they never taught me to dance.

"Did they get it right?" Tim asked.

"Not exactly. They've had twenty-odd years to work on their tricks. Still, it's a terrific movie."

What you might want to know. From the grave I can tell it without shame, the corny wind-up. Soon after that night at the movies, I caught Meyer Wolf on television—testifying, an unfriendly witness before the House Un-American Activities Committee. He was bald, still lean, and looked hungry as ever. Meyer was calm as he took the Fifth, betrayed no one. At times heroically silent, incriminating only himself. I remember he named Shaw a parlor socialist in the closed courtroom of the bungalow. When he bent down to the mike, Meyer blinked at his inquisitors, took off his thick glasses, that look of blind disbelief at garbage. Who would believe it? Meyer had done himself proud, with his scripts that mocked bosses and swells, same old story—the little guy wins—but moved with the times to the little guy loses, menacing stories. The inquisitor kept asking Meyer Wolf, *Meyer Wolf of Holmby Hills?* Holmby Hills, a good address, leisure class.

Lotte Grauber went back to Germany. Her husband produced

propaganda films for the Reich. It's the sort of thing you learn from documentaries watching television with your husband on a Sunday night. Lotte, romping at Berchtesgaden with Himmler, the Minister of Culture, was billed incorrectly as a star of the Hollywood silents.

Banks. I presume he disappeared, at least I never saw that name as the credits rolled. Oh, I sat through the credits, Gemma, till the screen went blank. The End. I loved movies. Years of silence and sound—in the Bijou, in the living room.

What more did you want to know? I outlived my marriage to the Murph. And my time. I loved my daughter, believe it. For too many years burdened with each other we sat down to supper, reviewed the day and often watched movies diminished on the little screen to one long reel of *Chatterbox* stories. If I emoted like Bernhardt or Alec McBride, the toast of Broadway, it was for Rita, my nightly performance cheering us on. On the last day allotted, I struggled from bed, such an old lady. I stood at the open window. Joe was not safe walking down the lane for his morning exercise, though he might be praying. Or not praying at all to accomplish God's will as a pilgrim. Knowing my son is through with the bribe of heaven, I called him back, "Jo-ee, Jo-ee." My final words wasted.

II
Excursions

There is no Frigate like a Book
To take us Lands away . . .
—Emily Dickinson

*He is seated comfortably at a desk on the West Side of Manhattan. We
need not know whose Georgian desk, whose handsome wall of books
behind. A woman with a zip cut brushes down his gray hair, attempts to
powder his forehead, which gleams under the lights. He is quite the gent
in a tweed jacket and green turtleneck that brings out the green in his
eyes, a good-looking man, mid-sixties, perfection of uncle.*

*"Use him in a pharmaceutical ad." This crack, Director to Print
Journalist, serious men making their documentary, segment of a series
on wars of the century soon coming to an end. Father Murphy toys
with a paperweight while the cameraman screens out the flickering light
from Riverside Drive. He's curious about the pictures on the faded
walls—paintings of fruits and flowers, Italian street scenes, photos of
grandchildren, must be, for the entry and this room, the study—so called
by the Director—are old fashioned, somewhat lifeless. All personal
items removed from the desk, just the paperweight and a student lamp*

with a green glass shade—*pleasing, authentic*. He has been told this is a pilot, low-budget, the apartment on loan.

The opening line of the Journalist: "You were hooded by the Nacionales?"

"Blindfolded."

"Subjected, as many prisoners were, to sensory deprivation?"

"No, I heard the guns and at times the grenades. They shut me in the stable behind the chapel. There was the smell of dead animals. They senselessly killed the mules."

"You were taken prisoner in March of '79. A political prisoner."

"No, they just left me. I was not important."

"Can you give us your perspective on how the war played out in El Salvador, Father, as a man of God?"

"I would not use that expression. As a servant, I was afraid they would come back and kill me, but I was not useful to them. You want to speak with Father Jerez if he is still alive. He was responsible for any political"—the paperweight cradled—"political agenda, no more than a village getting in touch with grass-roots democracy. We were labeled as Marxists, anarchists. Jesuits empowering the poor, throwing our moral weight against the imperial history of the country."

The Print Journalist with the recognizable name looks to the Director. The lights shut down. The Priest has been prepped. What they want is the personal story. Father Murphy is told to relax, tap into his feelings. How did he feel when chosen for Salvador? What were his sympathies working with the people? His emotions looking back on that time? The makeup girl has her way with the powder. He is brushed again, anxiously cups the paperweight until the lights go on.

"I felt blessed to be sent to the liberation. It was often a question of who's saving who. The peasants or the priests. Under the blindfold, I thought of my father in the War to End All Wars, wounded, battle of the Marne, 1918. I was no hero, and they might as well kill me. Be a patriot. Kill a priest. That was one of their mottos. The stable stank of mule dung. You see, I should have called up Bethlehem, the Holy Child settled on straw, not the comforts of our little house in Rhode Island. Jesuits had been central to the colonial enterprise, now we were giving the people back their culture, the land they once owned. Aguileres saved me, the best assignment I ever had. I'm telling it like a soldier come home from the excitement of military engagement. Call it the time of my life, the church militant. The uniforms of the Nacionales were made in the U.S. So were their bullets."

The Director is pleased. The Journalist flips through the pages on his clipboard.

The Priest laughs when he recalls being tagged a Marxist and goes into the details of torture, not his, the peasants'. "They only kicked me in the kidneys, bloodied my nose."

"Let's take that again about the Marxist."

"Marxist, Leninist? Who were they kidding? We were talking together—priests, nuns, campesinos. Such talk is not cheap. Our work to free the poor from their silence, to give them letters and numbers to fight for land distribution. Let me tell you about Loyola, the Saint who started out as a soldier, found the pen mightier than the sword."

"And the massacre?"

"There were two." He begins with 1932, the Matanza, low estimate thirty thousand killed.

"The massacre, El Mazote?"

"I wasn't there." Goes on to 1980, those good Sisters murdered, came to Salvador from Detroit, martyrs. There was a cover-up, then their graves found. Our Ambassador to the UN put them down as political activists. They were victims of policy, the last gasp of the Cold War."

But they are after his feelings, rage and sorrow, words that sound stale to Father Murphy. When the Director adjusts the little microphone clipped to his lapel and asks him to say it again, like a song, he thinks, take it from the top, rage and sorrow at the rape and murder of those good Sisters. For a split second the paperweight feels like a weapon in

his hand. He knows he will be edited, his voice spliced in with the voices
of others. From the top: "Martyrs, feeding and nursing the poor. Our
woman at the UN called it a regrettable incident in the course of normal
police activity."

"Thank you, Father."

It's in the contract, his words will be reviewed, a release from the dio-
cese.

"It is the diocese?"

And because he is a priest, they look respectful, the makeup girl and
the Journalist with his clipboard, the Director and cameraman helping
him over the cables. A car waits for Father Murphy at the door.

The next week he is walking round the courtyards of the Cloisters.
The mixed bag of twelfth-century monasteries looks nothing like the
Spanish-colonial cloisters of El Salvador. New York City schoolchild-
ren, transported to the museum for a cultural outing, are fascinated by
the cameras and arc lights brightening the day, the slow progress of film-
ing. The Director has asked the Priest to wear a black soutane. He has
refused. It was never the costume worn in Aguileres, or in San Salvador
at the Jesuit High School. The black suit, the white turn-around collar
will have to do. The camera tracks him on a path of lavender in bloom,
head bowed in contemplation. Schoolchildren hushed, bees busy at the
flowering thyme. He has been directed to turn at a bench so old the
public may not sit on it. The Director has been granted a dispensation.
Father Murphy sits, blinks the light out of his eyes.

"When you were hooded by the Nacionales . . ."

"Blindfolded."

· · ·

The kids are in the Buick, the car Isabel Murphy won for a dollar.
She took a chance. To her husband, chances were a questionable
way to the pot. "Gambling for Holy Name!"

Bel held the winning ticket in her hand. "First Methodist raf-
fled a set of bone china."

"Everyone's doing it . . . ," a maxim he need not finish. "The Buick dealer, a piece of work. How the hell does he come up with a four-door sedan idling on his lot?" 1943. Chrysler turning out tanks and bombers, Tim Murphy scolding his wife, but what the hell, swiping her cheek with a kiss. Talk was, the Buick dealer lived apart from his wife, kept a floozy up in Providence. "You better believe he wants more than a blessing from the Monsignor. Angling for an annulment from Holy Mother church."

The pity of it, Bel couldn't claim her prize. "It's yours for the asking."

"I'll stick with the Ford." A company car.

Tim, hot under the collar, inched the big shiny Buick off its blocks, where it had been displayed in front of the rectory. That Spring it sat in the lane, square in front of the Murphys' house. After supper Bel took her driving lesson, the only time the children remembered their father blowing his top.

"You'll kill us all."

On Good Friday she lamed the Pinchots' cat, which brought the lessons to a halt for a week, but Bel was determined, her body thrust forward like a figurehead on the prow of a ship until one day she sailed off, tooting at Meg Dunn on her tricycle, not stripping the gears. Hell of a year to win a car, gas rationed, so where, Tim asks, might she go beyond the school yard and her errands downtown, the few miles she walked each day before she took full possession of her prize? "The salt air will pit it." But when Tim called Phil Dunn to build a garage, never mind lumber was scarce, the fellow was off to basic training at Fort Dix.

"And where would we have put a garage?" Bel asked. The cottage hedged in on one side, on the other a chain link fence, Property of the State, the lane ending in a steep drop to the stony breakwater enclosing the bay from the sea. So the garage was a failed phantom of protection, and best Tim could do was insure the occupants of the Buick and the green elephant itself for all it

103

was worth. It was worth a good deal to watch his wife practice a perilous U-turn, till Bel, fully licensed, drove off on her own, clutching the steering wheel for dear life.

. . .

On her own was how he saw it, reminding Tim Murphy of Bel's departure when she headed out west, of her letter from Chicago, which he read at night, lying on his bed in his parents' house, plain people who had sharp words for Miss High and Mighty but came, along with the fans and *Photoplay*, to love Isabel Maher in the movies. The star, imagine that, who almost married their son, coming to terms with Tim's devaluation. On sleepless nights, he unfolded the letter and read it by the overhead light, the bright sterility of his room fitted out with pulleys and weights to develop his good arm, make it do the work of two.

I am not leaving you. I am off [blot on the page] selfish dream, never certain, [blot] testing my worth. . . .

There followed the encouraging words of a love letter, which he believed until it was folded away, placed in a cigar box with his honorable discharge. He could not imagine Bel's worth until, not to be caught sulking in the back row of the Bijou, he drove to New Haven to see her at Loew's and bought a ticket to watch her eyes flood with false tears as a cruel old father in wedding regalia, tails and striped pants, begged his Bel to marry the wrong man. The screen lost the amber flecks in her eyes, the wry twist of her smile. Her wayward black curls were pasted to her head in a glossy helmet. No feeling stirred beyond the numb desire to watch her, as though the shrapnel embedded in his left arm traveled to his heart, testing himself with her prancing in the frivolous one-reelers, with her melodramatic gestures in cranked-out serials. Watching the chill silence of Isabel Maher in the romance that made her a star, he chose to remember the warmth of her voice leading schoolchildren in carols, breathless as Juliet of the Ansonia Terpsichordians, the firm delivery of her responses at Mass. For three years he told himself he did not want this woman on the screen, and when she returned her few words overwhelmed him with pleasure, like a first gulp of Otto Sauer's beer, that's how Tim Murphy described his elation. She laughed at that one, Prohibition still in place, and all she'd said, dialing Murph's familiar number in the Brass City: *You there, Tim? I'm home!*

. . .

So the Buick sitting in the lane, despite the sure thing of two kids and no mortgage on the shingle cottage, presented a ghost of a problem to Tim Murphy. Where might his wife be off to? It was a brisk day at the end of April, the wind whipping the forsythia by the door. Joe and Rita already in the car when Gemma came panting down the lane, the Riccardi girl, all knees and elbows, wrists dangling from a coat too small.

"An excursion," Bel said, "back in time for supper."

Rita complaining. After school it was Homemakers' Club, she'd cook meatless macaroni with the simple girls she called her friends. Joe missing baseball practice.

"Not a lark." Bel pulled a stern face. "An educational journey."

Tim watched them drive off, Joe up front with his mother. When he turned back to the house he found the map on the kitchen table, her route marked in ink, and worried she would not find the way. Bel had left him behind. He soaked the oatmeal pot, cleared the table, homemaker's tasks, and thought how very sad, his daughter preferring instruction in meatless macaroni to her mother's adventure.

. . .

Low on gas, Bel stopped at the Esso pumps before heading out of town, gave over her ration stamps and, seeing the strapping young man was taken with her smile, begged for a gallon or two on the sly, wondering, until he tried to make change, that he was not off to the war.

Isabel Murphy reads. That is why her children and Gemma Riccardi are truants: each morning, when Joe and Rita go off to school, she settles in a chair by the front window with a book. After the early clatter of the milkman and the alarming radio news, after she sees Tim out the door with his assurance and persuasions, after the beds are made and the breakfast dishes stacked in the drainer, Bel reads in the quiet of late morning. She is a woman without friends, strange to say. Oh, the neighbors are kind, and there's Tim's partner at Prudential, the partner's gabby, good-natured wife, but Bel Murphy is content with her children, her husband and now and again that needy Gemma, who helps her in the garden, though the girl has no touch with living things at all.

Bel has been reading all sorts of novels from the Public Library, reading with pleasure as she did in *Chatterbox* days, as she did in the Hollywood bungalow when Lotte Grauber went off to endless parties. In Summer there is the garden. The rest of the year there are stories. What can be the harm of these stolen hours? Should she be at the hospital with the women rolling bandages for the wounded, or torturing herself with a tourniquet, learning first aid? These questions occur to Bel as she turns to the page marked with a shoelace where she left off when life began again—washing, ironing, meatloaf for supper. Bel settles in her reading chair, the Hoover plugged in, at the ready.

That Winter, confidence growing at the wheel of the Buick, Bel renewed one book at the library. *Moby-Dick*, last read with her eighth grade class in the Maplewood School, an abridged version watering the story down to Good and Evil, no wild flights in the language, a simple sea chase approved by the State Board of Education. Miss Maher had a flop on her hands—girls yawning, boys blubbering in the back of the class—and returned with a sigh of relief to the adverbial clause and the Paragraph that must contain the Topic Sentence. Picking Melville's novel off the library shelf, she felt the heft of it and remembered teaching the lightweight fake. Each school day she sat by the front window and opened her book, marked by the brown shoelace that had lost its mate. There was the next page with its many allusions, arguments and arabesques, the writer teaching her how to read it, though at times a passage was so odd she lay the book aside, looked out at an even tempered bay shimmering in cold sunlight, Bel Murphy cast away in the comforts of the living room, clinging for dear life to the worn arm of her chair. This is where she has landed, safe as the rinky-dink plane set on the studio floor, no monkey to challenge her performance. And it seemed once again that her round trip across the country was more about leaving than arriving, setting off like the sailor Ishmael, who survived to tell the story, while she must be silent or tell only the fraudulent version. What might she call her Hollywood days—a dumb show, false start?

When the kids came down with heavy colds, seriatim, *Moby-Dick* sat like a brick in its brown library cover by her chair. She missed figuring the urgent sentences and her own melancholy thoughts in the winter light. In truth: there were days when Bel stumbled on the writer's puns and fancies, the big book open on her lap while she gave herself to the gentle whitecaps decorating the bay and to sighting the boats that patrolled the shore. PT boats, Tim could name them. He'd brought Joe a chart that identified battleships and carriers, drawn circles round the ships that plied Rhode Island waters. On the chart they looked like gray toys, less dangerous than the billowing sails and creaking masts of the *Pequod* in Melville's story, which would end badly, all seamen and mad Ahab dead; only the writer left to set the record straight, which was partly about commerce, wasn't it? Whale oil. Getting and spending. She knew Melville had spent himself on this work. Bel wanted to mark this thought on a page, but it wasn't her property, a wild book that nobody read, last borrowed seven years ago, D. Littlejohn, signature of the reader next to the date of return in the back of the book. Littlejohn, like a hearty fellow in Robin Hood's forest, had returned *Moby-Dick* in two days, perhaps finding the whaling yarn overburdened with facts. Bel drifted in the pages, waiting for the kill. The phrase she committed to memory, like a line in a script, was the warning of the ship's master before Ishmael signed on for the dangerous voyage: . . . *before you bind yourself to it, past backing out.*

She wondered if she was bound to finish this book. She'd never bound herself to the movies, counted herself a failure in the whirling spin of projection. A hard Winter of earaches and sore throats, measles. *Moby-Dick* was overdue when, one day, Bel lost her voice. The kids taunted her gently, their mother's silence awarding them liberties, no homework, Mallomars and Cokes. That night she wandered down to her reading chair while her family slept above. The distant wail of a siren, the sky streaked with beacons of light searching out enemy planes. Making it up, she thought, Hollywood. She pulled down the blackout shades, turned on the lamp but did not read, hearing her mother's voice pleading with her, how Maeve's spirit had possessed her so she could not cross over to sound, would never be heard by millions worshiping her in the dark. Now she had no voice at all. She gave her passing infirmity a few tears with a little choking sound, the book open on her lap to yet another flight of fancy, the whiteness of the whale. She heard the creek of the stair tread, "Tim?"— whispering to herself as though rehearsing.

But when she turned to the shadow in the hall it was her son, tall as his father.

"Mom?" Not calling her Bel, the name she assigned herself,

backing out of plain Mom. She rose from her reading chair speechless, gave him a broad smile, hand at her throat. With a theatrical gesture she swept all worry away in the middle of the night, turned off the lamp, snapped up the blackout shades. Searchlights were skimming Orion's belt from the sky, tracking phantoms in the sea while the town slept. Her son took the book from her, laid it aside, steered her toward the stairs in the dark. She thought: *Children do not want to see us troubled, wandering at night.* She thought to say: *It's the war. Look what war did to your father.* But of course she said nothing. Then planes swooped like gulls, followed by a muffled, watery blast. She felt her son's arm around her shoulder, his pitching arm, strong for a boy of thirteen. Together they skip over the squeaking stair, Fred and Ginger gliding to a hesitation at the landing. Bel thinks, *I will never love anyone as much as this son, partner in a midnight dance.* And then: *But this is not the movies.*

During the night a German U-boat is chased out of the waters of the bay in view of the Murphys' living room window. The news is on the radio as Bel sets out jam and margarine for breakfast. "Christ," Tim says, "that's the front yard."

Bel's got back a raspy voice. "And we slept through it." She looks to her son, who says nothing.

. . .

Years later Joseph Murphy, S.J., will wonder why his mother lied. In a dark hut in Salvador, hidden under a blanket infested with rat droppings, he will think about the safe enclosure of the living room, that distant war. Across the dirt floor the *campesino* that brought him to this refuge is dying. He hears the butt of a rifle against a scrap of corrugated metal, poor excuse for a door, then a soldier is in the shanty, ready to kill the American priest. The soldier is a kid in a paramilitary outfit many sizes too large, the sleeves of his jacket turned up, cap slipped down on his ears. The priest thinks to shed his cover, take the M-16 away from the boy in a paternal gesture. The boy sees only a lump of filthy blanket, or maybe he is just scared. For a full minute he crouches in the dark as though playing hide-and-seek, before the distant sputter of machine-gun fire, then silence, then an urgent voice calls him away. Now the *campesino* is beyond the last rites. He is not of this village. The priest can't distinguish his face from the many weathered faces of the workers who travel from plantation to plantation during the harvest. When he lifts the man's head he notes the parched mouth of dehydration. Father Murphy remembers *N.* on the printed page of the rites for the dead, *N.* where the name of the Lord's servant was to be inserted. The man unknown to him; this is the home of a woman he's with for the season. The *campesino* had led him safely into the darkness. If the priest had guts he would have asked the dying man to make his peace with God before he hid under the blanket. Through a hole in the thatched roof, Joe Murphy looks on a bright constellation of stars and remembers his mother's lie. Bel had not slept through the night but wandered downstairs to confront some personal demon—not Germans, not the page of the big book that he closed, took from her. He is shamed by this memory of a blip in the tranquil beat of family life. White lies, secrets at the breakfast table do not belong in this country of mass graves, of coffee-bean / sugar-cane culture feeding pickers a starving wage. The *campesino* has a string around his neck dangling a scapular of ragged cloth with the picture of a dove, symbol of his *confradías.* Lately the bishops encourage these confraternities of men mixing native beliefs with the laws of Rome. *Espíritu Santo,* Joe whispers to N., administering the last rites, anointing him with the oil of his sweaty brow. He takes off the dead man's clothes, covers the body with the blanket, discards the peasant outfit Bishop Grande has dealt his priests urging them to be one with the workers as too obvious, too gringo. He will wear the bloodstained shirt, the trousers of the dead man still damp with urine, and go safely on his way.

Or not safely.

In the first light of day a woman of the village comes in with her silent children. She is wearing a long, flowered skirt, the costume of an Indian worn in defiance of Ladinos and landlords. Her silence is terrible. They might all be deaf and dumb, the inhabitants of this tin-and-cardboard hut. The children, there are four, never speak, though Father José knows the oldest, a girl he has taught to count up to twenty centavos, to add and subtract with beans. The woman uncovers the dead man and begins to dress him in the priest's proper peasant outfit. When the man is laid out for burial, the woman goes to a crock set beside a broken water jar and ladles out cane whiskey. She brings the tin cup to Joe Murphy, raises it to his lips. For a moment he will not take it, then gulps the raw stuff, which brings tears to his eyes. Only then does she ask the American for his blessing. Together they lift the light body, carry it to a patch of dirt that served as a small communal garden, now a cemetery. When they are done, they cover the fresh grave with straw. *I have witnessed the affliction,* he begins, hears that he is speaking English, what matter, *the affliction of my people,* then words clot in his mouth. A few women stand at the doors of their huts as he makes his way through the village.

He is taken by the next wave of soldiers, blindfolded, locked in a stable, where the padre of this place once kept his mules, their bodies decomposing on the path to the desecrated chapel. At times it is deadly silent. At times machine-gun flak or the pop of a grenade. Again he thinks of the black shades in the living room in Rhode Island. His father brought them home from the hardware store, hung them in each of the windows, not to alert the enemy. This memory is an aberration. Or a sin, call it sin, to comfort oneself with the anecdote of how the Germans were chased away, how it was on the radio and in the *Providence Journal*, even naming the Murphys' lane that looked down on the bay. Stargazing with his mother in her flannel nightgown, he had watched the Coast Guard scour the heavens, then the depths of the sea, heard the torpedo blast. In the morning Bel lied, a secret with her son, their pact of concealment.

When he is out of this—that is, after the soldiers in the uniforms stamped *USA* mess the Jesuit up with a kick to the kidneys, bloody his mouth, break his nose, abandon him in the stable, after the archbishop ships him back to San Salvador—Father Murphy will write to his mother that he is enjoying some weeks of R&R. No need to say more when her letter that has followed him miraculously to the Jesuit High School tells him that his father is dead, gone with no warning. *Your father's heart gave out. I buried Murph from the house. We do not rent a commercial parlor.*

· · ·

Bel was right. After her death, he mourns in the rooms of the house with the couch on which his father died and the double bed of her silent departure. Each empty room is haunted by the dead, though when at last he cries it's for the living, for Rita. When had they set her aside? The little sister at the edge of their story. Rita grown large yet not counted, now bound to her criminal. And the best he could do was scold her, belittle her connection to this Manny, though he knew nothing of love, not for years. Find fault, make fun of her holiday costumes, play the role of sententious brother. Or of the celibate, even now thinking of his useless body, not hers. Why, of all the human wonders we are granted, is it not possible for his sister to lie down with her nameless lover in carnal bliss? *The way you talk, Father Joe, since you went off to the seminary.* Her big golden boobs in that T-shirt, the smooth, round face twisted with her store of resentment. He stands in the doorway of his sister's bedroom, a girlish place with a harmless menagerie, the big panda staring him down. *I was a child and she was a child, / In this kingdom by the sea*, one of Bel's lines drifts into his head, a poem about love and death by a tortured man. In their innocence they heard only their mother's way with the rhyme, the swell of her voice passed lightly over the poet's meaning. *Suffer Bel's little children*. Not Rita Murphy. Suffer the old and infirm. When did she leave? Not a day or two ago. More likely she departed the confinements of this house when she was fully accredited to manipulate the bodies of her patients, prop them with canes and crutches—that working life all her own. When had he loved her, if ever, the tag-along sister? Snapping the comic book out of her hands to read out the savvy lines of Dick Tracy. Posing with a cod he fished out of the bay while she tangled her line.

Murph—who's that? Who's *we* who do not rent a commercial parlor? The Murphys of Land's End. The perfect family of four constructed by Isabel Maher and the patient man who loved her, who heard his wife steal out of bed on winter nights to read. She was a reader way back when she taught at the Maplewood School, and as a girl with her mother, the woman from Ireland who subscribed to *The Chatterbox*, Christmas books still up in the attic with their old fashioned stories, Bel padding downstairs in her nightgown. Tim setting the thermostat high for her prowling, but would she pull down the blackout shades? On a night when the sirens went off, that was the question kept him tossing until he looked out to the searchlights plowing the sky, heard the squeal of the stair tread, then Joe following her, sensing the night trials of his mother. Those two who read each other without benefit of a book, love their conspiracy. He never wanted his son to be a man neutered by the black cassock. Lost to his mother's wishes, the boy's hand dealt. Wasn't Joe already shepherding one of the faithful back to bed? Only his placid, plump daughter slept through the lights and the siren wailing.

You will be happy to know he died watching the Red Sox. The casket was strewn with flowers Rita picked from my garden. It was a perfect summer day like the day you pitched the no-hitter. He never pitched a no-hitter, only came close. She wrote that her garden was no consolation. He tried to imagine Rita clipping flowers for the bier. His sister disliked their mother's attention to the garden, Bel's exasperating care of her roses. Pacing the courtyard of the cathedral in San Salvador, black book in hand, he mourned Tim Murphy, the insurance salesman and perfect father, the good man who rescued Isabel Maher. *Wasn't I the lucky girl?* His mother's lighthearted version, if she spoke of her days in the movies at all. When his calling was determined, his father had asked, *Sure it's your choice?* Never saying that his son was about to give over his life, ante up for his mother.

We do not rent. We of the safe haven, Land's End. Each day for his hour of contemplation in the Spanish colonial courtyard, he turns to Loyola's *Spiritual Exercises. I will call to mind all the sins of my life . . . first to remember the place and house where I lived.* They were on the front stoop, Tim Murphy and his son, who had wanted to sign up for the navy. The war was over. The town was building a promenade to run along the shore with a refreshment stand and pavilion. *The whole thing will be wiped out in a storm,* his father said.

To please him I said, *They had better insure it.* The little house where we lived was weathered shingle. We sat on the front stoop, which my father made when he brought Bel down from Ansonia, ripping out rotten wood steps with his strong arm, pouring the cement himself in a mold of his making. On the beach below we heard the pylons slapped down and the tires of the lumber truck spinning in the sand. My father said: *If their pleasure palace isn't washed away, our cottage will increase in value for the girls.* The girls— my mother and Rita, figuring his daughter would never marry, never move away, and knowing that he would be gone. *Next to con-*

template your relationship with others. With my father I can remember only this one talk, man to man, his probing to see if I had the spiritual go-ahead for the seminary. His embarrassment, the way he shifted on the stoop to take out a pack of Camels, offer one to me, flip the matchbook, strike the light with one hand like Bogart did in the movies. *Sure it's your choice?*

My choice. In Loyola's discussion of the sin of words, he finds *slander, lying,* but it's *idle words* that best suit Father Murphy's reply to his father. *Idle* will do, or *unfelt,* which the Saint never mentions. He reads the letter from his mother announcing his father's death when he is assigned to teach in the high school attached to the university in San Salvador, teach English to privileged kids whose parents did not trust Jesuits who might very well be commies, still dealing the best education for their boys. Many will go off to colleges in the States. It is expected that Father José will write stellar recommendations to Georgetown and Notre Dame for the student, son of one of the Fourteen Families who own this country, its land and its people. The boy brings him French brandy from his father's cellar. Such is his need. *It is profitable to make vigorous changes in ourselves against the desolation.*

. . .

He is back in New York, about to be assigned to a teaching post at Loyola.

"You're good at math, Father Murphy."

"My work was in literature, with the poets. . . ." He knows his superior doesn't give squat for the poets or contemplation.

"That was a while back. What we need at the school . . ."

"I was at Fordham. . . ."

"It's the youngsters who need us, Father. Our ranks are thin. Math shows up as excellent on your record."

What record? Scores from the novitiate? GSATs? So math came

easy, but he knew the record was the embarrassing politics (not Salvador), the ashram-cum-commune confused in his superior's programmed head with Woodstock, LSD in the desert and the nights he dropped out, slept over at Anima Mundi, his lapse, his love for Fiona O'Connor, who disappeared, took herself out of his story, for the booze and a widow of sixteen, his house girl who lived with him in Aguileres, who bore a child, not his, out of wedlock. The superior knows perfectly well that many children in Salvador are born without benefit of matrimony—the sacrament of matrimony, this curried man would say, a real gent in his blazer and headmaster rep tie. Father Murphy is now fifty years old. He has been recalled to New York after the murder of Archbishop Romero. On a sunny morning, he went with a group of priests and nuns to the chapel in the hospital where Romero celebrated a Mass for his mother, dead just two days. The murderers wore dark business suits, not their military regalia. Three of them approaching the altar, three shots and Romero was dead. Only one man fired the gun. Later it was said that the mayor, Bobby D'Aubisson, staged a lottery and the lucky man drew the long straw for the privilege of killing the priest who spoke for his landless, impoverished people.

In the wake of this martyrdom, Joseph Murphy, S.J., finds himself reassigned to the province of New York, reclaimed like lost baggage. Best not think he's unjustly demoted, get into the martyr game. He's had the love of a beautiful girl and a war, what more does a man need, a cynical thought to put aside. Better to believe that he is perceived as spiritually untalented, like his mother he's returned to what is granted day by day by day. Math shows up on his record. For a season he is tutored by a young woman with sleek black hair that reminds him of Bel's in *The Silver Screen,* a movie magazine hidden in the dark recesses of his mother's closet. Unlike the sweetheart of the silents, his teacher is awkward, prim at their worktable, an uptight girl in Brooks Brothers suits, floppy foulard ties. A tax lawyer, she comes to an empty schoolroom of Loyola two evenings a week, puts him through his paces. As it turns out, she's a member of the congregation. Father Murphy is her pro bono. He perseveres in his assignments, testing his obedience, accepts the cloak of humility. One evening, his tutor's hair is frizzed, uncontrolled. She wears jeans and a sparkler, third finger left hand. He offers his congratulations, and when she smiles—twittery teen—she's radiant, his mathematician. He holds her hand while she reveals that the lucky man, a litigator, has made junior partner. Then it's back to algebraic operations, $5x + 6 = 3x + 12$, variables and constants, then on to the mystery of negative numbers, but when, as the weeks go by, she moves on to the two-pancake problem, *there exists a linear knife bisecting two pancakes*:

"It's simple geometry."

"Yes, only high school."

"Easy, but take three pancakes, one knife, unless the centers are collinear." Her playful hypothesis leaves him behind. "See, there's no proof."

"Take the pancakes on faith?"

"Not exactly!"

Her advice when their course is over: "Stick to the books."

That very summer he begins his work of the next twenty years, his first students repeating courses they've failed. He visits his mother and Rita bringing a bottle of sweet non-alcoholic wine. Bel gets the message. Each morning Father Joe walks down the lane before breakfast. His mother leaves him be, steals about the house as though not to interrupt his thoughts. He reads the crumbling pages of Ovid, amuses himself with *The Sultan of Swat*. In the evening, when they assemble in the dining room no less, with the fuss of gold-rimmed plates and heavy linen napkins, Joe edits his stories of El Salvador, adjusting the horror to network news. Going her rounds each day to the sick and dying, Rita asks how many died in his village. Her throat a bleating red, waiting for his answer and his praise, the chance to say that she too has administered mercy. For the first time he sees the pit of resentment seated in the soft bulk of his sister's flesh as he gives an estimate of the dead and the missing. It becomes all one on these visits: the body count of nuns and priests, of villagers at El Mazote, Rita's delicious apple pie. His mother is past seventy, though he believes she fibs about her age, a rearrangement of time dating back to her Hollywood days, acting the girl, a showgirl when she'd grown to a woman, taught school. She asks after his poets as though Donne and Herbert were school chums, inquires into his readings in theology, *now that your missionary work is over.* He lets her play that game, even while he marks up exams, writes encouraging comments on student papers. Back at Loyola, he speaks of this deception to Father Flynn, his chess-playing buddy, who sets up the board. "Oh, the Jesuit mothers! True believers, you bet." Flynn sacrifices a pawn to gain some advantage. Joe Murphy contemplates his next move, never speaks of home again.

The books by Bel's chair are now paperback thrillers, mysteries. The Summer visit—he admires her garden, blue iris by an unconvincing cement pond of his father's design, roses and peonies blooming. What she has made of a half-acre, her solitary Eden. Land had been taken from the peasants in Salvador for the vast plantations. They were dealt small plots that would not feed a family, yet at times carnations grew in the rich volcanic ash, stray flowers valued for their beauty. Bougainvillea spilled over the wall of the Spanish courtyard of the cathedral where he contemplated the sorry state of his soul, the scarlet blossoms of hibiscus too much for his eyes. Lovely, he says as his mother dusts poison on a delicate rose, genuinely glad that she has this pastime or passion. Bel drives a Chevy, bought cheap from a patient of Rita's, deceased. There is nothing sad about her, nothing defeated. She drives him to Providence to catch the train back to his classes and walks in Central Park, dinners with an aging, dwindling cast of priests—Flynn, Collins, Massinio, Burns—the occasional treat of *steak frite* at the bistros newly arrived on Carnegie Hill. So many have left the priesthood since Humanae Vitae, the encyclical carving birth control in Vatican stone, though the Council had voted to revise the church's position. Still he does not leave the order, though he thinks of the children in shantytowns of Aguileres—sores on their mouths, swollen bellies of malnutrition, their lethargy as they drew the letters of the alphabet in the dust—and of swayback women swollen with the next child and the next. He does not leave because this is what life had in store for him. For a while he believes he will work from within, go up against the Curia, against authority handed down, but that's all talk with Paul Flynn. He's checkmated by conservative bishops and cardinals, unable, as his father might have said, to put the money where your mouth is. What money? He is silent, plotting the next clever move though so often defeated by Flynn's wild gambits that pay off. For a short season he takes up squash, then heart fibrillations kick in, the flutter he will live with for the rest of his life.

He is invited to a screening of the documentary, not yet funded, on the ravages of many wars. Salvador is sandwiched between Vietnam and Iraq's invasion of Iran. He hears that as a political prisoner he had been hooded by the Nacionales; he sees himself looking hot under the Roman collar, strolling in the Cloisters as though a branch of the Metropolitan Museum with a busload of schoolchildren looking on, was a fit place to bare his soul. *The possibility of a communist agenda? As a man of God*, the journalist asks. No need for embarrassment, the documentary is never funded. He is more comfortable responding to scholars unraveling the American involvement in Salvador. They are infinitely more knowledgeable about the final offensive, the power of the President to fabricate details of approaching danger, of the State Department's covert machinations; and as he attempts to answer their questions, he senses the black cloth of the blindfold across his mind. He will tell all that he knows about the alliance of peasants and priests, of the popular struggle and the preference for the poor, but not about the man he should have shriven, or the frail girl, already a widow, who took lovers in his house. He will tell what may be only a story—D'Aubisson having his men draw lots to kill Archbishop Romero, and the anecdote of how the soldiers picked him up wearing the *campesino*'s rags but he forgot to take off his shoes.

"You see, the peasants had no shoes."

When he reads what the scholars have written, he can't recognize himself, denies their account of his heroics. The history of those years passes into the books, truth-telling studies with documented revelations of that prolonged war. Reading of the injury to himself, he thinks of his father wearing a suit on sweltering days so the dead hand tucked easily into a pocket, and of the one-armed stroke he taught his children to swim in the bay, and of Tim Murphy pitching a baseball off balance, yet never telling the story of his wound as an honor or disability, just getting on with life, never marching with the Veterans of Foreign Wars, selling them insurance on their lives, never trading war stories at their picnics.

When he is sixty-five, his mother sends him the watch his grandfather made. A bit testy, he thinks Bel should have given this treasure to him when he was a boy. Now he must screw up his eyes to see the spidery numerals, hold the watch to his ear, a new quirk of Father Joe's. Its metal case weights down the pocket of the cardigan he wears to class. Though there is a clock on the wall above his desk that sounds the end of each period, he places the watch on his desk to see the hour passing. It is a token of a forgotten time when a man, Patrick Maher at the foundry in Connecticut, figured from scratch the works of wheels and springs, made this useful timepiece with his hands. He listens to its gentle alarm go off at the same moment as the school clock's liberating raspberry. His watch recalls to him lines by one of his poets, and from the closet with the old books of theology he takes down Thomas Campion's *On a Portable Clock*.

> *Time-teller wrought into a little round*
> *Which count'st the days and nights with watchful sound;*
> *How (when once fixed) with busy wheels dost thou*
> *The twice twelve useful hours drive on and show.*
> *And where I go, go'st with me without strife,*
> *The monitor and ease of fleeting life.*

He thinks to send this verse to his mother, then thinks not. It will only encourage her talk of his promise way back when he paraded the love of his contemplative poets, when he had a fastball, fast for high school, when, as a scholastic in the novitiate, he jumped the meaningless hurdle of a standardized test in math. And Bel never reads the likes of Campion. There was her Melville season of memory, the borrowed book by her chair made famous by an excursion *to a point of interest*—the tired phrase given life by the expectation in her voice.

As they drove out of town in Bel's gleaming new Buick, she sang. Now, this was news to her kids and Gemma Riccardi. "Toot, Toot, Tootsie (Goodbye)" in a cheery soprano that swung into a series of old popular songs as she tooled down the state highway, which was no more than a two-lane road with a shoulder. *Button up your overcoat when the wind is free.* Clusters of houses made up small towns with a few stores, then back to farmers' fields, billboards for Pond's Lotion and War Bonds, Wheatena, Ivory, everyday fare. Cotrell & Sons, a brick factory by the Pawcatuck, "Take note, Gemma, those wonderful machines print your magazines, *Harper's, McClure's.*" Then, perhaps thinking not *your* magazines: "Mr. Murphy's *Life,* my *McCall's.* There are *never* enough stories!" *By the sea, by the sea, by the beautiful sea.*

Really going somewhere, they had been prepped, going to visit the chapel in Melville's book where sailors prayed before they headed off to dangers on the high seas (only Bel has read that adventure), to a site so near, so famous, though how was it famous when Tim Murphy never heard the likes of visiting New Bedford, a sleepy small city on the shore.

"Massachusetts!" Declaring his alarm, as though Bel was heading off with his children to Hindustan, Gay Paree.

"Not the end of the earth," Bel said, "I've mapped the miles." The map left once again on the kitchen table, so she stopped a state policeman on Route 1, did her charming bit about losing the way, Officer. A big bull-neck man striding over to the Buick from his motorcycle, gleaming black boots, and, don't you know, pleased to escort the lady with her kids to the Seamen's Bethel. His hand on the pistol in a leather holster—that was the excitement of the day. The rest, well the rest was finding a small white building in need of paint, the door bolted, then a caretaker come to their aid, a weathered man with a sickle hacking a rim of weeds brought on by the sudden warm weather. He spoke a strange language, which Bel said was Portuguese, but understood this lady wanted to enter the chapel, a cold, musty place with smudged windows, nothing as nice as Holy Name with its stained-glass saints and crucifixion. Rita put a hankie to her nose, the air heavy with mold, but Gemma, reading the plaques with the names of dead sailors—*never enough stories*—thrilled to any project of Mrs. Murphy's invention. There was the pulpit like the prow of a ship, and the engraved testimony to the deaths of so many who did not prevail against the perils of the sea.

MAUREEN HOWARD

This is what Joe Murphy will remember when, at last, he reads *Moby-Dick:* He is a bright scholastic, crackerjack at Latin and rhetoric. He is being schooled to teach, but before he will be allowed total devotion to his poets (he knows his superiors know, that spiritually speaking, Joe Murphy is a borderline case) there's the whole ten yards of Lit. before he gets to a dissertation—*Beowulf* to home-grown American classics, and one term it's Hawthorne's dark stories and *Moby* revived. After years of obscurity, admiring scholars are all over Melville and his masterpiece with analogues and sources. All he can think of is Bel, the big book his mother was not reading, the black shades drawn against the enemy, not reading the book that launched the excursions, that season beyond fixed limits. When he is called to prayer he sees not the paneled walls, the high arched windows of Shadowbrook, not Loyola brandishing the cross in the chapel, but the dank Protestant place of no account to Bel's children, sees her disappointment in Rita thumbing through *McCall's,* the homey magazine she's brought from the car, sees her hope in Gemma Riccardi with her box camera—though what picture worth taking in the dim chapel, after all? Joe sees the spot not as instructed in the first exercise of Loyola to visualize Christ scolding the moneylenders or healing the leper, never gets to the jangle of coins in the temple or suppurating sores—sees the chill Protestant walls, hears his mother's voice cracking as she reads Melville out loud in New Bedford, then her repeat of a line, a quick recovery. She's a trouper, script in hand, reading from the book renewed again and again from the library. She tells her children and Gemma, *Never fear when you don't understand,* confesses she once lost interest in the difficult work, then read she does, skipping about, *but there are no dull parts.* He experiences his first flush of discomfort, then awe sets in as words spill at him, as they settle to her performance while the Portuguese custodian stands by the side of the pulpit with his scythe, a grim reaper. *Better to see the page*—Bel threw aside a green felt hat with a bill that shaded her eyes—better to play to the children, her voice inflated with Melville's words, *Methinks my body is but the lees of my better being. . . .* Lees? *Yes, the world's a ship on its passage out* and so forth, a disturbing show. They did not want to know this about her, that she seemed, well, kind of nuts reading from a famous book for three kids in a row who could not meet her expectation of an audience. Had she brought them to this musty place hung with names of the dead to show them her cap and trench coat were not up to the performance? Many years later, her son reading Melville, would recall his mother exposing herself as an actress, her desperation as she slapped the book closed. Pricked with reality, she came down, down, down, put on her hat and shrugged, *"Well?"* Begging their review. Her costume, her delivery?

"Well?" A question never answered—not by Joe when he put on the amice, recalling the blindfold soldiers tied over Christ's eyes, performing the proper rituals until he ended up at Anima Mundi, where that communal life chucked the trappings of authority for their priest done up as a Buddhist in a saffron T-shirt—not in the humble costume prescribed by Archbishop Grande to be one with his people; not answered at his mother's funeral in the chasuble chosen as though out of wardrobe, penitent purple for the theater of the moment in an empty church. *Well?* Perhaps answered by Gemma—given to piracy and flamboyant disguises, nothing so modest as a perky green hat or seductive as pearls falling on the breast of a star in a silver gown. *Well?* Answered at last by Rita, her tart replies to Joe after a lifetime of silence, her pluck driving off to points unknown in the costume of a clown. *Well, Father Joe, what do you think of my show?*

No answer, but on the day of Bel's theatrics in the Seamen's Bethel, there was only the stunned look of three kids at a middle-aged woman carrying on as though on the stage of a Bijou, their wondering faces seen, really seen by her son, who goes back to his cell eager to get at *Moby-Dick; or The Whale,* but distracted by the memory of his mother's excursion, Spring 1943. Sharp recall of Gemma's murky photos. One, a carved wooden plaque:

In Memory of
Jorge Montera lost at sea
Steward of the Whaler Ambrosia
In the North Atlantic, October, 1933

The other, his mother lolling against the lucky Buick, though the day had its misfortunes. They must wait by the side of the road, *Yes, we have no bananas,* while a convoy of jeeps and open trucks passed them by, personnel being moved to a port of debarkation, waiting impatiently with the lure of Howard Johnson's frankforts and twenty-eight flavors on the other side of the King's Highway, the convoy trailing on and on, so only time for a pit stop, popcorn and soda, *It's only a paper moon,* the dark coming on, the gas gauge wavering toward empty when Bel let Gemma off at her house on Cotrell Street, "Thanks for the ride."

But home in time for supper, Tim Murphy discarding the evening paper, embracing his family as though they'd been where? Timbuktu, not New Bedford. As his son, in the discomfort of his student chair, finally opened *Moby-Dick,* burning the midnight oil in the Berkshires, he could do as Loyola bid, visualize the rewards for their pilgrimage, cube steaks, Rita's favorite Franco-American spaghetti, and recall from the dregs of his being the betrayal, wasn't that part of the deal? Hearing Bel proclaim Melville's fierce sentences, he had prayed, Let her stop the dramatics. Dear God, let my mother be ordinary. *Why,* as the Saint asked, *has the earth not opened up and swallowed me?*

. . .

The Murphys' house and its contents sold to Damien Forché, the fashion photographer. Father Joe's heart thumps into its arrhythmia as he waits at the kitchen table reading once again the arrangements. For the signing of papers, he wears the seersucker suit and a narrow knit tie, a straggler in his father's empty closet. His canvas sports bag zipped to go. It has been less than a week since his mother's death. He has wandered the small rooms, slept in his boyhood bed, walked down the lane as of old, breviary in hand. The girl who came to Bel's funeral runs out to meet him each morning modestly dressed, what a back number to think that, the sweet thing scrubbed clean, her face brown from the sun, generic pretty, blond, blue-eyed, the twitch of her uncertain smile.

"Joe," she calls, told to discard *Father* first day.

"Pet?" Her name, Pet, and she is that, a golden pup of a girl nipping at his contemplation. Not seeking the role, he has become her confessor. Pet, a model, celebrated, though he has never seen her on the cover of *Elle* or *Vogue*. Pet, strangely alone in her summer rental.

"She was like kind," Pet says. "We talked, you know, it was only a few days. I mean, your mother, I didn't know she was gonna die."

What was like kind those few days? Bel listening to the girl's story, how Pet had come to this newly discovered town with a purpose, how she had rented down the lane and found Mrs. Murphy still sleeping in a rocker when her house had been sold to Damien Forché. Before it is portioned out, he gets hold of her story, that the man had been her lover, how Damien wasn't into real estate and how she had this arrangement with him, you know, casting her eyes down, an arrangement, how Damien was swift, made her like famous—her face, her body. How they traveled together. Latvia, Kenya, a shoot on the Isle of Man.

"Rome?" she asked. "Ever seen Rome?"

MAUREEN HOWARD

No, though the week before she died his mother told Pet he would be sent to the Eternal City for his studies. Grant Bel her shopworn dream, for after all, she listened to the pathetic tale of this girl, whose limbs had been sanded, painted, primed, whatever they did to her breasts, thighs and that sweet face for the camera.

"It was like Mrs. Murphy knew I was celeb. Like you said in church, from her time in old movies."

He did not believe it was like. Under her bronze skin Pet looked washed out, celeb glossed with cosmetic health. How easily she cried and tried not to. As they walked together to the end of the lane, the serial of her sad love story was interrupted with news of the Mangiones' house, in which a popular novelist now lived, of the Dunns' renovated by an anchorman, NBC. He had not noticed, as blind to the stunning renovations of *Safe Haven*, *Done Roamin'* as he was to fashion on Madison Avenue. So—they were both waiting for this Damien Forché to claim his prize, the shingle cottage. Each morning Father Joe spoke to Pet of the vagaries of the human heart, the power of love to forge connection. *How you talk, Father Joe, since you went off to the seminary.* His sister's admonition in mind as he worked at his pastoral role. And where was Rita now? Registering in a false name, a motel stop on her way to a husband with a deleted history? Or had she already arrived at address unknown?

"Where you from, Pet?"

"Springfield, Illinois."

After the morning consolation of this lovesick child, he walks through the rooms of the house—*Were they always this small?*—dazed by the passing of this fragile family life so carefully constructed. He wants nothing, not his catcher's mitt or the *Gallic Wars*, certainly not the sanitized letters written to his parents, then to his widowed mother from Salvador. He riffles through Bel's closet for the movie magazine with her picture, always stashed beneath a moth-eaten shawl Maeve Maher brought from Ireland.

The forbidden text gone, but there's a puzzling tin skeleton rusted at the joints, and the road map with the inked route of each excursion, the blue veins of his mother's enrichment program. No longer her bright boy, yet he recalls the grand staircase of Mark Twain's house in Hartford, the mahogany porch, the fancy furnishings of a boy from Hannibal, the mother of all pool tables and Twain's failed typesetter inhabiting a lofty upper room. She never came close to the Melville performance, just said how they should read the adventures of Huck if they hadn't, and wasn't it something that he wrote about the Mississippi right here in Hartford, so close to home. That was her theme, close to home, the Greek Revival arcade in Providence, with its quaint shops under glass—*so Parisian*; the mansions of Newport—the Corinthian columns of Marble House, the Great Hall of The Breakers—*Do you think the Vanderbilts had fun?* Bel driving off with her crew, leaving home for the Pier at Narragansett, closed for the duration of the war, a bucket of fried clams to stave off disappointment. Dipping into the ketchup, her son, missing school and baseball practice, wondered, What's wrong with staying home? The blowout at a railroad crossing after the carousel at Watch Hill—for kiddies, what was Bel thinking?—bumping across the track on the rim, shredding the tire. *There's a long, long trail a-winding,* her plaintive song while he rolled out the spare. He was thirteen years old, jacking up the Buick, the work of a man.

Not home in time for supper. "You're lucky to be alive." Tim Murphy pounded the kitchen table. A cup spun to the floor, shattered, one of Maeve's teacups from Ansonia. Where to place the blame? It was referred to as *the accident*, soon forgotten, or maybe it was Spring, daffodils fading, baseball in earnest—the excursions came to an end. Bel sacrificed a plot of roses to grow tomatoes, squash, peppers, settled into a Victory Garden. Father Murphy, deed to the house in hand, figures that was it, the season of discontent passed. His mother settled.

"You're the *prêtre.*" Damien Forché, come in the front door, found him dreaming. Forché in black—silk and leather—top to toe. Shaved head gleaming above a clever face, nose and mouth sharp-edged, eyes scanning the location, retro American kitchen—Formica, metal dish rack, leatherette chairs, Aunt Jemima cookie jar. "Wow!" Moving about the set, taking possession, a touch to Rita's embroidered dishtowel, the frayed cord of the pop-up toaster. "The *prêtre.* Well, hellooo, Father!"

To Joe Murphy it rings like the refrain of one of his mother's favorite musicals, cheery and false.

"Hell of a situation, view of the bay. Prime. You travel the East Coast, how many, I mean, shorefront properties aren't crapped up with condos?"

"Not many, I suppose."

"You got it. Now, this is Carlo." Carrying in the equipment, Carlo. "Vintage Hasselblad, Stereo Realist in there you wouldn't want to leave in the car."

"The lane has always been safe."

"Always isn't now. Nothing in the car, Carlo."

Carlo, a choirboy, soft cheeks, rosy mouth. Joe Murphy, *prêtre,* sees him in a white surplice, the apple of many a priest's eye. Underage, still in that category? Carlo this year's celeb? There's a good deal of touchy-feely butt tagging while Carlo stows the equipment in the pantry. Yes, there is a pantry with the last jars of Rita's apple butter, strawberry jam.

"Cute," Carlo says, "is very cute."

The Murphy house with all the old furniture is to be photographed black and white.

"Before and Aft. Documentation. Print to the family."

"I am the family." Joe holds out the papers to be signed.

"So when we do the story. Stick around. Take. Take whatever."

"After you shoot?"

"You got it. Stick around. I mean, no hurry. Sorry about the noise, they start drilling for the pool. Carlo likes a lap pool. Stay in shape. You got that wasteland out back."

"The garden?"

Damien Forché is not limited to fashion ops. "Scotland, Louisville, Provence, maybe fifty gardens." He has produced maybe fifty gardens, cut the ultraviolet light, filter the haze. "A pool you get the flora droppings. Bluestone the grass. This whole garden thing's had its run, twenty years—lilies, lavender, bugloss. Parterre. *Japonaise. Basta* hosta. Bluestone to the garage."

"There is no room for a garage." Joe speaking as to a child.

Before and Aft. The cottage overlooking the bay is a tear-down, an expression new to a *prêtre* not into real estate. Neither is Damien Forché into it. He's on the road, click-a-dee-click, but with a keen eye for a growth investment. In place of the cottage, a tower, three stories, get the prime view, lots of glass. Shingle, stick with the vernacular. The garage goes urban, underground, bike rack, mini-gym, stay in shape.

"Leave the hedge, totally Hamptons." Forché unrolls the architect's plan, weights it with the Belleek teapot so light it skims across the table. Joe clasps it to his breast. It is the only thing he means to take with him, the teapot from Ireland, and, yes, the cigar box with his father's honorable discharge and the letter with tear blots in his mother's hand. He holds out the agreement, the last page to be signed, relinquishing furniture and personal possessions.

"If you will be so kind."

"Finalize, you bet. Where's the notary?"

The notary? He's been living out of the world too many years. A trip to town in the open Corvette, Carlo shouting at the low brick and clapboard buildings on Main Street, "Cool, is so . . . ," cool erased by sea breeze. When all was signed and sealed in the Pawtucket Bank & Trust, Joseph Murphy having affixed *S.J.* to his name, legal or not, thought to leave on the next train. He has his sports bag with Tim's cigar box, Bel's teapot rolled in his black suit, but feels beholden to Pet, his pastoral duty. He turns down a ride on the pretense he has some business in town. A digital display over the bank reads July 9, 12:00, 95°F. 35°C. Forché sucking up the heat.

Presuming these are his parting words to the fashion photographer, Joe says, "Consider light-colored garments."

"Padre Simpatico, you know who grew up in this town? Riccardi, that's who."

"Gemma. We graduated from high school together."

"That is totally amazing. Know where she lived?"

"I have no idea."

Riccardi is essential, grand duchess. Her series of the clapboard two-family house she grew up in. Wow, fifty years ago, secondhand Leica M4-2, is totally sad, totally beautiful. Move in close with the rangefinder, you gotta be a genius. The great late period: absence of material content, totally void. If Damien Forché had that talent and so forth, fuck commercial. A disciple of Riccardi, Queen of Tarts. 12:05. Joe Murphy enduring a lecture in the parking lot of Pawtucket Trust, loosens his father's tie. Padre, *prêtre*, feels the steamy pavement through his shoes. He will walk back to the lane, as he did each time he came on his visits. The town has smartened up, it's true. Espresso and T-shirts silk-screened with pictures of the pier, antiques shops, Brandle's soda fountain done up as Café Venezia. The trek home, not home, in the heat is exhausting—past the New England granite of Holy Name, past the rectory, its squat tower aspiring heavenward, past the yellow brick grammar school, sites which seem fixed, if not immortal. When he arrives at the lane looking over the bay, he knocks on the Pinchots' door. Mrs. Pinchot delivered him on a hot Summer day, helped him out of his mother's womb, that was the bloody story. Pet comes to the door. Empty of tears, her waxen prettiness dissolved, sallow flesh melts under blank eyes. Lifeless straw hair. Yes, she saw him drive by with Carlo. He was like speeding to get to the house now so totally his. Her nameless tormentor. She knows Carlo from the Armani ads, the Versace runway in Milan. From the bus posters, Calvin Klein. Like androgynous. She'd been a fool and run after them, ran round the high hedge, he (Forché) swiveling away from her, his swift backward smile dismissing her as he dismissed his models at the end of a shoot.

The priest has come to tell her she must leave this place.

"The old lady, that's what she said. She said go home. That's what I did, only home was Connecticut, not Illinois."

· · ·

Cotrell Street runs off the end of Pleasant, the end that runs into Price Chopper Plaza, with the dollar store, a Laundromat, McDonald's. Cotrell is a distance from the lane overlooking the bay. Gemma Riccardi ran it in ten minutes when she was a girl, ran to the Murphys'. It takes Father Joe a half hour by the workman's watch, stopping to rest in the heat on the steps of Holy Name and again on a bench fixed to the sidewalk in front of Handmaiden, its shopwindow displaying a three-masted ship in a bottle, ceramics and baskets by local artists. Cotrell is two-family houses built in the Twenties, respectable rents afforded by millworkers, mostly new immigrants. He had thought to call ahead, but Pet, reduced to tears, could not find a local telephone book. He has no notion if Gemma will be at that house on Cotrell but thinks there's a chance, while there's little hope of finding Rita, thinks how odd that he's tracking down women, first the sorry girl, now the icon, totally genius, that Gemma. Odd, but what's off the game board is his firm decision to stay in town, not slink back to his summer course at Loyola. At long last, the mule not choosing the way. Dizzy with the heat, it occurs to Joe now, or was it when leaving the lane for the last time, that his superior will recommend psychological counseling given his bereavement. He knows the doctor on 96th Street who will not cite him for disloyalty to the order, will not remind him of his vows. Depressed, deranged, perhaps the many deaths witnessed in Salvador never dealt with, and now? Now he reaches for a handkerchief to mop his brow, finds the skeleton in his pocket.

Now my mother has gone to her heavenly rest, her reward.

He knows the doctor, confessor to priests who damage little boys, a worldly man who quotes Augustine's confessions easy as accessing Freud.

I am less certain of my calling.

Only less certain? Not exactly a revelation on the road to Damascus, this long festering of doubt. He will not mention Rita, not give her away. He must be at liberty to find her. Reparation is now his calling.

We all live with uncertainty.

Let's not argue the point. This heroic retort plays well as he heads down Cotrell, what may still be Gemma's street.

Dunphy inscribed on a tarnished nameplate. He remembers about the Dunphys, not much. Memory calls up a fussy small-boned woman in the shadow of her daughter. Who really cared about the parents of classmates in the self-enclosure of adolescence? He knows this from the kids at Loyola—doctor, lawyer, merchant chief, custodian. Dunphy, a bookkeeper at the mill?

But here's Gemma, larger than life.

"Joe, you're a shambles."

"What's left of me."

· · ·

What's left of Joe Murphy is a backroom boarder sort of man, a quiet fellow coming and going through the cluttered rooms of

Gemma Riccardi's house. He has moved beyond less certain, is much occupied with the first anxious step to leave the priesthood. They will not keep him on, a teacher of math at Loyola. He has never sought work in the world. Can he live without privilege? That's what it's been—the boy, the man set apart, in no need of intimacy, not with family or his fellows, Bishop Grande plotting his ministry in Salvador, Paul Flynn allowing himself a second beer over his next move, always the chessboard between them, their talk guarded. Padre, granting absolution for the *campesinos'* sins, spirited away from their shanties to the safety of the classroom. His birthday passing without notice, he is now seventy-two years old, a man with a fragile teapot, cigar box, tin skeleton, workman's watch.

Flynn is called in this moment of crisis. "It has a name, Joe, accidie, a sort of spiritual melancholy, loss of grace. A little too late to quit, Joe. Take early retirement. Play golf. Permanent retreat."

"Be taken care of?"

"It's like getting a divorce," Gemma says, having twice signed on that dotted line. Riccardi professes to live in the present, cooks hearty meals, tends to the small plot of lettuce, herbs, the tomatoes Bel advised. It's pleasant having a boarder, though Joe is often glum. Stuck in the past, his talk sounds to her like faulty translation, or jacket copy spilling the beans without the full story. Or the hidden details of a negative. In fact, she finds him undeveloped. This man with the full head of gray hair and set jaw is scared to death of his shadow, scared there might be someone still there. He once loved a girl—well my goodness! And solaced himself with the bottle. Cowardly lion, while she's in need of a heart, hers numb as the tough nut of her ambition. And there is the missing child, Rita, sullen in the back of the Buick studying her lady magazines, the chubbette lurking in her bedroom while she turned the earth in Bel's garden. Rita is somewhere baking pies for her husband—granite counters, Cuisinart, no trace of the dumpy kitchen on the lane. Working in the darkroom of the Riccardi-Dunphy kitchen, Gemma invents the rewards of Rita's disappearance. She develops the film shot during the day when she prowls the neighborhood in a caftan, gift of the Minister of Tourism, Morocco. (*National Geographic*—sand ripples, camels, mounds of dates and figs in the bazaar—Kodak color Land 55). The days come on hot and humid, so she wears the caftan with gold braid to the amusement of her neighbors, the Wakowskis. She writes down their names, Sue and Henry. They sit on the front porch for their picture with Sandy, mixed breed. And the kids running naked in the spray of a fountain and the grizzled vet with the track marks running up to the dragon tattoo of his outfit in Nam and the pierced poet chalking the sidewalk with verses. And Joe, she takes him in a moment when he looks up from his papers, startled as an animal new to the zoo, then he smiles to please her and she snaps him again.

She will not go near Land's End to report on the demolition. "Spare me the kudos of Damien Forché." Riccardi taking her pictures, her gift or limitation. Hometown, nothing fancy, nothing new, which after all is her signature. The plot of earth with the first picking of basil, the hard green tomatoes keep her in one place for the season. Who would have thought it would be the Murphy girl got away? Not a question to put to Joe, heavy with this loss when he should be mourning his mother. He's launched himself into a detective story to track Rita, married to a squealer, imagine! A shotgun wedding, that Rita unable to testify against her husband, the lucky couple packed away. Gemma never asks her boarder how long he will stay or what he's up to in Phil Dunphy's bedroom. She doesn't expect a little brown envelope with the weekly payment. In the evening, she sets their places at the kitchen table with the oddments left behind by renters she never set eyes on. Her glass of wine, his iced tea. The upper floor is now empty, and she thinks to settle Joe in a place of his own. He has never been on his own, passed from his mother to Mother Church. In Salvador there were poor women to wash and cook for the gringo sent to save them. Then again, she likes to come in from taking her pictures, from weeding the garden to find him writing whatever he writes to the authorities that run his life, and to the office of the U.S. Attorney begging for news of Rita. Plea bargaining, she calls it.

. . .

What he's up to: writing on Gemma's laptop to his Provincial in New York, that's one project, a letter of his departure from the Society rewritten each day, which will be sent, he vows it. Writing to the U.S. Attorney in Providence, he uses *S.J.,* Rita always in mind, the wife of Manuel Salgado, the union boss who ratted on his partners in crime. Somewhere in the fifty states, Rita is monitored by a U.S. marshal to assure she has contact with family in the eventuality of crisis or death. When he arrives at the State House, he is shown into the upper reaches, which look over a city all new to him, an impressive mall, the river buttressed by a highway, in the distance the gilded dome of the Old Stone Bank. Bel had parked right in front, and they'd watched students in sculls racing downriver, then crossed the bridge and found the Arcade with sad little shops—tobacco store, shoe repair, millinery. His mother had made them climb to the top. There was no view, just a dirty glass ceiling. Nevertheless, an excursion. He takes his workman's watch out of his pocket, black suit today, wonders if it is part of the game, keeping him waiting, time to consider he's an old fool.

"We took a chance, you know." This from the assigned contact, an assistant state's attorney who looks twelve to Father Murphy, flustered going up against a priest. "A chance letting the wife stay behind. We understand the crisis is over, that is . . ." At a loss for words.

"The death of our mother?"

"Well, yes."

"So I must wait for another crisis?"

"A medical event, it would have to be major. In a federal case, we get reports from the marshal. Of course, they could come out of the program, the Salgados. It happens if a party can't adjust to the situation."

"What sort of gamble would that be, reverting to Rita, to Salgado?"

The attorney offers no answer, contemplates the mall, swirling letters—Lord & Taylor, Sears. "Could be the climate, the change. Times, they're lonely."

Joe endures a long moment of silence, then asks, "The charges? What do you have on this Manny?"

"It's not nice."

"Beyond fraud, extortion?"

"Nothing to tell you. Forgive me, Father."

"No need. It's your job. We are in the same confidence game."

. . .

He finds the Salgado children. No problem for the contact giving those names, though the son has been legally Brett for some years. He grants the priest an appointment, not his office, his home on Saturday, gives directions to a gated community on the Connecticut shore. Joe Murphy last drove a VW bus in Aguileres, before its tires were stolen. He fears death from a semi tailing him on I-95. He scoots out of control drawing up to Brett's mega house, sets off an alarm. Manny's son steps onto the circular drive to speak with this old party rutting his perfect lawn, prying.

A trim middle-aged man, wound tight, small as a jockey, Mr. Brett is scrappy, "It's actually none of your business. Have you ever lived with a fuckup for a father? A turncoat?"

Joe can't say that he has, but notes *turncoat* and the Boston College sweatshirt. Brett is an educated man, his harangue of sharp words carefully chosen to address this priest who might have taught him. It's good riddance to Manny wherever he is. "I'm not without sympathy for your situation. If you'd like a second opinion, call my sister."

He leaves Father Murphy in the scalding sun of the driveway, returns with the telephone number written on his card—

Anthony Brett

INVESTMENTS • REAL ESTATE • INSURANCE

A curious Mrs. Brett now stands in the enormous double doors of her house, doors fit for a church on a New England green. She is wrapped in a towel, still dripping from the pool. Stays in shape, Joe thinks, wiry body, a sharp nose sniffing out fear. A vagrant, a beggar come to her door, seedy old man unsteady on his feet, a threat to their comfortable life, to their disconnect from Manny. As he pulls away in Gemma's rental, he gets Brett in the rearview mirror, stroking the ground, healing the tire tracks in his lawn. The interview has taken less than five minutes, Joe checking his watch against the clock on the dashboard set for another lease, another season.

• • •

He calls Mimi Salgado at Bon Soir, in Boca Raton. Two phones: one for the boutique, one unlisted. When the phone rings, the one she dreads, she leaves a good customer trying on satin sailor pants that won't zip. She hangs up on the man who's calling. When she answers again, Mimi whispers, "Father *who?*"

"Murphy. It's about Rita, my sister."

"I don't know any Rita."

"The woman who married your father."

"That slut? Killed my mother."

She slaps down the phone. Pooch yaps in his little bassinette made for a doll. He knows when his mistress is upset, but does not stir from his nest. Visibly shaken, Mimi prays, *Jesus, protect the dear one*, smooths the Yorkie's topknot, goes back to her business with a woman from Venezuela whose husband got the money out in time. Mimi suggests ghetto jeans that are fashionably baggy, parachute silk in an 8, vanity sizing.

When the phone rings again, she lets it ring, *dear Jesus*, finally answers.

"Killed?" The man's voice unsteady, choking back sobs, "Killed, *killed?*"

Mimi hisses into the mouthpiece, "I meant with the goddamn massage, the manipulation. I don't care the doctor sent Rita. Leave her in peace."

"The massage?"

"Leave my mother in peace. She was dying."

Pooch is licking her hand, soft laps of love, *holy Jesus*.

The customer is thirty years too old for the parachute jeans. Very expensive, half the thrill of the sale. Not today. Today Mimi turns CLOSED on the door of Bon Soir, calls her brother.

"He's nothing," Tony says.

"So you gave him my number!"

"A sick old priest. It's a pathetic situation."

Not pathetic, she takes no comfort in her brother's cool consolation. *Tragic*'s the word, always the men waiting for her father. Cops circling the block. Little Manny with his buddies. When they were kids, they knew those guys were protection. *Let them be blotted out of the book of the living.* The neighbors knew, and her mother. Her father was a neat small man, dressy, that's where she gets the style, not from her mother, who married a fisherman wanting a simple life, not brick facing, three car garage, mink and the Elsa Perreti. Her mother prayed for Tony to go into the law, to have law on her side. That didn't work out; after BC with the priests, he threw in with his father.

"How's the pooch?" Tony asks. They have little to say to each other.

"She's the best." The best little doggie, her gift from God, with little wet nose sniffing her tearstained cheek.

Her mother's hands knotted with arthritis, unable to turn a knob, open a door, and that woman sent by the doctors, Rita, with the implements of torture, pulleys and spongy rubber balls, when all Carlotta Salgado wanted was to dwindle away on the hospital bed set up in the Florida room so she could be with her plants, the trailing lantanas, rex begonias, not even a little sweetheart, a pooch for companion. And her father laughing with the woman—fat thighs, plus-size 16—laughing at lines from last night's TV. *The mouth of a loose woman is like a deep pit.* The cheery Rita playing doctor with her blood pressure kit, her jars of salves and lotions to pound into her patient's brittle body. Rita from public service, a freebie when there was all that money, that filth. Always the deal, someone knew someone, tell me about racketeering. Mimi was married then, down the block in a Tudor. She stopped coming by in the morning, not to see her father looking spiffy, waiting for Rita to march in the front door with her dose of disease. Jesus knows when a person carries evil in their bones, like those two laughing and chatting while her mother wasted. Only once she said to her father, "You could do better."

Mimi Salgado leaves the boutique by the back door. Pooch in her pocketbook, a fresh ribbon in her topknot, biscuit for a good girl. What's pathetic, she will say that to Tony, she will call him and say pathetic is to let that priest in the door. Give out her unlisted number. Tonight she will go to prayer study. She will speak her heart to Jesus. The Lord is her protector, not buddies or her husband with his harlot in the Tudor, not even her son who threw in with Manny Salgado. Her boy, she will not let his name come to her troubled mind. She will ask Jesus to save her from the wicked and from her brother. The Lord will take her to His heart. He sees their evil, their killing kindness with weights and pulleys. Wherever they are, Manny and Rita, He hears their laughter. They will be silenced. Killers cannot hide from the Lord.

Mimi's hands tremble as she locks up Bon Soir, too early for study at the Tabernacle. Preacher, a man sent by the Almighty, has given her the lesson for the evening. It lives in her Palm Pilot: *The heart knows its own bitterness and no stranger shares its joy.* Proverbs 14:10. On this day of betrayal she has been dealt a hard text that she cannot as yet understand. There is an hour not to idle, to give to her nails that must be wrapped, lacquered, the better to serve customers, the better to honor her Lord. Our bodies are His vessels that we inhabit for a season. Though we be bent and shattered, we are His children. The manicurist massages her palms, heats the soothing wax. Mimi's fingers find peace in the lavender balm.

"That's one adorable dog. What's his name?"

"She. She's my girl."

On cue, the Yorkie is adorable, sniffing the perfumed air.

. . .

Gemma says, "Stay on. You're no trouble."

"A trouble to myself." He longs for his sleepwalking days at Loyola, the bare room of his wakeful nights, the correct answers of the classroom, the kids making fun of Joe the Murph. He daydreams of being farmed out to a parish, shooting baskets in the driveway before dinner with a suburban family. When the kids are out of the way, the parents will ask him about the abuse of children by the clergy, the unavoidable subject. He will advise that celibacy, part of the problem, was only written into church law in 1215. Read the *Decameron*. He will say it is unfortunately very old news, these sinful secrets, the betrayal of our bodies. Or not sinful, which brings to mind Fiona. Though he prays for loss of memory appropriate to his years, she lives on, ripe and ready. He was the virgin. Fiona brushing her dark red hair. He takes the brush out of her hand, throws it aside, hears it skim across the floor, then the breath of their silence. His fingers in the tangle of her curls as she gently pulls him to the cot. He wears the saffron robes of a Buddhist monk, a false claim to the simple peace/love of Anima Mundi. He explores the drift of freckles on her pale face, God's perfect imperfections. He is stunned by the details of this recovery, the floral scent of her shampoo, the scratch of a two-day beard he wore to please her, the soft padding of their Chinatown slippers, Italian macaroons dipped in red wine, total recall of his desire for that girl. *Our one desire and choice should be what will best help us attain the purpose for which we are created*, his crude appropriation of Loyola's lesson. He looks out to Gemma's backyard on Cotrell Street where a little garden flourishes, a letter from his superior in hand, a kind pastoral letter from an ambitious boy he once taught at Fordham. He is asked to reconsider, take time, recall to mind and heart his vows.

. . .

"Stay on," Gemma says, but thinks he will go missing. They speak of his mother, Gemma recounting the predictable plots of Bel's silents she's seen, Joe calling up excursions in the Buick, bedtime stories for children, simple one-reelers.

Or he will not go missing. There is no detective story, no clue beyond his sister's bright summer clothes. For three weeks he's been seduced by the notion that in his pursuit of Rita he is choosing the way.

"Summer—she might be anywhere, Vermont to Texas."

He rules out Oregon and Alaska as chilly. At the end of July, Gemma drives him to the train that will take him to Grand Central, back to Loyola.

III

Dog Days

Let faith oust fact; let fancy oust memory;
I look deep down and do believe.
—Melville, *Moby-Dick; or, The Whale*

Rhus Toxicodendron

Tomatoes hang heavy in Gemma Riccardi's garden, hard and warm to the touch, still green as she stakes them. Perhaps planted too late to ripen. She takes their hard pale skin as a sign that she will fail again, this time as a gardener, though the basil is coming on bushy, the lettuce perfect as the tender leaves you might buy at a farmer's market. It's hotter than she remembers this town on the bay. The Wakowskis have said she must water early or late, not in the heat of the day, so she's in the muddy compost with a hose, seven-thirty, not every morning.

Overwater and your crop will have no taste.

What crop? Who's she kidding? When she turns to the house, she sees the empty eyes of the windows upstairs and the shade pulled in the back bedroom. On the day that Joe Murphy left, she did the strangest thing, pushed Dunphy's bed and dresser aside, moved her equipment in, pulled the shade, never in her life felt so lonely. It's hotter than hell in there, and the heat speeds up the developing bath, prints with no depth, no contrast. The expense of an air conditioner means nothing to Riccardi, it's as though she's bound to stick it out for more than a few leaves of lettuce and hard green tomatoes, for control over the photos she's taking of life on Cotrell Street, once her home.

. . .

Pet (Elizabeth Strumm) stands in a tangle of poison ivy at the break in the old lady's hedge. The shingle cottage is gone. From the picture window of her rented house, she has watched its roof and walls being carted away in Dumpsters, hunks of plaster with strips of wallpaper flapping, sinks and toilets disemboweled, battered doors rent from their hinges. The place cleaned out by Goodwill before the demolition, the trophy of a stuffed panda tied to the hood of the yellow van. Pet knows she should pack up and leave, but stays on, punishing herself with a glimpse of the black convertible, Forché at the wheel in baseball cap, Carlo greased for the sun. Now they have departed. Why has she come to the old lady's garden in this heat without shelter? She lives alone with bits of wicker furniture, a lumpy sofa, like Goldilocks tries out each ill-fitting bed. The mismatched plates and spoons, totally grungy, belong to no one, summer rental stuff. Pet, who is not a reader, thumbs through the discarded best sellers and guide to the sights of Rhode Island. A picture book of Ferraris, Maseratis with the name Ricky Pinchot in a sloppy boy's hand, and a *Fannie Farmer Cookbook* stained with chocolate and translucent splotches of butter, seem to Pet totally sad.

Her red MG sits in the driveway. Surely he must have seen it.

In town she buys Doodles and Fritos, frozen enchiladas, Häagen-Dazs Cookies 'n Cream and a fifth of Stoli. As she gobbles forbidden goodies, Liz Strumm of Springfield, Illinois, suspects this life day by day without will is called maybe Clinical Depression. It's an effort to slip in a CD, someone's Motown or bebop or Schumann, an effort to turn off the hours of daytime TV. Time melts in this heat like that sick watch of Dalí's. Her thighs bulge in Comme Des Garçons jeans, breasts pop her Armani jacket. In the mirror she sees herself like, exactly like in the high school yearbook, corn fed, ripe for the picking; a robust American girl no prize for the runway or the cruel lens of Damien Forché. The house is sticky, stifling. Not to hear the noise of destruction, she shuts the windows tight till the wreckers finish their day. At night she sleeps a drenched sleep without drugs. In her gear, a model's vast store of expensive creams, paints and dyes, Pet that was has a supply of candy that might make her happy—Zoloft, Prozac. To pop one, just one, would be an act of will, a step in some direction. The trucks grind past her window, heavy with rubble at the end of the day.

Then it is quiet. A day of rest, Sunday? TV says that the temperature throughout Southern New England is ten degrees above normal. Flipping along in flipflops, Liz walks down the lane in the blast of midday. Far below she sees the beach is crowded, little ant people stirring up the water, scrambling in the sand. This is healthy, walking as she did to the old lady, walking with Joe, who listened to her sob story, that's what it was, total girl-grief. The silence of the day has calmed if not cured her. She stands in the break in the hedge, viewing the empty half-acre lot. There is nothing, not a tree or flower, not a shingle or splinter of glass, a hole in the ground where once a cellar. Liz does not trespass, just looks on as though this scene of devastation is framed, picture of war zone. But there is a cement wound in the earth, long and narrow, with stones placed round it like graves where the bodies are buried.

As she turns to run away, her flipflops come off in the thicket of poison ivy. "Leaflets three, let it be," Liz remembers from Girl Scouts, and runs barefoot back up Land's End. In the bathroom of her rented house she scours her ankles and feet with an ancient cake of laundry soap, a comforting self-flagellation, then anoints the scraped flesh with the dregs of the bottle of Stoli. That should do it, but driving through the night, when she is more than halfway to Springfield, the prickle begins, the rash flames. How long had she looked on at that desolate scene in Rhode Island? Time enough for the oils of *Rhus toxicodendron* to bond with her skin. She draws off the interstate at Columbus, tries to sleep by the side of the road. In an all-night drugstore in Dayton she buys peanut-butter cups, calamine and *Vogue,* the September issue, out early as always, with Pet (no last name) on the cover, wearing a glen-plaid bustier, Queen of Scots as classy rocker. One blond tress hangs to the meager mound of her right breast, wind fans the rest of her ironed hair to the sky. It had taken all day to get that shot, one of maybe hundreds. Hands on hips, pelvis tilted to right, to left, center forward, a pose he discarded. Her left hand idles at the lacing of the plaid contraption, itchy under the studio lights, while the right arm, sporting a Celtic bracelet, is flung aloft: daring, free spirit. Pet flaunts her chill touch-me-not smile on a million and a half *Vogues*. She buys three, cleans out the store. At this checkout counter no one will see her. The lens capped, end of a grueling session, the shuttered look of his eyes. It was like he'd stolen her soul with the camera. Dawn in the shopping plaza. A man with a jug of milk, a jumbo pack of diapers takes off in his SUV. Liz Strumm plunks herself down on a dewy island with struggling petunias, screws the top off the calamine, dabs at her raw feet and ankles. The blisters are weeping.

She drives out of Eastern Standard Time at the Illinois state line and on through Urbana-Champaign, where she should have

MAUREEN HOWARD

learned her lesson. She has gained an hour, may be home in time for supper.

. . .

Paul Flynn opens the chessboard, sets out the men. He is on the roof of the lower school, fitted out with a jungle gym and swings. The city is trapped in a heat wave, a brownout sucks the cool from the air-conditioned buildings of Loyola. The long summer daylight exposes the priest to his neighbors. Waiting for dark, he's brought vigil lights up from the chapel, cold beers and cans of Pepsi in a bucket. Waiting for Joe Murphy, who said he was up for a game, but said little else about the death of his mother. The silence of their play is always punctuated by groans at a stupid move, yelps of triumph. Perhaps there will be a moment to ask after the sister left alone in Rhode Island or the details of the burial. Joe has been away for more than a visit, and their only conversation was that blip on the phone, nonsense about leaving the order. He's sorry he made light of his friend's despair—retire, play golf. Weeks left of the Summer, he will propose they do a stretch of the Appalachian Trail. Perhaps one he's hiked before, the easy stretch in the Berkshires short of Mount Greylock. By his count, Paul Flynn has done a good half of the A.T., has plans for the Blue Ridge to Harpers Ferry where the Shenandoah and the Potomac cross, *worth a voyage across the Atlantic*—Jefferson, quoted to his class, who fake interest in Whistling Gap, Big Bald, Devil's Pulpit, the friendly shelters of the Trail, midges, cow pies. He'll stick the Summer out with Murph, stop short of Greylock, the mountain too high for Joe's trick heart. Below, the clever babble of hip-hop at the light on 89th. His students pretend they belong to that angry world. He attempts to instruct them in the false freedom, drugs and money, the commercial depths of the music business. Given the choice, they would rather listen to him on the slaughter at Antietam or the

Thru Hikers who make it to Maine. The light changes, dead silence. The city can't get its breath. He lights the vigils. Then the thud of the metal fire door shoved open, and Murphy comes toward his little altar of skill and deception. Paul Flynn takes the first game with a crafty rook ending.

Joe twists the top off a beer. "What harm?"

"None at all, a hot night."

"Otto Sauer"—Joe gulps from the bottle—"he was a neighbor made his own in the cellar. That was back in the town my parents came from. Prohibition. My father said it was the best, better than Guinness in the field hospital before they shipped him home from the war. But he drank Bud when I was a boy. It was cheap. He was barely making it till the next war came round. Did I say he sold insurance?"

"Murph, you never said a thing. Except you came clean about Salvador."

"Not so clean, but I was raised with these stories, just a few of them packed when they left Ansonia, Connecticut. The beer and the watch, the heavy one I carry, made by my grandfather on the kitchen table, and the teapot from Ireland. Did I show you the teapot I brought with me from home?"

"You did not." Paul Flynn is laying out the rank and file of their men. His friend has never spoken of his family beyond a mother and sister who dote, which was to be expected. There is something near sacred about this night, with the heat pressing down, and their lofty position in the playground with the sticky rubber surface so the children will come to no harm, the pilfered candles flickering. A beer-drinking vigil. "No teapot," Flynn says.

"Well, every family has one—a pot, a plate, a spoon—the memory totem with a story that tells you where you come from, though not one of us ever got back to Ireland." He puts the beer aside, not the solution. "Though many families do not have the revered item, nothing to show if the shanty is torched and the men mostly missing. But I have this goddamn teapot."

Back in his room, Paul Flynn stands at the open window watching Con Ed work a pit, the men stripped to the waist. Wearing their safety helmets, they carry their lamps with them to the underworld. A connection has frayed or blown right at the doorstep of the school. On this extraordinary night, he has witnessed something like a confession. So out of practice with the sacraments, he did not say *go in peace* at the end of Joe's story, or drama, that was it—a drama to break your heart, like a movie that brings you to tears and you're ashamed when you go out into the night. The shame that he bears at open emotion, as a man of his time, as a priest. Lying in his room with the power outage weighing on the city, he figures they are of an age, an age that kept the family secrets, Murph's self-effacement presumed to be the mark of a humble man, almost holy. And all the while he was part of this extraordinary family with a movie actress mother, his sister gone to the bad, the heroic father. Insurance, the man sold insurance against the demons—a bent fender, disability, death. Tim Murphy seemed like the father in a family movie pitched high. He suggested as much—Dana Andrews, Jimmy Stewart?

"You've got the wrong war," Joe said. "You're the historian."

True, but the Murphys' epic skimmed time, like the links his students get on the Net, doughboy to U-boats to militant Jesuits, Mack Sennett's Bathing Beauties to the tearjerkers of post–World War II, Melville to Manny, a Portuguese fisherman after all. He's a throwback, warning his kids the links are too easy, back to the books, the whole story. Upon the roof they had played lightning chess, swift careless moves played so badly Flynn folded the board. The night was thick, noiseless. Joe walked to the roof's edge as though he needed a breather before going on with The Murphys of Land's End, the last bit: how he botched his mother's wake, laughed and sang as if to please her, in his eulogy had carried on about day trips to keep her truant spirit alive. Flynn wanted to say, Why did you come back? But said, "Take more time."

"That's what they all say. I've had my time. More than allotted for the yearly visit."

They were standing at the door of Murphy's room, that bare cell he chose to live in. In the flicker of a vigil light, he held the teapot up for view, cream china with little shamrocks. "*Our mother feedeth thus our little life, / That we in turn may feed her with our death. A fragment, not one of my poets.*" But he's never told Flynn about his poets of contemplation. His pal with the chess set in hand now had the burden of his incomplete story. He had left out Fiona.

At dawn the air conditioning kicks in, a blast of cold air stirs the papers on Joe's desk. His copy of the notarized agreement with the flourish of Damien Forché's signature, letters with Loyola's crest *in the hopes that you will take counsel.* . . . The psychiatrist on 96th Street to be considered, and a note in Gemma's bold hand. They had been laughing at excursions, the fancy word Bel used. When a boy, he had looked it up in the big dictionary at school. *Escape from confinement; progression beyond fixed limits.* And the treats—twenty-eight flavors, fried clams and franks. They had been laughing at Bel declaiming *Moby*. Gemma handing him her scribbled note: *Pick up Ball Park Mustard.*

"Yes, home in time for supper."

Dead letters, still, he must deal with a note from the young attorney who patiently explains once again what constitutes a crisis under the Witness Protection Program. Terminal illness permits the bedside farewell, or death by natural or unnatural cause. Joe Murphy's heart flutters with something like joy at the prospect that he must give his life to spring Rita. Then considers the chance it may work the other way round. Place your bets: the route is not perfectly clear, not inked on a map of Rhode Island.

BON SOIR

"I opened with nighties, lingerie. When I went into casuals, I'm thinking, *Night and Day,* but by then I had what you call a following."

Mimi Salgado talking to Preacher—holy, you can see by his eyes, dark orbs of wisdom. Lean as a saint who prays in the desert, though pale as an angel of the Lord. The miracle moment. Mimi is early, alone in the Tabernacle with Pooch at her side, and Preacher is just there in a white Nehru jacket, just there, placing Bibles on each chair. She is stunned by his humility. How many pilgrims would gladly assist.

"*Soir* is fitting." His voice has that blessed conviction, just gabbing with Mimi. "Night is good. When the day's work is done, night is the Lord's blessing."

Mimi now distributes the Bibles while this Messenger of the Gospels lights the candles for prayer. Helpers in blue robes come to test the mike, set up the system. She can't believe she has mentioned nighties to this chosen man who fasts, cleanses his body for Jesus. Pooch trails Mimi chair to chair, nipping at her heels, just as helpful. Sweet thing must stay in her bag with Bow Wow Biscuits when prayer and study begin. Only now does Mimi notice the ribbon marking the page in each Bible. Matthew 6, though how was she to tell which verse, her eye running down the page settles at 6:19—*Do not lay up for yourselves treasures on earth, where moth and rust consume and where thieves break in and steal.* Perhaps that is this day's text, and if not it is a sign. She has missed the last meeting, fighting with her landlord who won't ante up for hurricane insurance. Costs a pile! So? It's his mini-mall, right in the swank heart of Boca. Her father could handle that bastard, one visit from Manny Salgado would cook that slime's meat. She fears water damage, moth in this season devouring cashmere, shoplifters, spiraling winds, the vacant eye of the storm. There are four named hurricanes swirling in the Caribbean. Settling Pooch in her bag as the flock straggles in, Mimi repents: she would never seek the aid of her father.

Preacher, wand of the mike in hand, marches the length of the stage, flips the page: Matthew 7:6—*Do not give dogs what is holy; and do not throw your pearls before swine, lest they trample them under foot and turn to attack you.* Now, that is a lesson hard to figure. Pooch has occasionally nibbled at her toes. Bow Wows are little treats, not manna from heaven. She prays for understanding. Jesus meant beasts, not Yorkies. Preacher now raising the mike to heaven, His grace to descend.

"Someone give me a hallelujah." In a mighty chorus, men and women, old and young, cry out the response. Preacher urging his flock to recall how generous they have been to a son or daughter, to a neighbor or husband. "*Pearls before swine.* And were you not trampled. Did they not turn to attack you. . . ."

One side of Mimi, a woman's face is washed in tears; the other, a boy trembles, his whole frail body shaking with the truth of the Messenger's words. She sees Rita Murphy by the side of her mother's bed, Carlotta smiling sweetly, asking her daughter to bring the nurse, calling the intruder nurse, a cup of tea as the heavy woman lit into the ruined flesh that fell away from her mother's bones.

"Maybe tea's not her thing," Manny said. He did not even know the pounder's name.

When Mimi returned, the woman had flipped the patient on her side, so her mother could not see her daughter rejected with the porcelain cup and saucer, sugar and cream.

"I like coffee, I like tea. I like the boys and the boys like me."

Her father turning from the window, where he watched for the thugs, laughed for the first time in months. "Maybe coffee?"

"Coffee, you guessed it."

Which began their mornings of feeble jokes and the stout woman's muffins, coffee cake, feasting while Carlotta wasted.

If she had known then that sickness was not of God. There is only one Great Physician, Jesus. If she were granted another moment with Pastor calling for a Moral Crusade—"Give God a hand!"—she would tell how she came to Boca, trampled by her father, then by her husband, who lived with a whore in her Tudor, paid off to get out of the way like she was still standing there with the tea set. How Tony Brett, that bullshit name, her brother said get out, get out long before the investigation. If another miracle moment was granted with Preacher, Mimi would tell how she built the business, how at Bon Soir she discovered her gift, advising concealment or exposure, seeing each body in her boutique with its soul.

That night the tides rise with Hurricane Edith. Pooch whimpers as Mimi tapes the plate glass windows of Bon Soir. The lights flicker, go out. In the dark she touches the fine linens and silks on their hangers, lace nighties, cashmere sweaters and shawls in their Frenchified cupboards, every garment so fragile, defenseless. She sits on the Yorkie's little chaise longue. If the shop goes with its goods and her precious girl, Dear Jesus, let them go together. By candlelight she reads in Matthew: houses built on stone which withstand the storm, or houses built on sand, *and the rain fell, and the floods came, and the winds blew and beat against that house, and it fell; and great was that fall.*

Edith falters, blows up the coast. The storm is played out by the time it hits Rhode Island, flapping the awnings in town, watering Gemma Riccardi's basil and tomatoes, wetting the fresh concrete in the lap pool that runs at a stylish angle in the sandy earth at the end of the Murphys' lane.

IV

The Tontine

For the man whose house is insured may thereby be rendered less rather than more careful with regard to the risk of fire.
—Josiah Royce, "War and Insurance," August 27, 1914

Insurance on Lives

Come all ye Gen'rous Husbands, with your Wives
Insure round Sums, on your precarious Lives ; —
That to your comfort, when your Dead & Rotten
Your Widow may be Rich when you're forgotten

What could be better? The canvas lounge by the side of the pool, the sun not yet high in the sky, no question of a burn with straw hats and the lotion. Ray likes to dip and dry off, then finish his second cup of milky coffee, which she brings along in a thermos. He's all over brown, the darker frown on his face looks drawn in with lead pencil. You have to squint against the sun, but the frown comes when the mommies appear with the splashers, the squealers. Then Jen packs up, smiling—you want to be nice, to be friendly—and they hightail it back to the townhouse, theirs among so many, taking care at the steps leading down from the pool. Turn at the purple hibiscus, count down five units on the left, go round the greyhound trembling in its cage, frightened almost to death by the scrape of the lounge chairs against the walkway. The dog's high, plaintive yowling.

"They starve them for the track, hungry to chase the rabbit. It's a rescue operation. I was never into dogs." Ray knows about the track—horses, not dogs. "Punks run the dogs."

Seven on the right from the gas grill chained to the fence and they are home, nine-thirty in the morning. Nothing could be better.

When the sun climbed over the lone date palm left at the edge of the parking lot, the depth of La Cumbra Terrace vanished. Units stuck one to another, row upon row, appear flat as cutouts, the paper decorations—Santas, hearts, angels she pinned on the bulletin board in the rehab back home. But early morning is good, each patio with an umbrella or a picnic table, pots of flowers and statues, each owner making their townhouse home. Early is best. The day follows.

Only he doesn't look like a Ray who sold his business, small appliances, and came out here for the weather after angioplasty and a stent in his aorta, a risky operation. He will tell you about it if the talk is health talk, often the case when visiting with elderly neighbors. Ray still up for a game of golf, weekdays you don't have to wait till hell freezes over before you tee off.

"Well, it's heaven out here." Jen laughs, tapping her husband on the wrist. Another glass of wine with folks from St. Paul, then it's home to supper. She's some cook and will tell you about it at length, about fusion, her spicy black-bean sauce, her blowfish risotto. Up to the minute—well, you have to be, nobody's going to find Jen, that roly-poly, playing bingo at the Senior Center. Three days a week yoga at home when he's off to the course, lays out her mat, slips in the video, mutes it, and what could be better than the gentle stretch, the slow bend. Jen knows about the body, the story it tells of anxiety, cramped muscles that won't give in to pleasure, to the extension of life.

"We never had kids," she says, "that's why Ray's such a grouch with the splashers."

This evening they are having a cookout at the Mortons', three units from the greyhound whining and scratching at its cage. Ray sneaks down the walkway with a hunk of lamb off his kabob and feeds the poor thing.

"Do you think you should have? With the curry and all?"

The nights are so long in the Summer, just like back home, "Only in Vermont you could use a sweater."

The Mortons, native Californians, have done New England, been to Vermont, but not up past Brattleboro, where Ray had the store. He doesn't look like a storekeeper—gnarled, you would say, knots big as tennis balls in his legs. Always looking around on the course, kind of a tic, tight swing and a dash for the golf cart like it's leaving, last bus out of town. He's, you would say, swarthy, with a gut over his belt no bigger than a dirt-bike tire. A nervous guy, wisps of black hair—does he dye it?—rough features, the old wood-carver himself in a storybook not for children.

What could be better than having a husband who gets out of the house, plays golf with a bunch of old geezers? She is splayed in the half cobra position attempting stillness of mind. Thing is, she is hefty, no longer young, though she doesn't show her age—the henna wash, the contacts, the clothes California-gaudy after all those years in woolly Vermont with the pancakes and maple syrup. Cobra pose, she's a beginner—stretch, aim at union. She knows the body, worked with every muscle, bone and tendon, while Ray kept the store. Famous in the rehab, Jen's gentle massage and the vigor of her manipulations. Now she would like to get beyond body, beyond body type, which roots her as earthbound, dependable, persistent, all those cold years unable to imagine her life. Now she imagines every day on command, imagines a town north of Brattleboro, Vermont, which is not unlike a town in Rhode Island, only there is no bay, no shore, no prospect. Quilts and maple syrup, inventing herself each day, she leans heavily on snow, on black ice and the brick mills of New England, which might be the textile mills along the Providence River, or the foundries of Ansonia, Connecticut, where she once traveled as a girl, an excursion to a cemetery, her dad driving the company Ford. Before Bel won the Buick.

Jen Peebles aims for clarity, but it's old dog new tricks, and with effort she flips to the corpse position. Clarity of mind in which she selects from Ray's stories. Not the store in Vermont with the convection ovens, juicers, bread makers, microwaves, and why he never went in for the hassle of fridges, TVs. His fish stories, how you advise your customers of the warranties, "You'd be surprised, they don't send in the warranties."

No half-told tales of graft and corruption. "You get started as a kid. There's no turning back, Rita."

A slip when they are alone. Alone in the townhouse with leased furniture and climate control. Alone with her thoughts, knowing she will never know the full story, Manny turning state's evidence, facts—figures, dates, names, names spilled out with a plea for mercy. That he came clean, witnessed, went straight to her heart.

"Quit school. Out in the boats. What, are you going to bring your children up in some Portuguese shack, like it's old time fishing? Catch of the day?"

There is no turning back.

She is certain of their present safety when the marshal comes by, a young woman conventionally suited for a bank, for the office. Not a looker, dull brown hair, serious and pale like she lived somewhere else, not sunny CA. Ray assures their keeper they've had no contact, their cut-off complete, finito. The young woman—niece? possible daughter of friends?—affects an air of concern.

"Oh, we're doin' fine."

"Never better."

Which means nowhere near death or disclosure, drinking iced

tea this day, something of an occasion. It has been a year since Rita Murphy Salgado handed over her car at Bradley Airport and came out to join Manny.

Ray and Jen visiting with a young neighbor from Vermont. The cookies are delicious, a touch of anise. On the financial side, Jen holds the cards: "You know my father was in insurance. He provided." This announced proudly at each visit, so they may have attached Ray's house, the car, left him flat broke where he began as a boy going out for the cod, but she's clean, standing pat. She could almost laugh at the clever transfer of her money. Ray says it's like those scams you read about. "Slippery bank accounts some Caribbean island, but legal, set up by the feds. They get away with murder."

"Not funny," Jen says.

Every visit, the marshal suggests there are occasions when a witness in the program gets a bit gabby, self-destructs, or occasions when the old life spills over, that's to say recurrence of unhealthy habits.

"Nothing like that," Ray says.

The marshal's cell beeps. She talks in short, coded sentences, takes her leave, and Jen wonders how many clients, if she calls them clients, will she call on in a day, like a social worker, like the women who sent her out on assignments, sent her to Manny's wife, thinking of that poor woman lying in a hospital bed set up in the Florida room. Official, checking them out, Miss Marshal made her visit.

"A tough cookie," says Ray.

"She was only speaking of unhealthy, a way of life." Now, why did she say that, when they are here in the sun, free and easy, safe as townhouses? A phrase which might amuse her mother, dead this past year. Funny thing is, when the marshal comes round to check out the present, both Peebleses are overwhelmed with the past.

Ray stands guard at the front window waiting for his buddies to circle the block, escort him to a meeting in Providence or Boston's North End, the fishing business extended to construction, money in urban renewal, like he said to the feds, he was middle management—dispensable, that's the word. On the record union boss? So tell us about the structure of the company, they said, nature of the contracts, tell about accidents. All very polite until, sucking in his breath, the young U.S. Attorney got rough about maybe drugs, a little medication dealt on the docks, and listed charges which if you thought about time away would add up. *How old are you now, Mr. Salgado? So you have something to tell us?*

"You feel she didn't want chat today with the tea and the cookies." Manny packs the cell to call from the course. What could be better than a thoughtful man who calls home to pick up whatever for supper?

And Rita, why be drawn into the make-believe of their plot, *Rita* moons about the empty living room with the lean sofa and comfy modern chairs, arranges a vase, a statue of the Little Mermaid on a shelf with a Sessions clock bought at an antiques fair, an old Bakelite clock made in Connecticut. It lost time. Manny laughs when she winds it.

"Don't say it."

He says not a word about the clock on the stove, or the battery clock on the bedside table. Kind to her always, that was how it started, Rita falling for—*low-life*, her brother called him—hood with a dying wife who wanted out of this life. Settled in the cocoon of her silk coverlet among flourishing houseplants, Carlotta Salgado smiled faintly at the plump woman who came to massage her body as though to awaken it in a story that cheated death. Manny so obliging, ate the muffins she brought, though no need with the housekeeper and the disapproving daughter who lived down the block. A neighborhood of fancy houses, the new breed of lawyers, dentists, bankers who commuted to Providence, using the old mill town, the fishing port, as a suburban refuge from city life. Well, small town was enough for Rita Murphy with her work, bringing life back to the atrophied limbs of her patients in rehab, driving out on assignments which were seldom as useless as working the blanched legs and arms of Carlotta Salgado. She remembers placing the soft rubber ball in the slack hand that refused this little gift of possible improvement, the bright red ball dribbling across the tiles of the Florida room, and Manny scooping it up, throwing it to her, their smiling together, the situation hopeless. She knew that the men waiting for him were thugs. If her father had been alive, but what use Tim Murphy's moral fiber, as her mother called it, a breakfast food promoted by God, or her brother, the priest too good for working with bodies, or Bel, who abandoned the tempting image of herself in satin and pearls. No use at all, and what could be better than a man who needed her comfort? She'd never see sixty again.

"You're my babe," he said, his sweetie pie, doll, Manny's talk out of date, out of innocent times gone by. Times when he talked about his business she didn't get the lingo at all. Didn't want to know, that's the truth of it. He was kind, calling her after Carlotta died for sympathy in short supply, his kids disconnecting years before the investigation. One night he took her to dinner in Providence, fancy steak house in town, a spot once known for seafood, now steel and glass with college-kid waiters. She laughed at every little invention, the fluted napkins, lilies floating in water, the water eight dollars a bottle, the pêches flambées, laughing together as though she was free of Bel and the shingle cottage, as though he'd washed his hands of fishy business. That was the night he drove her home. Seeing that her mother's light was out, they prowled the house like thieves, took the risk of stealing upstairs to her room with the stuffed animals and the photo of her brother in a black cassock. They stood apart, these awkward lovers, for their strange mating had taken place in an airport hotel off the highway, no need for words now as he touched the pristine bureau scarf, nail buffer, beads and bracelets spilled on a china tray, the trinkets of a girl, which is what she finally heard, *girl*, "That's my girl," in his hoarse male whisper. She knew it was her innocence he fell for, hook, line and sinker. Her big panda's glass eyes shone with blank gaiety, her own eyes brimming with girlish emotion.

Their romance had flourished, an undercover operation right through the investigation. And what's wrong with saving yourself? A new page, Father Joe? Deep breathing, clearing her mind, the yoga instructor thin, young, agile, her body twisted in a pretzel. Rita, still a beginner, closes her eyes, a year in this valley that spreads out from Los Angeles. She remembers the day Manny picked her up at LAX, the sun through smog as expected, heavy traffic and, set up on the dry brown hill above La Cienega, the famous HOLLYWOOD spelled out, a bit dusty, w tilted. Was the sign there when her mother lived in this city of dreams? That night when she unpacked—the furniture motel-modern, bed and dresser of pale laminated wood—she set *The Silver Screen* under bright T-shirts bought back home while she waited patiently for Bel to die, bought for the new life with Manny waiting for her on the patio with a bottle of wine. The fan magazine had always been hidden in Bel's closet, off limits. At the door of this bright impersonal room, she turned and retrieved it. Show it to Manny, that was her thought, Hollywood, the connection.

"Look." She flipped to "The Sweethearts of Yesteryear." "I wasn't kidding."

"Never thought you were."

He studied Isabel Maher in the fading California sun. The pearls and white couch had yellowed on the cheap paper; the star of the silents' glossy cap of black hair dimmed to gray. "Ancient history," he said, not unkindly.

This was their first night in the new world. The jet lag, the wine made her giddy. *The Silver Screen* lay between them. "Wasn't she swell?"

He had ordered in Mexican. Manny in the kitchen a sight to behold, juggling tortillas and salsa. She found her way back to the bedroom, tucked Bel out of sight in the dresser. In the morning she would learn the details of Ray and Jen Peebles, the childless couple who fled the cruel winters in Vermont. Ray had come out to La Cumbra Terrace to settle in. Months back it seemed plausible, what with the bypass, stent in the aorta, that she took on the stress of selling off the house and the store.

The yoga instructor closes her eyes, brings it down, mouthing words of inner beauty and peace. At the end of the tape, her hands come together as Joe's hands in prayer, a few words of grace before supper at Land's End. Their parents' laughter when the town actually named the lane, by order of the U.S. Post Office. With some difficulty, Rita gets up from her exercise mat. She is sixty-nine years old—now, isn't that something—flexing and stretching in the promised land. Press rewind for day after tomorrow, when Manny plays golf. Suppose she went to the phone and called Joe at Loyola. No, went to the Mortons'. Manny's belief: their phone tapped.

Suppose she called it a crisis, her need for ancient history, or called simply to hear his voice say Rita, her name. Four o'clock back east. He'd have finished his lauds or complines, whichever came after noon. What a natural way to keep track of the day, Bel said, "Sunrise, sunset, call of the bells!"

"But the clock factory!" She'd said that to her mother as though to argue, then fell silent. She would only provoke the story of the quartz watch that killed her grandfather Pat Maher, who died back in mechanical time.

And the Russians are coming to supper—Nina and Ash, who live directly across the walkway with a grape arbor over their patio and little white lights left up since Christmas, though they are Jews. Young people, transplants like so many of the old folks in townhouses that go on and on in the Valley. There's always an awkward moment when Ash asks about the store in Vermont, why Ray stuck with small-time appliances. Wal-Mart move in, sell the techno, read manual, easy as pies. Language breaks down. Ash does something advanced with computers. The Mirskys are blond and hearty, happy with their lives, all aspects—the Mexican tiles of their temple, the shopping, deli knishes and rugelah they will bring in a pastry box from Bel Air, not clear what Nina does there for a living. That's how it is at La Cumbra, the woman who owns the greyhound works for a studio, something to do with costumes, away on location. Why rescue the starved dog only to cage him? Ray and Jen Peebles have their script in hand, but in the shower, work and lives reel in Rita's steamy head: Mangione's hardware store; Phil Dunn, carpenter; the Dunphys keeping books at the mill. A clear memory of Henri Pinchot slipping her foot into the measuring device, 6B, a dainty foot for a large woman. Daddy, the provider: insurance. A heavy burden of the past when the marshal comes by, and today marks a year of the plausible life, a year and a day since Bel's death, that would be. The pock-pock of firecrackers in the parking lot sets the greyhound keening. Fourth of July.

Rita runs for the phone decently wrapped in a towel. Lemongrass and wasabi, any market along the way. What could be better than a man who picks up what's needed for supper? On her knees, the familiar position of prayer, clear in her mind, she tells the Hail Marys of childhood. Praying for the phone to ring, for Father Joe with no crisis, just her brother and their mumbled words of forgiveness, the way they made up when they were kids after a row. She was not herself those days after Bel died, not poor old Rita, second fiddle, good soul. Possessed by the dream of departure, she refused Joe's counsel, his priestly advice. Her future all planned with such care by Manny and the U.S. Attorney. That youngster, what right had he to ask was this her choice? He could see she knew next to nothing about her husband's affairs. Twisting the new ring on her finger, there was no turning back. What was she, femme fatale, schemer like Stanwyck in *Double Indemnity*? Well, her dad didn't buy the insurance agent in that movie, poor chump come to the door to renew the lapsed policies on the Plymouth and La Salle.

"Couldn't keep his pants on."

"Now, Tim, he was vamped by her ankle, that's all the Hays Office let by." Bel allowed the end of the book was better. "They're stuck with each other till the end of the line. Like the schemer says, can't get off the trolley." Her mother, such a reader.

Rita prays, the old formula of repentance, *heartily sorry,* begging forgiveness, then slips into the palms and parrots, the bright muumuu her husband loves. The pock-pock of firecrackers, whiz of a rocket. One year to the day, Bel laid out in a violet silk dress never worn, bought years back as though for the occasion of death. Rita's hand trembles as she dials Father Flynn, Joe's friend at Loyola. Joe won't have a phone in his name, inviting hardship not required by the order. The phone rings, then Flynn's firm classroom voice: *Leave a message.*

To speak, speak to my brother, her words gobbled, *No crisis,* in tears, *a year and a day. Can't leave my number. Tell Joe waiting is gruesome, like Daddy's Tontine.*

Why bring up family stories? Father Flynn could never guess their embarrassment when Dad talked insurance—false claims, swindlers attempting to pull the wool over Prudential's eyes. The Great Fire of London? Did they know that tragedy was responsible for houses of brick, safer than thatch and wood, like the third little pig's—couldn't blow down? Marine insurance. Didn't they live right here in Rhode Island? Insure the ship and its cargo. Slaves were cargo of value. How many ships sailed out? How many lost at sea, not to mention mutiny, pirates? That was exciting when they were children; later, sighs of boredom, their father, spare with words, revving up for what Joe called his claims for insurance. The Tontine! Then they were in for it, Lorenzo Tonti, the Italian who made his way to Paris to sell his scheme to enrich the bankrupt King of France. The King wasn't buying. Tim Murphy called Tonti's partnerships a scam. Yearly contributions and the money of whoever dies first is thrown in the pot and so on, death upon death until the last man standing gets the prize.

Gruesome, Bel's word, waiting for others to die. Waiting for the crisis promised by the marshal, the young attorney? Rita's only prize—her deathbed reunion with Joe. Tonti was on the take, yet couldn't feed his family. His system might tempt you to murder or fraud. Betting on lives, such gambling was not assurance. Oh, you can insure against invasion and rain, insure the twinkle toes of a dancer. Seventeenth century, you could insure against going to hell. Joe said he got it out of newsletters, the Insurance Society of America, their father no student of history. Dad's lesson, thrusting his good arm forward to make the point, the power of human control over the accidents of daily life. He believed in his product. More than his daughter believes in the double bed in this room, or the woman in the mirror with mahogany hair, a pudge draped in bright flora and fauna, crying over the spilt milk of the past. She has not made the connection to her brother, the only living soul who can laugh at Daddy's Tontine. When the telephone bill comes, Manny will discover her call to Loyola.

· · ·

"Io. You're Io," Joe said, as though assigning her to a part in the make-believe of little children, but they were in high school, the first years of his Latin studies, already acknowledged to be preparation for his calling. His teacher had rewarded him with the translation of Ovid's Meta-

morphoses. *Joe latched on to the pagan tales, wild stuff. "Io, it's the name of a cow."*

"Thanks a lot."

"I mean, a cow can't speak, speak our language." *He was standing at the door of her room, recently gone teen-girl with lace bureau scarves and ruffled curtains, a fringed lampshade that cast his sister in a forgiving light. On the crocheted bedspread, a rabbit in a peach satin gown clutched a celluloid carrot between her paws. He stood with the Metamorphoses in hand, his finger marking the page where Io, a lovely nymph, is transformed into a white calf by Juno so Jove can't have at her. That's not what he meant to tell Rita, not that love stuff of the story. Balanced on the threshold, Joe was reluctant to enter her world of fancy toys not meant to be played with. Photos of smiling girls who could do no wrong in the movies, Deanna Durbin and Gloria Jean, were stuck in a mirror. Why her crush on goody-good stars with show-off opera voices? Rita couldn't carry a tune; besides, he'd come to say something about how she doesn't talk anymore, not walking home from school or at supper, not in Bel's car.*

She laughed. "I'm a cow. So what's your problem?"

"Forget it, no problem." *He went back to his room, lay on his Indian blanket. He turned to the page where Io's family does not know the beautiful white heifer, sadly mooing, to be their daughter and sister. With one forefoot she makes an I in the dirt and an O beside it. Perhaps he had only wanted to read that story of the mute calf to Rita. In his godless book so many stories within stories to believe while you were reading them. Not all nymphs come to a happy end. Joe was fifteen, not ripe for preaching, for speaking in parables about the end of childhood, of filial affection. In the end Io is claimed by her family and awarded a lover. Her mooing gives way to speech.*

•   •   •

As Rita's blubbering did to Paul Flynn long-distance. Her husband will see the telephone bill, or the call to New York may be picked up by the marshal. Suppose she were to retrace her steps, get a plane out of LAX to Bradley Airport, take the keys to her car from a plainclothes official, bit player in the film run backwards until she was once again hauling her suitcases—thump, thump, thump, up the stairs in the shingle cottage, a comic rewind. Then Father Joe would be strolling down the lane, breviary in hand, never play the bitter scene with his sister. Alas, her departure is as frozen in time as Isabel Maher's in *My Darling Daughter*, though Rita was never doomed by a bankrupt father to marry a slick Moneybucks, yet she was surely Daddy's darling, like the innocent American song says—*a boy for you, a girl for me*—that's how the Murphys sorted out into teams—*can't you see how happy we would be*. She's not simple, never was, just grounded like Tim Murphy, no flights of fancy, no artifice to her at all. Miscast as Jen Peebles in her adventure with Manny.

On the day her father died, a Saturday, she'd been on duty at the rehab coaxing a patient to take a few steps free of the walker, a gruff Vietnam vet in a black T-shirt with an emblem of crossed bones, tibia of both his left and right leg shattered on the road that led to Newport Beach, a bikers' rally. A sweet man broken in spirit by the war he'd not won. He took a step, then two, then fell against her strong body.

"Pisser!"

"Try again."

"Give up on me, Rita." He wanted the walker, the wheelchair.

When she drove home that day, there was Bel in the garden, naturally, a flowing skirt and crisp apron, head tied in a kerchief, the idealized peasant—not her daughter's thought, yet a flick of recognition went through Rita's head. Where had she seen such a costumed worker? A bright summer day, the windows of the house open, the unmistakable patter of a Red Sox game. Her father would be watching. She'd sit by his side, rooting for the team as she did often, once till late at night—a spectacular overtime. Her mother, puffed with pleasure, held a pot of brilliant red flowers, smiling as though posed for a snapshot. Yes, Bel, I see you. Who could miss that grin of satisfaction?

Her father stiff as a pillar on the couch. She knew at once that he was dead, not sleeping through Yankees 2–0, ninth inning, Yastrzemski at bat, two men on for the Sox. She marveled at the death grip of the beer can in Daddy's good hand, the hand he'd trained like a magician's to do everyday tasks, beat the odds. She stole across the carpet and sat beside him. His eyes were fixed on the screen. She lifted the injured arm, no pulse. These fingers had always been stiff, now she caressed them, father and daughter breathless as the crowd in Fenway Park. The first pitch low, inside. Yaz tipped off, fouled again and then the miraculous crack of the bat, the ball sailing beyond the distant Green Monster, out of earthly bounds. The crowd went wild as she closed her father's eyes, turned off the set and went to get Bel, her tears silent, not sharing the homer. The next day she would read the score to her mother, Bel, a picture in widow's black. Then Rita remembered the three of them, late show on a Saturday night, the long skirt and nurse's white apron of 1916. *Farewell to Arms*, Helen Hayes wiping the brow of Gary Cooper, an injured soldier she loved, though in the end it's the angel of mercy who dies.

. . .

On her way to the kitchen, Rita slaps the fan magazine down on the glass coffee table for anyone to see Garbo's head thrown back in abandon, eyes half closed in cool seduction. The star of stars clutches a richly embroidered shawl round her shoulders, which might drop at any moment, any moment on the set of *The Divine Woman*, 1927. "Where Have They Gone?" Hollywood looking back on its short history, nostalgia for sweethearts of yesteryear at the outset of the Second World War. Bel was beautiful, but even in satin and pearls just the girl next door, or so her daughter thinks as she hacks away with the poultry sheers, severing duck breast from ribs, thighs from legs. The marshal's visit has brought on such grieving for the past, yearning for the present, let it come down to this year and a day. Tomorrow she should be at Bel's grave with a tribute—a book, a flower. Her every move now extremely dangerous, recklessly chopping bok choy, the blood runs free from a cut on her finger. In the drone of climate control, a touch of vertigo. Rita Murphy finally gets it: she's not leading her own life.

Manny finds her crying with a giant Band-Aid on her wound. "Babe!" Kiss to the injured finger, she's his cutie, knows nothing beyond what she's told, nice Catholic girl with stuffed animals who came to work over Carlotta, didn't know she was coming on to him with the muffins, with jokes circulating in the rehab. "Sweetheart, sell it as a leaseback," he instructed when they could figure with some accuracy Bel was not immortal. Crappy little house. Quaint, that's what she called it, fisherman's cottage, view of the bay. What did people like the Murphys know of fishermen, two families to a shack? Miss Marshal inferring, that's the word, he'd lucked out living off his wife's money, off her care, no one else gave a damn. Rita, kindness itself, asking after his game. He'd whacked, sliced air, run for cover under the awning of the golf cart. Righteous, that's the word—bitch of a woman's talk of unhealthy habits. What's unhealthy thinking about the boss he put away, man he worked for not exactly going to the office, though like he said, middle management, bastard kept him down. Tony and the grandson came along for the ride, smart boys bailed out well in advance of the investigation, don't give a hot damn he's dead or alive. Plain Jane comes in her navy blue suit for iced tea, upsets Rita. Finito, no connections.

"That cap!" OK, she's laughing at him with the Korean chopper in hand.

He's still wearing his cap, makes him look like Jimmy Cagney, *Yankee Doodle Dandy*, twenty years watching old movies with her mother after the provider passed on, straight arrow with the busted arm.

"Sixth of July, I came out here."

"It's the Fourth."

"So not quite a year in L.A." She knows it's nine o'clock in New York. If Joe is home, no chance he is reading theology in the dreary cell he calls home, viewed once on a trip to the big city, a conference on sports medicine, therapists from the sticks, demos on new tricks with the body. The mind. She was not supposed to be in priestly quarters at Loyola—an aging population, her brother said, showing her his iron bed, straight chair, faded Kodachromes of family. Nine, he's playing chess with Flynn, a gentle addiction. On this day he must be remembering Bel, maybe even his sister, how she had gone sour and feisty. Following her heart, wasn't that the idea? She hears Manny in the shower singing; now, isn't that fine. What could be better than running her life, wok on the range. A year and a day since her mother called out for Joey, who never got the message. When she ran to Bel's side only silence, the blessing of a hand shooing her off. To let her go free, that is how she thinks of her mother's last gesture. Free, she goes to the coffee table, looks Garbo in the eye, a beauty who left the business. Rita is running her life. She has called Flynn, set out *The Silver Screen*. Let it come down.

· · ·

Nina and Ash arrive with grapes from their arbor, who would believe it? Little red grapes sweetened by the sun. The Peebleses are their American neighbors they treat with respect, as they would old people in Georgia, where they were raised, by the Black Sea's side, Ash explains. He calls the Peebleses Ray and Jen, is the California way. Ray mocks his L.A. enthusiasm for traffic on the freeway, exhibitionists parading the beach at Venice. Nina, an aficionado of everything Disney, has been twice on the studio tour. Tonight, Fourth of July, they have come with a dry white from Sonoma and the rugelah Nina picks up in Bel Air, each stuck with a little American flag. Dinner is otherworld, nothing Jen cooked up in Vermont—sweet-hot dishes surprising the jaded palate. From down the walkway a char smell of barbecue.

"Please!"

Ray closes the sliding glass door. You have to savor faint perfume of basmati, scent of ginger honey on duck breast. Not U.S. of A. for the glorious Fourth. Amazing what she has picked up a year away from pancakes and sausage. Fusion, the men sit outside with vodka and counterfeit Cuban cigars. Battery of pock-pock-pocks like gunshot in movies. The greyhound yelps, his cries high pitched, constant.

The women wash up, then drink dainty cups of black coffee. There is nothing to say, once Jen's called up the parade with the mayor of Brattleboro, with war vets and the high school band. Neighbors without gossip, without talk beyond weather, television news. Nina picks up the fan magazine. "So old! Is who?"

"Garbo!" Doesn't know Garbo? Can she be that young, that foreign? And then, why not when dealing with such a blank slate? Rita Murphy turns to the picture of Isabel Maher.

"This is my mother." She speaks slowly. Nina will understand: "My mother, she was a star."

"Is true?"

True to Nina as murky photos of czarinas, as Snow White bedding down her dwarfs, as Tinker Bell or Pocahontas, as sipping black coffee in La Cumbra Terrace, township of Tarzana, San Fernando Valley. True and amazing, an American story, figuring the silent star born before Revolution, before Stalin in Politburo. Language breaks down. Eight o'clock Pacific Time. The Mirskys and Peebleses watch the Los Angeles Philharmonic in a stirring salute to America, security tight in the Hollywood Bowl. The capacity crowd assured by Kenny Rogers, hardly your dad, still fatherly, mellow, tried-and-true singing *the rocket's red glare, the bombs bursting in air,* sing along, get it rolling. Bring it down to *Lonesome Road* and all through the philharmonic Gershwin, Copland, *Grand Canyon Suite,* Jen is fine allowing herself a sip of Ray's vodka, a second sweet pastry. The light show super—red, white, and blue projecting Old Glory all through the Cole Porter, she's OK, laughing at the maestro's dip to "Love Me Tender" as though the wrong score and a wave goes through the crowd, *His truth is marching on,* fine during the commercials and a switch to Coke, to beer, enough with that vodka. Fine until the medley of Sousa marches, then she breaks down, holding Garbo to her breast, sobbing softly, but who can see in the last blue hour of a summer night? Who can hear with the patriotic pyrotechnics?

Be kind to your web-footed friends. The Sessions clock reads ten, that's the next day in New York. Joe will sleep in peace, having said his lauds in that cell with two crossed sticks on the blank wall. Or may not sleep, having received her message. There is no crisis, no deathbed scene this day or tomorrow, L.A. or New York.

"Just so moving," dabbing her eyes, bear hugs from the Russians. If she were home in Rhode Island, she would choose a book to lay on Bel's grave, foolish, as though the story could seep into earth, the pages never yellow or blow away, a weight never finished, Bel's book they laughed at, *Moby-Dick; or, The Whale.*

· · ·

Manny, a little tight, stumbling into his pajamas. His calves knotted, lower back cramped. She has failed with every manipulation of his body, every laying on of hands. He lies stiff as the dummy she practiced on when first learning her therapeutic trade. What could be better than a pat of his hand? The night follows. Pock of the firecrackers, screech of rockets. Carousing up by the pool. The greyhound's cry endless, caged poor thing. Nine o'clock in New York. Joe may not be at Loyola, the season each year of his visit. She prays he is off on retreat, will not hear a word of her gibberish, weeping to Flynn. That would buy time, go back, rewind, a blessing. Sleepless hours go by till she steals out of bed. Moonlight plays its tricks, white as snow on the roofs of La Cumbra, little peaked roofs of a village in Vermont, setting for a simple tale instructing children in good and evil. She steps out onto the warm bricks of the patio. Endless Summer in this place, dry heat they claim good for you, never a breeze. Rita waits, that's how she will tell it, that she was simply taking the air when the blast went off louder than the rockets heard all through the night. The greyhound keening just broke her heart. She will say how the lights all down the walkway were off. Inside you don't hear the yowling, with climate control, but she had stepped out, then turned back to her kitchen for the poultry shears and did not know what she was thinking, or was not thinking at all, as she found her way in the dark toward the purple hibiscus. The dog was trembling in his cage as though cold, no, afraid, the whole body alive with fear, poor scrawny thing, his coat smooth as silver when she put her hand in to comfort, just a touch. The woman who did something with costumes was not home— seldom home, she'd heard from the Mortons, three units down. Why rescue an animal you did not care for? Save it from chasing the mechanical rabbit? Cutting the wire that confined him, like severing duck wing from breast, leg from thigh, it was that easy. The dog's heart thumping at a frantic pace in his narrow chest, stilt legs shaking. She will say, I thought to take him by the collar. There was a fancy collar with brass studs. And what did she think she would do with a stolen greyhound?

"Quiet him. Feed him. Take him to our condo, here in La Cumbra where my husband, Ray Peebles . . .

"But he bolted?"

"Yes, he ran free."

Her husband slept through the disturbance, but a mother nursing her baby, that would be directly across from the Mortons, light from her window stretched to the patio, where the greyhound cowered and whined. Looking down from above, she saw the old lady in a nightgown. Yes, that nightgown with floppy sleeves like white wings. Crouched down on the walkway, clipping at the cage, that old lady she was sure of. The dog's owner in Santa Fe on a picture. Someone fed it, walked it, a nuisance. And when the dog ran wild, the old woman ran after, tripping where the steps lead up to the pool. A dead dog on the highway, the identifying tag on his collar. In the morning police were taking pictures of the mutilated cage. The mother came with babe in arms to tell them, a witness.

. . .

It is ten by the Bakelite clock on the knickknack shelf in La Cumbra 63C.

"Anniversary, that's the word," Manny says. "Tell them, sweetheart, about the anniversary, your mother's death. She was upset. The dog drove her crazy."

Nursing her bruised knees, Rita speaks in her own defense, innocent admissions against self-interest, exhibiting the page with Isabel Maher on the MGM couch, 1928. "A year and a day my mother buried, not here, in Rhode Island." She will repeat this down at the station, after she has been escorted past curious residents of La Cumbra. Mothers protect the squealers, the splashers from the sight of the woman who made nice every morning at the pool. In the parking lot, the faint gunpowder smell of firecrackers in the air. Though her crime is no more than a misdemeanor, the dead greyhound, poultry shears, Jen Peebles, née Murphy, is tabloid news, or no news at all, another looney-tune, but Area of Dominant Influence is L.A.; local item: Silent Screen Daughter Goes Nuts.

. . .

Upbeat woman at the news desk: You've got to love this Hollywood story. Swaddled in fox fur, tears in her eyes, Isabel Maher in My Darling Daughter, *mother of the accused, Rita Salgado, the seventy-year-old resident of La Cumbra Terrace who came to Los Angeles to write her own script. Rita on the courthouse steps, a sober blue suit for her arraignment, waving to the delegation from the ASPCA noisily supporting her. The commentator mourning the greyhound.*

Salgado, Witness Protection scrapped, an editorial decision.

The miracle of magnetic restoration provides a clip from the archives: Bel in a bathing suit flirts with a famous fatty, gives the camera the blink of an eye. Silent Screen Daughter, a thirty-second spot.

Limos arriving at the Getty Museum: a fund-raiser for the restoration of the Frank Lloyd Wright house in Griffith Park brings out the upper crust.

Rita's moment prolonged by letters to the *L.A. Times* from the animal people: the perpetrator was kind, brave, that dog illnourished, starved for affection. The negligent owner of the greyhound protests, but dare not press charges. Rita Salgado is sentenced to community service in a rehab, the sentence suspended given her age.

Iced tea, but no cookies for this last meeting with the marshal. Turning to the young woman, who wears the gray uniform of her profession upon this occasion, Rita smiles, hoping for what? A

MAUREEN HOWARD

frayed net of protection. Malicious mischief is not the marshal's territory, but she is sympathetic to her clients, Rita and Manuel Salgado, suggesting they move to safe quarters, perhaps the Pacific Northwest. They must understand they are no longer in the program.

"Finito." Manny sits next to his wife. "Thanks, we'll stay on at La Cumbra."

The Salgado story falls quickly into place with the neighbors: how he aided and abetted the investigation back east, turned in the boss and his buddies, went straight. Now Rita is free at last to call Father Flynn, who reveals with slow and deliberate care the news that Joe has been, indeed, at his post this past year at Loyola, but never got the message that all is well in California. He's been gone now for some days. Gone off, call it a crisis of faith. Off, God knows where, leaving the address of a woman in Rhode Island.

"That Gemma."

Yes, Gemma Riccardi, who apparently knows nothing, yet the note with her address signals some intention. Flynn thinks to say people disappear—in wars and natural disasters, in ordinary life— then thinks the big picture is worse, no comfort. Each night he calls Rita in Tarzana, California, believing it's his way of grieving for the loss of his friend, the passing of their communal life. He plays chess against himself on the computer. His backpack and hiking boots sit by his door. He walks miles upon miles in Central Park. Its artificial rambles, heavy traffic of joggers round the reservoir can't compare to nature untarnished or the solitude of the Trail. Involving himself in the Murphys' plot, Father Flynn reports to the superior: Joe is away, settling his mother's estate. Each night he calls, "Rita?"

Who else would be waiting by the phone? "Paul?"

They console each other. It has been three weeks since her appearance in court. Five nights since she first spoke to Joe's friend without fear. "Manny's so kind, right here by my side," her throat clogged with tears. One night, visitors and Manny in the background, she whispers, "I don't think he gets it, about Joey, about family."

Father Flynn wonders how long they can indulge in their conspiracy. At the end of each call he repeats words that tell her nothing: "The Lord works in mysterious ways. Every day has its mysteries, Rita."

She'd never let her brother get away with that. "Every day has its sorrows."

• • •

Sirius, the dog star, is in the decline. The worst days of Summer coming to an end in an election year. The entertainment of political conventions consumes the country, though not Gemma Riccardi in her air-conditioned studio, working in a frenzy printing the photos of the neighborhood she takes each day. The Salgados do not venture out of climate control to the pool in the heat of the morning, each day a sizzling color-coded scorcher on the morning news, hovering near a hundred degrees. Manny switches channels, politics to last night's Yankees, then comforts his wife with a cooking show.

"Come on, babe, he's making the meatless lasagna." Which for some reason sets Rita choking back tears. She has lost her taste for adventures in the kitchen, serves up microwaved Lean Cuisine. How Joe loved her home cooking when he came for his visits, pancakes and muffins, bloody steaks, home fries. The common room of Loyola is comfortable as Flynn checkmates himself in a thoughtless move, picks up the pieces and turns on a game, Red Sox 0, Yankees 3. Love the Sox, Murphy said, and you get your heart broken. There is need for fillers, harmless curiosities, sidebars of information to alleviate the domestic tax plans and global prospects of the candidates. At the loping end of a dull baseball season and in this political climate, the story of the greyhound does not go away.

In North Dakota an albino bison is born, one of its kind in the world, romps with its mother. A school of beached whales, gasping for air, wash up on the shore in Santa Barbara. Since the fables of childhood, animals are proven items, more often than not tugging at the heartstrings with the story of their dependence on our curiosity and our kindness, their mute wonder at clever creatures who built the Ark. Unlike the genetically bleached bison and flapping whales, the greyhound, unfortunately dead, lent itself to human interest beyond the thirty-second spot of local news. *Never enough stories.* Let the public consider the court's indulgence to this aging woman who freed a caged dog in an act of mercy, a woman recently retired in Los Angeles, where strangely enough, her mother, a forgotten star of silent film . . . So it spins, and the dog struck down on the highway lights like a feather along with the droppings of Canada geese devastating golf courses across America. . . . *Her mother, forgotten by the public*—a clip of the Bathing Beauty vamping the famous fatty, scene set up by a gagman, then Rita in her courtroom suit waving to her supporters.

RERUNS

The sweetheart of yesteryear was not forgotten by Victor Szabo, a scholar hungry for any scrap dropped from the banquet table of silent screen lore, among his files the photo of Isabel Maher on the white couch, satin and pearls. He has read the untrustworthy piece in *The Silver Screen* that reveals the actress "romanced" by her director as well as other bigwigs in the business. In preparation for "The Hermeneutics of Silence," he has studied the restored film of *My Darling Daughter*, lip reading to determine that Maher spoke every line of the script, that she could act had she not been in the heavy hands of William Banks, an uninspired director. Flirty and

185

fresh, with a wry little smile, Maher was a sprightly comedian in many two-reelers, but no one of note in a list of lost sweethearts, not a snuffed candle to Garbo, Louise Brooks, but useful in a paper Szabo has in mind: "Mutations of Orality in Late Silent Film." Isabel Maher's precise delivery of her lines was a footnote to the work of Chaplin, Keaton, Harold Lloyd, the greats who resisted crossing over, who got caught up in the trials and errors of synchronized motion and sound.

Never enough stories: Victor Szabo has been working up the silents for years, a slight fellow with squint eyes, oversized ears; looking and listening to silent film his life's work, his calling. He can tell his students that Lloyd hangs from the minute hand on the clock in *Safety Last,* that the audience gasped aloud at the thrill of the bespectacled hero dangling high above the city street, a composite shot—four cameras, stunt man standing in for the star. He can tell them how many frames make up the sequence, but they are into random-access, non-linear systems, not a flicker of interest in ye olde Moviola—chitchat, filler—digerati waiting for Szabo to get off his hobby horse, get on with the lecture: "The Dialogic Speech Act in the Materiality of Ambient Sound." Szabo is unashamed of his passion, sifting through re-recorded mixers, restorations; anthropology of sorts, with all the dangers of the natives dissembling or turning against you. When he calls the daughter of Isabel Maher, the husband says she's upset with the death.

"The dog, that's understandable."

"Of her mother."

Manny slams down the phone. He's had it with the dog, the mother, the brother, with skimpy portions of Swedish meatballs, mac and cheese. Rita is fading on him, drooping, her complaints much like Carlotta's. Now that the feds no longer pay up for the condo, now that they own the unit, nothing pleases his wife—the rented furniture, recycled air, never an ocean breeze. Enough—the old lady's sofa, dining room chairs, like that was some palace, squat house end of nowhere. The yoga mat stuffed in the closet. Times when he's watching the Yanks—who plays golf in this heat? Her old man hated the Yankees. Manny thinks how she blew his cover, the dog and her mother all over TV, how the boss could send someone out or make contact, some obliging contact in L.A., middle management, come to finish off Manny the Mouth. But that's the old habits, old fears, finito. He looks at his wife waiting by the phone, remembers the good times, even Miss Marshal checking them out. "Sweetheart," he says, "the weather breaks, we go up to the pool."

. . .

Pluto, god of the underworld, keeps his wife half the year, the dark Winter half. So can he be cast as Rita Murphy's husband? They live in climate control, a netherworld neither Summer nor Winter, comfort level A/C. She has followed him to this sunny place of her own free will (how free in the throes of love?), so the myth breaks down, as they mostly do when transcribed pagan to Christian, book to life, novel to film. Yet Manny is bewildered as many gods by his fate or his crime, a poor boy wanting to get the stink of fish off his hands, transformation on the waterfront, an American story. What did he do but make it nice for his wife, his children? What did he do to deserve their contempt? No longer acknowledged as their father when he calls, now that he can call, now that he's out in the cold, so to speak? The son dusts him off. The daughter talks Jesus. He blames Carlotta for that, the Virgin in the garden, the rosary clutched in her dying hand. The good people of La Cumbra adjust to Salgado, one of those stories, you come out here from Russia, Rhode Island, Vermont. The wife caused the trouble. The cage is still there, the sharp flaps of its escape hatch a reminder of negligence. The dog's owner off to the next film—wardrobe?

Pluto, god of death. Is it fair to paste that on Manny? What he spilled to the young prosecutor sealed, finito. Graft, robbery, murder suggested by the priest, Rita Salgado's brother, who as a boy read Ovid, loving those stories that morphed one into another, as Peebles segues to Pluto, racketeering to small appliances, maple syrup to iced tea with the marshal. In Ovid each body is buried with a coin to pay the ferryman who crosses you over the river of death. Pay up, there's no freebie, but not even a fair coin in Manny's pocket. It's some kind of hell in the townhouse with his wife on the phone for her evening consolation with yet another priest, and his daughter taped on TV declaring for Jesus, sickness is not of God, middle of the night Pacific Time, cheap time, the comics and reruns over nights you can't sleep, his little girl lost in the crowd of weepers, wailers for their sins and forgiveness. "Some Catholic girl! A good thing your mother is dead." Shouting at the screen as though it's a lousy call at second base, and his wife, a ghostly apparition in the doorway, bleary-eyed. "Come to bed." Pluto is not even a planet, just a dark icy star. Pluto, a Mickey Mouse dog, digs in the dirt for a bone.

· · ·

In the spirit of scholarly intruder, despite the turnoff by Rita Salgado's husband, the professor of silents makes his way to La Cumbra 63C, digital camera in hand. Rita steps out on the patio for yet another interview with the animal people. 100°.

Szabo spots Mr. Salgado putting on a felt green.

"Don't mind Manny. Please, no pictures."

"No pictures." How to put it to this woman trapped in her own small story? "I admire your mother's work."

"She never worked."

"Her work in the movies."

"Bel never spoke of her time out here. She liked movies. We all do."

He backs up. They gab about movies: how his mother took him

MAUREEN HOWARD

as a kid to an art theater, the Thalia, Upper West Side of New York, showed the old pictures, the foreign films his mother didn't want him to miss and the old silents, all flickering movement and light; how Rita Murphy watched late into the night, top of Bel's hit list Hepburn and Roz Russell, Connecticut girls with lots of spunk, did he know?

"Watched late into the night."

"Alone?"

"No, we watched together."

"Bel, her voice? Can you tell me about her voice?"

"Oh, her voice was just fine. Daddy called it sweet, but I couldn't see it."

"Hear it?"

"Sorry I can't invite you inside. My husband has trouble with strangers."

A plastic golf ball pops against the glass door, Mr. Salgado's contribution to . . . what might Victor Szabo call the aborted interview? Disruptive discourse. A splotch of red stains Rita Salgado's throat, her eyes tear as she speaks of the greyhound and protection, how a cage is no protection. The professor is witness to a meltdown in the intolerable heat, thinks she could die right there on the simmering bricks, helps her to collapse in a hot metal chair. What comfort can he offer in this unfortunate pass?

"I have a print of *Kid Tilly,* one of her nifty two-reelers. You might like to see it."

"Once. Not now. Let her rest. She wouldn't want to know he's a hood—Manny, I mean—or that Joey is missing in action. That's my brother, the priest. Why let Bel see what's become of her children?"

Szabo dizzy with the thought the woman has fallen off the bridge between then and now, living and dead, as though a close-up of Isabel Maher, hearing her daughter's upset, might speak back, scold or comfort from the screen.

189

"She sounded, you know, like my mother."

Manny at the sliding glass door, putter in hand: "Get what you came for?"

"He came about Bel."

"Ancient history."

"You said that before. You said that the night I came out here."

Finding himself in a domestic dispute, Szabo is down the walkway, round the corner by the purple hibiscus, the turn to the Mortons', finds his way to the pool, when she catches him up.

He takes the tattered copy of the old fan magazine from her politely, gossip by the yard. "Thanks, I've seen it."

"How could you?"

The professor spells out archives, cultural history, leading to the interview with Isabel Maher in *Classic*. "Now, that picture of your mother is superb."

"*Classic?*" Clutching *The Silver Screen*, the sacred text, "It's all here about the director. And the other one. Wolf. She talked about him, not the movies."

"Wolf?"

"Someone who made it out here. Watching the credits, Meyer, she said, Meyer was a bright boy."

Not a bad sort, Szabo leads her back to 63C.

Her husband stands sentry at the glass door. "She's upset."

The scholar of silent trivia is dismissed. He'd like to say he'd come by with his photocopy from *Classic*, the studio shot of the young actress about to enter the star system, Bel, as her daughter called her, tousled, full of mischief in a fringed cowgirl skirt above her fetching knees, a live number not yet the dead meat on MGM's couch. The interview, recalled from Victor Szabo's trash heap of movie lore, in which Maher said her dad made guns back east, pistols not like the rifle she shot in *Kid Tilly*, and, believe it or not, she loved books, had no beaux. A peppy American girl—if they ever got the machine fixed up, she'd be happy to give talkers a go.

Before he is halfway back to the solitary viewing room of his apartment Szabo has figured Meyer as Meyer Wolf, who sure enough made it until he was blacklisted, then made it again, when all that was just history. Meyer Wolf: propaganda movies during the war, 1940s that war, Russkie peasants dancing, surfeit of balalaika, popular-front sentimentality, then ominous *noirs* of the Fifties, something gone rotten in the state of the nation. Meyer Wolf, the Oscars passed him by, yet a legend trotted out at Cannes some years ago, surfacing again at Sundance. It's all been a goose chase, this business of Isabel Maher. Stay with Fields and Keaton, the mess Lloyd made of sound in *Movie Crazy*. That night Victor Szabo is distracted as he watches *Monsieur Verdoux* for the umpteenth time, can't get his dander up about Chaplin abandoning the Little Tramp for this bitter French farce, anti-war, preachy anti-corporate script, not a moment of sublime footwork. Drinking Hungarian wine, the professor knows he will bore his students with the weak projection of Chaplin's voice, a melancholy thought, for how often he tells them of the gasps and cries of the audience who came together for the silents. Live, they were alive, part of the show, women audibly sighing at Valentino's kiss, yet he watches the serial killer, M. Verdoux, once again, unable to edit out the Salgados, that pathetic old lady, white roots striping her hennaed hair, the gnarled little husband dry as a prune, the dim shot of their unit, spooky as the motel room in *Psycho*. Szabo rewinds to the opening sequence: Verdoux clipping flowers with a comic twist to his mustache while yet another wife burns in the incinerator, a scene he forgives Chaplin, but tonight he ejects, gives in to his addiction. A helpless case, he finds *Wolf, Meyer* in the phone book. No longer a big deal, the writer is listed. It's 2 A.M. He will call first thing in the morning.

Yes, he is that Wolf, Arroyo Terrace. Happy to show the professor around. Meyer Wolf, a prim little fellow at the imposing oak door. Wolf, late eighties? Fringe of white hair, pale skin, an ascetic in a white Japanese robe, same robe on his wife, who might be his twin twenty years younger, museum pieces, ivory carvings removed from the surround of Pasadena high-rises on the Boulevard. All is serene, even Meyer Wolf's words spoken softly, not to disturb the dim religious light, the solemn perfection of beams, paneling, furniture and rugs, each exquisite hand-crafted artifact the work of Greene & Greene, 1908.

"Craftsman. Every stroke done by hand."

But Victor Szabo hasn't a notion about Greene & Greene which doesn't ruffle the Wolfs. Their house is on the National Registry. It's all in the books, and so, it turns out, is the blacklist, as well as the FBI file on Meyer Wolf—Young Communist League at Stanford, Spanish Civil War, articles in *New Masses*—all available to the professor. Not what this wound-up young man has come for. Young, Szabo not yet fifty, younger than Meyer's wife, a colorless man with tired eyes, slab ears big as Bing Crosby's. Not Un-American Activities, this small misunderstanding brushed away. Peace descends on the vast living room, which is cool in spite of the heat oppressing greater Los Angeles. Stop frame: they sit on uncomfortable low chairs in comfortable silence. Szabo thinks *aura,* emanation, time out of time.

He has come for further news of the inexhaustible silents.

Wolf says, "*I remember absolutely everything, young man. That is my curse.* Joseph Cotten, *Citizen Kane.*" Mrs. Wolf touches his hand. He need not go back there.

"It's OK, Maya."

Her beatific smile: we are here with the Van Eck lamps, the exquisite Tiffany inkwell, the prize Fulper pots.

Meyer turns to his interrogator. "Ask away."

Szabo has crossed into their set like Keaton in *Shylock, Jr.*, now must play out the scene, clears his throat to say her name. "Isabel Maher?"

Now it's Meyer's turn to smile, "She was one of the pretty girls. Socialist, working-class. Fond of reading George Bernard Shaw. Candy for the camera, but talented, whatever that means. They were about to gobble her up with a studio contract."

"Was it voice, her voice?"

"She sounded, you know, a touch phony, classed up, maybe trained for the stage. Isabel was a smart girl, left the business. I don't know what you're after."

Maya's hand on his knee.

"It's OK. Remember, Professor, sure you remember the closing shot of *Citizen Kane*. That big hand lettered sign, **No Trespassing.** Murky black and white."

Of course he remembered that magnificent jigsaw of a picture, the reporter's question never answered, the final piece only fit in place for the audience in the dark. He understood Meyer Wolf had posted his sign, though graciously showing him a silver beaker, hand-beaten.

"Probably Clara B. Welles, circa 1904."

So they were both obsessed, both demented.

· · ·

In the dark of his apartment, shades drawn, Victor Szabo turns from the blank screen. His mother had taken him to the Thalia, a Saturday afternoon. He was maybe twelve or thirteen. A revival of *Citizen Kane*, she said was a classic, and he knew he must love it, love this time with her at the movies stolen from everyday life on Riverside Drive. His father taught Evidence at Columbia Law and did he have to say it again: it was foolish to take in old movies with the boy, he heard himself called the boy, when the boy should be out on the ball field with his brother. Victor went to the bedroom shared with his older brother, climbed into the upper bunk. It was dusk, end of day in the Fall. If he closed his eyes he could see the shafts of light from the projector, hear the soundtrack, the clapping hands of Charles Kane at the opera—clap, clap, clap, denying his wife's screeching failure. A football struck the wall above his head. The Monkees sang on the transistor. His mother was quiet at dinner, then perky and false. Entering the dark Thalia on a clear October day, they had done something hidden, illicit. Yes, he remembered **No Trespassing,** but only now understands he'd hung it on himself, closed the gate. Victor could, if he wished, pronounce upon the vanishing point of his perspective. The only paradise, the one that's lost, was a ticket to the show at the Thalia. In the cave, only shadows. The boy should have been in the scrimmage, not collecting dusty phantoms of silence and sound, frame upon frame, so many, many should have been left on the cutting room floor.

The day after his visit in Pasadena, Victor Szabo greets his students with notes on the spatial primacy of the filmic object, no indulgence in Vitaphone, Movietone, no Garbo Speaks, no voiceless Isabel Maher.

V

Let Us Now Praise Famous Men

They were of a kind not safely to be described in an account claiming to be unimaginative and trustworthy, for they had too much and too outlandish beauty not to be legendary. Since, however, they existed quite irrelevant to myth, it will be necessary to tell a little of them.

—James Agee

Sharecropper's Bed, 1936
—Walker Evans

ON THE PORCH

Uneasy with the chipped rim, I set a glass of water on my bedside table for thirst in the night. I turned off the lamp. Sleep came quickly—cross out, that day over. The lamp is pink china. I have seen it perhaps a thousand and one nights and not seen it at all, the swell of its body capped with a tilting silk shade, a matron of cartoons gone by, the genteel world my mother aspired to, the pink lamp being hers, one of the many cherished possessions which furnished her life now mixed in with the discards of my tenants. To deal with the present untangled from the past, what an accomplishment. What a wonder it would be to see the houses on Cotrell Street undiscovered, emerging in soft morning light.

One thing about the lens: the view is always of the moment, never looks back, not even if you set up your subjects in artificial light with the apparatus of old studio photographs. The palm, the parlor table draped in a shawl, prop of a family Bible, etched glass of an oil lamp. Or set yourself up picturesquely as Juliet on her bier, or costume yourself in the clichéd role—housewife at the sink, bland office girl. The time lapse of self-portraiture is a trick of the present. I come back to this house on a street with the retired, the unemployed and workers of this town, come back weekends and Summers, as to a house in the country or on the shore. We are on a bay. Landlocked on the asphalt plains of urban life, you'd never know it. My neighbors no longer find me curious. I've abandoned the odd clothes which set me apart, though as I sit with the Wakowskis, August end of day, I'm burdened with the photographer's curse, gaining their confidence as I once faked interest in the festive Saints' Days of Argentina or the sumptuous fabric of a Park Avenue chair, or coaxed dew drops on the ripples and craters of a cabbage to please the jaded lens. Decades of such seduction, intrusion on faces, bodies, the body politic. Nature embalmed in my chemical bath. When not pursuing the down-home life on Cotrell, I return to New York, resume my professional life.

I will tell you of three families. Words as a medium are fairly new to me, but attempt to tell like James Agee (you do not have to know who that handsome drunk was, a man intoxicated with words that challenged his partner's photos). I step in the print of those who have gone before. Monkey see. Monkey do. I will tell you of the Wakowskis, Sue and Henry, and of the poet who lives alone, and of the Murphys, who lived on the right side of town, and as I tell, you may see me hiding behind the camera, Riccardi never in the picture. What a dodge. The photographer is always there—a father beheading his child in the playpen, the tourist shrinking Buckingham Palace, the pornographer selecting the erect member, the aureole of nipple from swell of breast.

I am on the Wakowskis' porch with Sue and Sandy—part Lab, part neighborhood mutt. In good weather Sue sits out, any season, takes in life on the street. There are sixteen houses, eight facing eight across the paved road and crumbling sidewalks, all alike when they were built by a local developer in the Twenties, built as affordable rents for workers in the mills and factory. Each clapboard house has two doors, two rents, upstairs and down. Each house has a narrow front porch and square plot of front yard, all the same though now different, amended over the years. Only the first and last houses on the block have a driveway. Autos were not envisioned for the workers. *Healthy walk to work,* that's how Sue tells it. She's fed up with Henry searching out a parking place when he comes home from the Bonanza Bus Station, where he's lucky to sell tickets to Providence, Boston, Hartford and small stops in between, happy to have the job. In the mill, Henry was union. *Didn't work out,* is how his wife tells it, though when pressed Sue can relate the whole story of the decline, the factories moving south for cheap labor, or show you the label, *Made in Taiwan,* on her cardigan, worn these evenings as the Summer cools down. Sandy rolling over for the belly rub, hard times not dwelled on as she documents her works and days, the good years when the children were small and she sewed for women on the other side of town in need of an adjustment of waistline or hem. *Now you throw last year's outfit away,* said with a tart smile, her bright streak of lipstick drawn on, everything shipshape, faint odor of lavender soap, crease in the pressed jeans, whitest of tennis shoes, permed white hair, polished pink nails.

My hair has grown out of its crayon black. I tell myself we look much alike, Sue and I, women of Cotrell. She is younger by ten years, has always been here and asks don't I remember her as a child, when she lived in number 12 with the front yard chained in? To be honest, I should say I had no use for this place. One season when first *professional,* I photographed the Riccardi house unpeopled. Working with my first Hasselblad while my mother and Phil

Dunphy were keeping the books at the mill, I made haunting desolation of the empty rooms with lifeless chairs, rumpled beds, the silenced radio, broken tiles of bathroom mishaps, the melancholy diversion of the kitchen clock, a black cat with hours on its white belly, tail wagging the minutes. I made a statement, not to mention a success of the pathos: *Factory Town Dwelling.*

> *Above all else: in God's name don't think of it as Art.*
> —James Agee, *Let Us Now Praise Famous Men*

I will only take snapshots of Sue and Henry holding hands like high school sweethearts. No need to ask them questions. They are primed for the interview, as we all are, wired for the mike, the TV van, more than willing to say they own this house, bought in the good times. Their children have gone off to Boston and New York, except for the one they call Bing.

Runs La La Latte. Raking it in, goes to show, he was the slow one.

With the pride of a city slicker, I bring the Wakowskis tomatoes and fierce little peppers.

There was a time, don't you recall, when the Italians had gardens took up the whole backyard you couldn't play in.

Frank Riccardi never had a garden in the house he mysteriously owned. He left us with crabgrass and gravel. My effort, that's what I recall, lugging in topsoil and manure after Bel Murphy died. The effort to stay in one place for a season. *Here's a heritage tomato and the jalapeños.*

Sue holds a small red pepper at arm's length. *Bing will like that one.* The slow son who still lives at home, the boy they are proud of, big as a linebacker but soft, his happy-face sweet and puffy as the muffins he home-bakes on the premises of La La Latte.

Henry's arrivals and departures are timed by the bus schedules, the Providence Express, the Boston Local. His stories of rude and pleasant travelers, the encounters of his day more alive than my many excursions. Henry's news is of weary commuters, the folkies still searching for Joplin at the Jazz Festival, the tourists to our exhausted town now converted to quaint. We sit of an evening and watch the street, the wobbly progress of a child just out of training wheels, the neighborhood dogs lifting the last leg of the day, teenagers with smokes playing at being somewhere else, the blue lights of television screens. We hear the distant voices and muted laughter that calls Sue and Henry in to their programs.

Night-night, Gemma.

I go along home, happy to have been awarded my given name. What is it I ask of the Wakowskis?

I have no contract to memorialize them. I have not been sent here like Agee and the photographer Walker Evans, to bring home the goods on tenant families in words and pictures. They traveled to Alabama during the Great Depression to tell the world of poverty as lived by the poor. I am on my own, can't pretend to Agee's passion, to Evans' perfection of cool. Riccardi no longer works on assignment. If I please, I can take pictures of Sandy, beloved creature's head in Sue's lap, little girls pressing their luck in sexy dress–up, cops in a squad car cooping, wasting the taxpayers' money. Snapshots of life on Cotrell are self-addressed, but I will tell you of the poet who lives at the end of the street with a driveway to park his car, a wreck of a Seventies Camaro. He is a youthful man, perhaps fifty, with a braid down his back of sandy hair, silver earrings, beads and Native American vests that mark him as once a free spirit. He lives alone. His children visit, two sullen girls pressing toward teendom. This Summer they wear strappy tops sold at our new mall on the highway, display their childish thighs, mosquito-bite breasts. Their father lives in the rent upstairs, but the girls choose to sit on the porch in Summer, ears plugged with their music, waiting out the hours until the poet drives them home to their mother.

He has given me a chapbook, a pretty thing of few pages with his poems. It was an awkward moment between us when he

THE SILVER SCREEN

handed me his work with a smile I will call complicit, signaling that we are different. I said I would be pleased to read his poems, wanted to say I long *not to be different* on Cotrell. The poet is handsome as maybe an aging actor in Westerns, the good guy with a checkered past. He is narrow-hipped, in my mind, his thighs sinewy, chest smooth, hair feathering a narrow trail down to the neat package of dick and balls. I have never seen him with a woman. My candid camera did not capture the deep lines etched in his long cheeks or the small creases sprouting round his eyes. His gray beard faded. Teeth need attention.

> *Most young writers and artists roll around in description like honeymooners on a bed.*
>
> —Agee

I am not young and no writer to speak of. My poet is still strong, but that's another story. When he gave me his book, I went home and read it at once. I wish his words were about wildflowers invading our patches of lawn, or the constant thrum of the highway that runs past the dead end of Cotrell, or the wetlands seeping in from the bay. They are about the mother of those daughters, small bleeps of disappointment. *She counted my pennies like love in a jar.* They are about what he wanted and did not get. *Wine and song in the fast lane pass me entire, knapsack and all.* So that I am embarrassed by his confessional verse when I see him get into the Camaro with, in fact, the knapsack to drive off to school where he teaches Language Arts, how to write the simple sentence; Communications, how to sell yourself to the prospective boss.

Why flinch when the poet insists we are different?

The poet is strong: that's the other story. He's built a ramp so the vet who lives downstairs can zoom out into the street, reckless in his wheelchair. What's he got to lose? A bad habit or two. When he has indulged, the sturdy poet grounds him, a parental arrangement. I admire the vet's tattoos and am tempted, but will not take a close-up of the Fu Manchu dragon rising in full splash from the high sea of a bicep, not exploit his grizzly male, useless male body. When our vet skids off the ramp of a Saturday night, the peacenik upstairs, *shithead, pansy,* heaves him out of the wheelchair, puts him to bed. Our vet nursing the bitter triumph of having been to his war.

If I were going to use these lives of yours as "Art," if I were going to dab at them here, cut them short here, make some trifling improvement over here, in order to make you worthy. . . .

—Agee

I will simply tell you about the Murphys who lived on the other side of town. The enchantment of their little house and Bel's garden. One day long ago, the way it is long ago in Victorian photographs set up in staged scenes, as the curtain went up in Brandle's Pharmacy, I twirled on my stool at the soda fountain and entered the Murphys' magic circle. There was the mother in a snappy straw hat, Isabel Maher, who had been in the silent movies. *Gemma,* she said, *you're in Joe's class!* There was Mr. Murphy, wounded in the Great War, petrified hand in his pocket, Tim Murphy decent and friendly to all, even to those on Cotrell Street who could not afford his insurance. There was the boy, above all others, who passed for a prince in this town. The girl, round and rather silly, miscast in the family story I wanted to be my own. It was the mother, Bel, who told me to leave town. Now, why did she do that, when she went out there, out there, turned around and came home?

Perspective, the easy answer. Back away from the scene.

Back away. *There will be digressions.* When *Let Us Now Praise Famous Men* was published, 1941, no one much cared. There was a war on. Agee had taken too much time with his words. There was further delay with the pictures. Walker Evans saw his photos, about to be published. They had been cleaned up: *Sharecropper's Bed*, 1936, no tear in the sharecropper's pillow, no wrinkles, no fleas on the sheets. He had taken care to capture the family's dignity as well as their poverty. Evans' photographs display emotional accuracy, a grand accomplishment for a city boy, a Northerner, something of a swell. Spare the expense, restore each wrinkle, the tear in the pillow. The fleas were etched in.

I developed the Murphys into a myth that couldn't hold water, the briny water of our bay stinging the cuts of my childhood. I'm attempting to clean up my act on Cotrell Street, ink each black speck on the white coverlet of memory. That's the best I can come up with in words without pictures. Enlarged: the Murphys of Land's End, who were not perfect in every way. Soft focus: Bel, the restless excursions; her beauty could not find its place in a shingle house or on the silent screen. Deleted: Dad of All Dads, the shadowy figure of the father, pleasant and dull, with the award of his wound in a war. Cropped: Joe, headshot of an old priest, his body among the missing. Posed: Rita, off center, startled, the red spot of my flash fixed in her eyes. I have a lot to answer for, taking my snaps of Sue and Henry, false testimony to the ease of our evenings on the porch.

I will tell of two places, long avoided. Cowardly, I thought to take the poet to Land's End.

Yeah, big shots over there. The tower, I've seen it.

So I went alone, as always, parked blind side of the privet. The lane has been paved. Rampant local color, loosestrife and goldenrod. I took up my post at the break in the hedge, where I hid as a girl watching the life of their house, the coming and going. Mr. Murphy with a worn briefcase, Bel clutching groceries to her heart like she'd won a pot of gold, Joe swinging a bat or book bag. Gemma Riccardi out of the picture. Where's Rita, skinning her knee, falling off her bike? This day that I speak of, this late Summer day on Land's End, I spied once again. A house rose above me, a silo, reference to New England farm that never was, not here, where fishermen built their cottages low against the gale. Or a lighthouse, could that be the feeble notion of one Damien Forché? The photographer I've never met, but swear I know him. He's of a type, his beacon lighting my way to disposable fashion, its shadow not reaching to the nude body of a girl grilling in the sun. He flips her, Forché dressed only in a planter's straw hat, shameless. Oh, the girl is that starved-down model Pet, alias Elizabeth Strumm. They lie on striped canvas lounges, so Fifties, so today. There is no garden, only stone, gray stone, as though the topsoil of Bel's half-acre has been washed away by a great wave and left only bedrock, unfertile. A boy, dime-a-dozen Adonis, rises from the slash of pool set in the stone. Forché calls out, *Carlos,* saluting the boy's *tremendos cojones.* Laughing, all three laughing. I wanted to see Pet and her pals as less than human, register scorn, but there was nothing I cared to portray. Damien's shingled post-modern dildo not worth a snapshot. If I back the car up, swing round—cross out, this day over. It's a bitch of a turn in the narrow lane. How merciless we were, taunting Bel, sure she'd drive off the cliff. With her kids and Gemma in the Buick.

That night on the Wakowskis' porch we speak of the doll woman who has disappeared from Cotrell Street. Some authority has claimed her, a daughter or son.

She was Bev Heany, married a Molloy. The doll in the window began, you know, when the kids moved away.

Sue no longer presses me as a witness, though I did see the big doll's clothes were changed each day, overalls, party dress, plaid skirt and warm sweater for school. Now—a week, ten days—she's in the same yellow sunsuit, sand bucket in hand. I'll miss her when I pack up to go away. Miss sharing the virtual child, miss Sue and

Henry. Miss Bing lumbering up on the porch with day-old goodies courtesy of La La Latte, the rattle of the busted muffler on the
poet's car and those awful girls cowering on the porch when they
see our vet, as though that ruined body could harm them. Our talk
turns to Land's End.

You finally seen it? Henry leans forward in his creaking wicker
chair, whispers. *Tim Murphy must be laughing in his grave.*

Mr. Murphy insured the Plymouth. That would be '68, the
Wakowskis' first car.

Over the years, fire and theft, homeowner's policy.

After his death they stayed on with Prudential.

First hurricane, that house'll go down like a bowling pin.

That erection on Land's End a curiosity. On a family drive
you wonder at the establishments where the notables reside for
their pleasure—TV anchor, shoe designer, fashion photographer—
much as we wondered at the Vanderbilt and Astor cottages in
Newport on a crazy excursion. Bel in her tour guide mode exhibiting The Breakers, the moral thrust of her lecture—*All that
money made them happy, you suppose?* So beside the point of Good
Humors and the elation of testing our toes in the icy Spring waves.

Sue seemed to know this was to be my last night on the porch.
Labor Day looms with the final influx of tourists. The shops and
cafés on Main Street will coast till the next Summer season; La La
Latte serve only the professional class from Providence making
suburbia of our town, now a small city. Up, out of my rocker, time
to go. Last lick of Sandy's rough tongue.

Wait, Gemma! There was a cake of Sue's making and tea.
Crumb cake. I thought of Bel, who attempted to bake and sew
with the best of them but never made it past her domestic failures,
or past the books she devoured, to really care. I felt honored being
served on the fine china, sipping from a glass that might have been
my mother's, no danger in the smooth crystal rim. Doubly hon-

ored when I heard the racket of their *Wheel of Fortune* whirling while the Wakowskis sat on patiently with their company, Gemma Riccardi, not one of them.

As I walked back to my house, my home, the vet careened down the middle of the street, headed to a dreary pub, his nightly destination. His accident was as a biker, not in his war. We nod, nod, smile, the acknowledged pretense of friendship between us. When it is finally dark, I go out my back door to look at the Summer sky's last shower of stars. It's all endings now. By moonlight, last plucking of peppers and tomatoes, snipping of basil and thyme. In the darkroom I develop my snapshots of dogs, bikes, cars of Cotrell Street, front yards with their quest for variation, Vet, Poet, sulky girls, all three Wakowskis and the doll abandoned in Bev Heany's window. Black and white film, true to myself in that way.

Now I will tell you of the cemetery, once exposed to the highway. This past year it has been hidden behind a mall so we can look upon the offerings of familiar chain stores, our comfort goods within reach. The motif of Pilgrims' Plaza is nautical, seaside New England. A Pawtucket in profile shakes Roger Williams' hand. Sailors' knots twine with lobsters in a frieze, so we no longer have to think about the grim repository of the dead as we drive to Providence or connect with I-95, but of the peace and prosperity that defies unemployment and the cost of our continuous wars. A new road cuts round the rear end of Pathmark to enter the Catholic cemetery by a wrought iron gate sporting a freshly gilded cross. The flatland is shrouded in spooky silver-gray haze. My mother and Phil Dunphy are buried here. I attended both funerals, perhaps to ward off guilt—for that thought forgive me—and made out a check for the monument, insisting their names be chiseled together in granite, reparation long overdue. There they rest, the grass nicely trimmed by perpetual care. The Dunphys, not who I came for, cruel, not as cruel as my years of avoidance. The plot, which Phil purchased, is defined with metal markers, and I see he's left ample room for me. There was no attendant, no map, just row upon row of gravestones, straightforward, not a maze. The Italians keep to themselves. I never thought to look for him here, my father with the phantom beard, the subject of my romantic stories. A Teresa Riccardi died young, died the year I was born. She would have been my mother's age. Once this would have thrilled me or set me in a rage. Now I leave such discoveries undeveloped. What would it prove, show or tell me that I had not guessed or imagined?

Oh, we have grown old; it has been a long, long climb. I've come to this cemetery on business. The morning mist has lifted, no ghosts, a clear view of angels, crosses, lilies, stone upon stone. Portuguese lie toward the marsh reaching to the sea. *There will be digressions:* a miniature stone temple with a low wonderland door, the resting place of Mary O'Brien Cotrell (d. 1873), buried in Catholic ground. Could she have been a housemaid or mill girl, an oiler of the multicolor press that printed our *Saturday Evening Post? Never enough stories.* Mary from the wrong side of town? Murphy will be nearby, center front with the Irish. Separate headstones of Timothy and Isabel, their dates scanning the last century. The end of Summer, Bel, not the Day of the Dead, no confusion with Halloween tricks, demons in Kmart masks. Just this day, an ordinary Thursday, no souls rising from their graves in the apocalyptic crowd scene we've been sold. I suspected you were mortal, that's the skeleton in the closet, though I shouted above the din, *the bombs bursting in air,* playing my shadow puppet stories against the blank white wall, which is only my fancy way of saying I did not want you to be over, like silent movies or the Keith Circuit, like beauty, like instruction, like belief that if I brought you crumb cake or my harvest of basil, *excellent for pesto,* stayed in one place for a season, you would call out to me, *Gemma, where are we going?*

Cotrell, naming my street, which did not prove to be the right destination. The course of nature was too slow for Riccardi. I didn't know how to manage with sun, shade or rain, couldn't alter the process with cow shit or chemicals, lime to sweeten the soil. I hung in for two Summers with a small crop, unnatural to me.

Nevertheless: Oh, nevertheless. I have been asked to take on an assignment, to deal with the present. An editor has asked me to take pictures *like Bourke-White's* (you do not have to know who she was, the woman who took the first cover—1936—for *Life* magazine, handsome, her picture in a high-altitude flying suit, a popular pin-up), but he knew, the young man schooled in photography's past, knew Bourke-White's *Night Bombardments (1943),* placing me back in the days of photojournalism, so pure, so Forties, though I would have been only thirteen. I dare not say the flat desert lit for an instant with Scuds and the flash of car bombs will not register like the gorgeous fireworks of the Italian Campaign. A job is a job, always was till the girl from Cotrell Street got into art. I'll use a Rollei and a peanut flash of yore, not tell the young editor—

> *The beauty of the past belongs to the past. It cannot be imitated today and live.*
>
> —Margaret Bourke-White, *Diaries*

I've brought you a photo, Bel, a graveyard thing they do in Latin countries honoring the Day of the Dead. Your picture will last for a while. Taken from a negative so old I thought it might not survive its glossy lamination. It was snapped with my Brownie. You shifted your hand slightly during the exposure, so it looks like you're waving *hello, hello there,* to me and your children out of the frame. A bright Spring day. You are propped against the Buick in a green cap and raincoat. The slice of white building behind is the Seamen's Bethel, New Bedford, in need of a paint job. It was the day you read to us from *Moby-Dick.* Later I laughed with Joe at your take on *The Whale,* the way kids laugh out of ignorance. I understood nothing of your performance, just heard your voice which could tell me any old story and I'd believe it, the whole Hollywood script.

I'm costumed for the porch, Bel, slacks and a matronly cardigan for the cool start of the day. For the porch of my neighbor Sue Wakowski, not the back porch where I plagued you with questions, where I reappeared as Riccardi exhibiting her wares. I went back to Melville, his big bible of a book, where I knew I'd find the words to say: *how is it that we still refuse to be comforted for those who we nevertheless maintain are dwelling in unspeakable bliss?*

Gemma, where are we going?

Off on my own, this time for good. Enough of one place for one season. Riccardi—Little Miss Echo, quotidian quoter:

How were we caught?

What, what is it has happened? What is it that has been happening that we are living the way we are?

The children are no longer the way it seemed they might be.

SEED UPON STONE

Preacher speaks directly to Mimi Salgado who is mindful of the privilege. Let us take Matthew: *Do not fear those who kill the body but can not kill the soul . . . Are not two sparrows sold for a penny?*

She has been admitted to his study, a place of infinite calm, so many books behind glass, a grand desk with photos of the wife and children, blessed with his presence every day. Pooch good as good can be, snuggles against the wild beat of her heart.

You are of more value than many sparrows.

Which makes Mimi weep, then unburden herself to Preacher, tell all, all about her father, the informer, her sainted mother, Carlotta, and Rita, the woman who killed a dog. How long must she take their sins upon her as though her very self was apprehended, disgraced on TV?

It is within our belief system to carry the weak. Charity is given to those who enter His Kingdom, praise the Lord.

Mimi responds, *Praise the Lord,* as she does in meeting. In the hush of his study her voice sounds weak and forlorn. How long must she carry the weight of their sins upon her? Pooch shudders with fear for her Mamma, not the everyday tremors of a Yorkie. She tells about the men who waited for her father, how she knew their evil as a little girl. *Spilling the goddamn beans like my father.* How dare she take the Lord's name in vain?

Preacher reaches across the big desk—*Surrender*—takes Mimi's hand. *Surrender. There is no torment He can't lift from your soul. Let us pray.*

Then silence all about, their heads bowed for the grace of the moment. Mimi looking down at Preacher's wedding ring, at the perfection of his long fingers and the soft sandy hair on the back of his hand, at a small crescent scar pale as the moon in ascendance. She is mindful of the healing half-hour of his gift, yet he has not answered. *How long?*

The Lord works in mysterious ways.

But that is a phrase of her mother's, an answer that was never any answer at all, Carlotta never saying, *I am sick unto death of his kickbacks and bribes, of the little gun not a toy in his pocket, the black car at the curb.* For the first time Mimi does not trust Preacher or does not trust herself, longing to turn back to a day when she was proud of Manny Salgado, who had drivers and buddies, her daddy in tailor-made suits, polished wingtips and always the silk handkerchief tucked in his pocket, who dealt out crisp bills to his son and daughter. *Make the good grades. Buy out the store.* It was Tony brought home all the A's, all the trophies. Manny reciting a poem he learned in school before shapeups on the docks. *You betta ya life, Mia Carlotta, I gotta.* Wanting to say he was a champ, welterweight, did you know it? Good grades, trophies, the poem finito and now her time with this Preacher is over. *Those who kill the body?* She doesn't get it about the sparrows, or the text for future study, mustard seed sown on a stone. All she has asked, how long must she endure the shame of their evil? Preacher has not answered, now begging for her pledge—not calling it cash—to carry forth his crusade.

When Mimi returns to Bon Soir, the gravel voice of her father begs her to call. Delete. Delete that message. Twice she's changed her number. Twice her brother has betrayed her. Why does her father sound pitiful? *Sweetheart, all is forgiven,* silly words used on her mother when he came home tanked, big business with the boss, the scum he handed over to the feds. Grasso, doing twenty to life. A nasty cough cut off her father's plea for mercy. *Mimi, give us a call.* Us. That would mean butterball Rita, who pounded a dying woman, overwatered the rex begonia, killed it with kindness before her mother's eyes. The boutique that evening is lively, Mimi's ad bringing them in for a sale, mark down the caftans, half-price the thongs, even in Boca Summer ends, time for the twin set, the shawl. Pooch in a sling chair, they love her, little head wagging, chewing her Petpourri ball. Mimi, thank you, makes her own money, no need for Daddy's allowance. When she unloads the last of the Betty Boop T's, flop of a novelty item, she packs up Pooch, drives home to their condo, orders in Thai—how her girl loves it, the milky sweet with touch of piquant.

You little monkey. Tonight Mimi knows she talks to a dog. Sometimes it all falls away. What to believe? Alone in this world. Parables she can't understand.

She must take stock: precisely what Mimi does next day, puts up a notice on the door of Bon Soir, Closed for Inventory. *Those who kill the body may not kill the soul.* She's on a plane to L.A. Pooch her co-pilot in the pretty net basket, good as can be. *A girl. She's a girl,* Mimi tells her seatmate plugging numbers into a laptop, though the man never asked. Well, it's no novelty, Mimi having no one to talk to. When did her angry words, mouthing off, turn to something like silence? When her son threw in with her husband and Manny. When Rita worked over her mother's body each day. When her brother went off to Boston College, all A's, so where did that get him? Threw in with Grasso and Manny. Tony with a new name, leopard changing his spots. No one to talk to way back, back before the marriage, in the marriage, in the Tudor on the street with doctors, lawyers and the phony businessman, her father. When did Mimi Salgado drop her married name? When discover silence and shame? Back, way back, a day when she went to Providence with Daddy in the back seat of the big car, a Caddy, not quite a limo, with walkie-talkie, jump seat and bar.

Special, her birthday, going to see a show. Her mother ailing as always. No parties with the neighborhood kids. She had on the pink A-line, that she remembers, the grown-up style of that dress and white tights. They were driven to a restaurant, dark wood, heavy curtains, real dim though it was noon. No customers this time of day. She sat in a booth waiting for her father to talk upstairs with Mr. Grasso. In her purse she had lipstick, not allowed by her mother. The first greasy feel of that redness streaked on her mouth. When they came down, her father and the boss, they were laughing at her. *Wipe it off*, Manny looking at his little girl, handing her a napkin, the bright smudge on the white cloth. They ate big steaks, talked business. Side orders of creamed spinach and home-fries. No cake, no candles, Boston cream pie.

A little something for the birthday girl. Grasso took a Kennedy half-dollar from his pocket. *There's more where that came from.*

The men talked for a long time, ordered more wine. She kept thinking, *How great to be out of school on my birthday.* The other kids were at math, after recess Dina and Val changing into gym suits. No school, but Mimi was not dumb. Grasso was talking about *our friend,* about someone can't play ball, a man who *needs hurting,* talking that way as if she could not figure hurting meant harm. Old enough to know they did not want her to understand. Their waiter came over with a message, the only waiter in the empty, dark place, lots of brass, big mirrors. The green glass lamps hanging from the ceiling were not lit, just a small shaded light at the booth like the one her mother turned on to play the piano. Grasso's driver came in with a message.

Her father said, *Sweetheart, see you back at the ranch.* Nervous, rapping his fingers on the table, wiping his face with the silk handkerchief she'd never seen him use. He was halfway out the door. She remembered the bright shaft of sunlight and how he turned, came back to the booth to kiss her, a big smooch, not like him at all. Turn back to that day when she smelled the wine on his breath, felt the tremble of his hand. *Sorry to miss the show, darlin'.*

She never knew what movie was playing at the Strand. *Thanks,* but she'd just as soon not see it with one of her father's buddies.

Take the girl home, Mr. Grasso said. *So—wasn't it nice to have lunch with your father?*

Almost the same words her mother used when she found Mimi hurting, poking right through her white tights, splotching her leg with lipstick in oily red wounds.

Wasn't it nice? Only her mother's voice was more like a cry than a question. *Carlotta, I gotta,* in a worn chenille robe, fingering the rosary beads in her pocket.

• • •

Torment remains. She will lift it from her soul.

Mimi has planned. Reserved their room in an airport hotel, researched the kitchen shop on Google. Room service with Pooch. It's ten o'clock back in Boca. Early to bed, the California sun still shining. In the morning a cab. Fearing a dumb driver, she's not had time to map her route with red marker to Tarzana, to White

Oaks Boulevard where the greyhound's body was crushed by a car, to the starred destination, La Cumbra Terrace. Pooch not abandoned to a soulless hotel. That was the hardest to figure. They are in this together, Pooch secure in the net basket. No gate, no guard, Mimi in the maze following numbers down pathways with bright flowers so much the same, same as Boca. The chlorine smell of the empty pool smarts her eyes as she descends step by step to a giant hibiscus. The C line, 54, 55. There is no one about, then a baby's cry, cartoon babble, the hack of a morning cough; 60, 61 C inscribed on a *Home Sweet Home* placard. *She will carry the sins of the weak no longer. The worth is herself, not a sparrow.* At 63, a patio like all the others.

They see her through the glass door, her father and that Rita, their shock and confusion, then their disbelieving smiles. Their welcoming arms. And she is in this sunny room imagined as a cell, a dark place of hiding. She is pulling hard to unsheathe the kitchen-shop weapon, to hurt or be hurt forever. The knife tangles in the netting of the dog's basket. A wild yapping. What was Mimi thinking, not to leave her girl out of this? The knife cuts a tuft of pale hair from the Yorkie topknot, poor little girl. A puddle on the carpet. Pooch scampering under the couch in shame.

Rita mops up: *That's the dearest little dog.*

Manny taking the knife from his daughter's hand: *She's cute as a button.*

Yes, a little girl! He did not even have to ask. Her father looks old, so old in his tattered pajamas, his hands, mapped with blue veins, in a constant tremor. His body, always so tense, has gone slack. He pulls her to him in a timid embrace, but his kiss on her moist cheek is firm, what she's been waiting for how many years, a smooch and the open door with a flash of sunlight. Rita scrambling under the couch is a sketch, that's the kind way to see her, slimmed down to a 14 Regular, the henna hair not too bad. Then Mimi is drinking coffee with her father, catching up on golf and the sales figures at Bon Soir while Rita fashions a little nest of pillows and towels. Pooch settles in with a Bow Wow Biscuit. So does Mimi settle, surrender to this weepy ending, its laughter and release—immoral, entertaining—like how many movies seen or only imagined in which killers and lovers are granted their reprieve.

"Chris?" Her father asks, "How's the boy?"

Chris, *Christopher*—the name of her son finally surfaces. Then the floodgates truly open.

"Oh, a boning knife! So useful." Rita, comforting Pooch, still wonders at the nature of their visitor's intention. "Useful, but you know it's bad luck to give knives as a present."

The Salgados did not know.

"It's thought the blade cuts love, but if you give the giver a pin or halfpenny . . ." Rita tells the undoing of that spell imported from Ireland by way of Ansonia, Connecticut, to a shingle house on a bay in Rhode Island. In her purse she finds a bright penny, places it in Mimi's hand. She withdraws from this happy reunion to the kitchen, puts the boning knife in the drawer next to the poultry shears, ruined when she hacked open the greyhound's cage. She routs about on the shelves for flour, baking powder to make muffins. It's been a while since Rita's thought of comfort food. Hard to say whether it's the father or daughter no longer among the missing. Tonight she will call Paul Flynn, tell him of this extraordinary occasion, hoping for news of her brother. Surely one miracle may beget another. Isn't that how it goes—loaves and fishes, raising the dead, walking on water? *Never enough stories.*

THE LITTLE MERMAID

She's been missing, long gone. Imagine her dead. Give it a try. Sample her, bitter and sweet, Fiona O'Connor. In his version, that's the priest's, her hair is burnished copper as it was when he knew her—loved her, we want him to say. One thing is certain: her story can't be simply another account of adolescent rebellion. Else why did she cut out her tongue?

Begin on upper Fifth Avenue, a good address. Her parents were happy to have her, the child of their polite disaffection. Cyril O'Connor adored his girl as only a father can. Banking on her promise, he never looked back to the happenstance of personal history that brought him to invest himself in Wall Street. He sure enough loved his irreverent child, made light of her every spill on the carpet, stain on the furniture of his wife's proper life. Mae was the mother.

They were kind, good people.

Mae pulled the girl's unruly hair into tight braids, dressed her in plaid skirts and navy blue sweaters. Sent to school in this disguise, she was always discovered. A note sent home. *Fiona has laughed, hummed, will not follow the lesson.* The girl's rosebud mouth spewed forth *inappropriate language.* She was expelled from one school, then another. Daddy's reprimands sounded like praise. The child's moxie was what he'd lost, moxie his word lost in time. A bleat in her mother's voice called her to account for homework not done, teachers sassed, unsavory companions.

Mae's scolding was hesitant, shy. *I will pray for you, Fiona.*

Imagine the girl's fury at all those saints and angels tracking her wicked ways.

Fiona ranted against her mother's choice of evening entertainment.

Simmer down, Mae said.

Cool it? A retort to please her father.

They were patient people.

Cyril O'Connor made money, that's what he did, but never brought the business home to Fifth Avenue. At night he read history against television white noise. His concentration was a presence, a giant thought balloon with old stories running. Lincoln's letters and *Personal Memoirs of U.S. Grant* in sober covers were stacked by his chair, his leather reading chair by the window. When Fiona was in high school, he told her, *I should go back, start with the Founding Fathers. I'm stuck in the middle.* His briefcase, Mark Cross, a gift from his wife, sat unopened each night in the front hall. Fiona was not above riffling through the Annual Reports of Hess Oil or Xerox, the wonder stock, to find evidence that he really went downtown each day, played with these numbers. A lovely name she discovered, the name of a Spanish knight. *Who's Cerro de Pasco?*

A copper company that's failing. Are you interested in the market, Fiona? He smiled at her poking round in his business, went back to his reading.

Cyril, Mae, and their girl carried on in that cavernous apartment on Fifth Avenue with the extra bedroom waiting for another child or the guests who never came, until Fiona discovered lust. Not lust like the doorman's salivating pass at her ass, the elevator boy's moist breath on her nape. Oh, you will think she was into BODY, exciting explorations of tit and clit, of boy smell and facial fuzz—incidental. She lusted after someplace far from the privileged view of Central Park, from the potted parties of private-school snots, quested not after the holy land of A-list colleges.

Fiona's smart, Mae said to Cyril, *smart, not bookish,* a little dig as he looked up from, maybe, the Reconstruction, if he'd got that far.

Arrive at scenes with the priest, make quick work of family, Fifth Avenue. Yes, Fiona went downtown. She was studying at the New School, those walk-in courses, dabbling in art and music, strumming a guitar like how many kids. This guy in Pottery I invading her with talk of Redemption on the Bowery, the ultimate show, which sounded like *Jesus Christ Superstar* warmed over. Still, together they went down to Anima Mundi. That was the first night Fiona didn't go home.

Well, it's your HOLY Catholic Church.

Mae could not stop her wailing.

That's where I've been, where they CARE about the poor, the homeless. Care and *humility* figured heavily in the lecture delivered to her parents, undigested material of a one-night stand. For a week she did not go back downtown, then that guy found her in the auditorium there on 12th Street, listening to the professor do the Alan Lomax folk, *Bad Man Ballads* so peaceful after "Light My Fire," her favorite oldie. They held hands listening to the blues, this nice guy with long blond hair she'd talked to through the night, slept with incidental, then went down, made the scene at Mundi. Poverty, community, much to learn aiming toward the good life or good death. Children to feed, drunks and druggies to care for. Searchers checking out of a material world. Fiona felt loved. Loved, not by the nice guy throwing pots at the New School, growing the beard of an apostle, loved by this family who fed her the lines to say on Fifth Avenue, instructing her father about the sins of Dow Chemical, her mother about the massacre at My Lai, as though Mae couldn't watch it on the evening news. When his daughter launched her attack on the covert operations that led to our invasion of Cambodia, Cyril attempted a course of instruction. He had been a captain in the undeclared conflict in Korea, led his soldiers to defeat in a brutal ambush. What disturbed him? Fiona's high on this war, her embrace of the drama without the dull backdrop of history.

Fiona half listened, not wanting to know her father might have reason on his side, pressing her half-baked argument, loud and clear, "As a pacifist, I am called to LOVE my enemy."

Mae, working a Celtic cross in needlepoint, pricked her finger. "Please!"

They were tolerant people.

Fiona's apostle deflected, took off for chemical inspiration in Bombay, leaving his parents' address for Fiona. He was Gerald Kalb of Shaker Heights, Ohio. In case, they said, all tolerance and understanding at Mundi, she might want to reach out to *Shah*, as we knew him. The girl thought for a moment about loss, about the transient lesson of that apostle, their trip on the Broadway Local downtown. Now she was sought after by all—the mothers, children and naturally the men of Mundi. Leave sex out of the picture. It's not about the body, is it? Though to continue we must see her: abundant hair, terra cotta or color of a tarnished penny, the violet-blue eyes wide open, the serious upturn of nose dusted with innocent freckles, a brave beauty long out of date, Girl of the Golden West, not the early Seventies, upper Fifth Avenue. Fiona cleaning toilets, baking pies, mending shirts like Sister Suzy, barely knowing which end of the needle was up. A thick slab of wood lovingly polished was the Mundi altar from the Tree of Heaven. As though to counter her mother's rote *Aves*, she lulled herself poor and needy with mantras. Cyril admired this wacky independence, more moxie, which pissed off Fiona. She moved out. First time Mae came downtown decked out in kid gloves and pearls to find her daughter, the girl spoke to her harshly.

No. No, that was not the anima. All were welcome in the old schoolhouse.

Mae put down her purse, began to ladle out soup. The children took to her, hungering for the very indulgence that once set her daughter to letting her hair go wild, hiking the plaid skirt to a mini, selling her school ring for the bong abandoned with psychedelic posters in a back closet. Mae was just as nice as could be to those kids, some with mothers at Mundi, some not. Mae had a life.

Good works downtown, two days for the hospital shop, one as a docent at the Metropolitan Museum: Fiona sloughed off the caul of her embarrassing birthright, came to believe her mother passable, never laughed when she clipped notices out of the Mundi Newsletter, number of GIs dead and missing, Watergate tidbits, Nixon with Pinocchio nose.

Arrive at the priest. It was over that altar of precious wood she first saw him performing his duties. He came from uptown where he taught, wearing civvies not to offend, Mundi being free of clerical attire, though at Fiona's urging he donned the Buddhist saffron of renunciation, still a good look. They sat cross-legged on the destroyed linoleum of a schoolroom. She recited from the *Gita*—*I am the fire and the offering.* She was eighteen, might have been one of his students. *I am the goal, the upholder, the witness.* . . . Enchanted with the freckled girl as his guru, with the intensity of her quest, not her lesson, a confusion of selflessness with self-proclamation, he whispered, *Shantih. Shantih. Shantih.* About love, he never doubted. The peace that passeth understanding was far from his mind, though hadn't the poet monk, Thomas Merton, gone off in search of Hindi Masters, Nirvana, Zazen? At his university, the enrollment in Sanskrit was up. Up to five. A time of theological tourism, he thought to shatter Fiona's mindless chant, tell her stories of Loyola's fierce concentration or the mystical apparitions of St. John of the Cross. Pursuing the Void, Nirvana or Heavenly Rest, it would be unfair to say their mind game gave way to the body game. About love, he was certain. In years to come, the priest would never consider himself a fakir for his silence, for simply devouring the sight of her face turned up in meditation to the water stained ceilings of Anima Mundi.

She asked, "What do you teach?"

Such a simple question. He thought to devote the rest of his life to an answer, but said, "This week Donne's sonnets—

"When I died last and, Dear, I die
  As often as from thee I go . . ."

She put a finger to his lips. "I'm not bookish."

About love: He was, yes, good looking: the sculpted high forehead so promising, crisp hair going early gray, the stringy build of an ex-athlete and no, not fumbling with her body, just never been there. Tender, will that do? Those consecrated hands discovering her thighs, stroking her tangled hair, *Suppose we were Fiona O'Connor and Joe Murphy, just a couple of ordinary micks?* All first names at Mundi; O'Connor and Murphy edged toward personal, prehistory. As O'Connor and Murphy they broke the unstated rules. *Ordinary,* that's a lot of supposing. One night when Joe did not go uptown to the clean cell where he lived, actually had his life with the Jesuiticals, a boy, maybe six or seven years old, came from round the corner, from First Street, called for a priest to come quick. Father Joe took the girl along. That was his mistake. Fiona's mistake was listening to him coax the woman's sins, his whispered absolution. The boy who had come for the priest knew they were too late. His mother was dead, couldn't he see? Bruised, wasted, her face still glistening with overdose sweat. Father Murphy wore the saffron shirt, the purple stole of his calling round his neck, *In the name of the Father and of the Son* insisting on the sacramental moment, never doubting the woman's soul had not yet departed. Fiona O'Connor saw the hovering Holy Ghost of his belief steady as the flame of the blessed candle she held at the bottom of that urine-soaked, bloodstained cot.

They'd never be just a couple of ordinary micks.

When she knew the child was coming, she more than supposed he would do the right thing. They would marry.

One Spring day Mae came downtown with a camera. *To show Dad,* she said, snapping the improvised kitchen, the slab of wood altar, assorted Mundi children in a tidy circle game. Then to snap Fiona with her friend—a young Jesuit, imagine! Mae ushered Fiona and Father Joe out into the sun. Then along came Russo, the ghetto priest from New Jersey who had discovered the cool world of Anima Mundi, who leaned on the darling redhead, everyone's sweetheart. Smart Fiona made certain a couple of micks would not be documented as a couple. She grabbed Russo's black leather jacket, the hip getup he wore into the big city, and they posed, all three, in front of a noplace brick wall. Mae clicked one exposure before Father Murphy called a halt.

A photo Fiona never saw, never wanted to see. Straining the waist of her bellbottom hipsters, costumed by the Sixties, hair blowin' in the wind. Priests were coming out of orders. The Great Exodus. Well, didn't they know that downtown embracing real poverty, not a vow. Suppose the right thing. Marry. The right thing was to go uptown with her mother, home to Fifth Avenue, no parting kisses. Where had she come from, the enchantress? Who would know on that first-name isle of downtown innocence? Was it ever entirely clear in that dreamy old schoolhouse that the priest had been sent by some higher authority to check out their belief in the system? If so, he was an undercover agent, or a lost soul not finding his way.

The right thing for Fiona O'Connor was never to see him again, having seen him blindly greasing the dead woman's eyes with oil like the holy ghee in the *Gita*. The right thing was to forget the ambulance that took away the body, to forget the child in the back seat of the cop car and the cops who didn't believe Murph in the Moonie outfit.

"Father!" Handing back the priest's ID. "How about that!"

The right thing was never to have cared. And then to be silent.

In Hans Christian Andersen's tale, the Little Mermaid rescues her prince from drowning. Poor fish-tail girl yearns to be human. Here's the hard bargain: if she's to stand pat, maybe dance at her wedding, she must cut out her tongue. In her rewrite, Fiona went silent to abandon Murphy to his belief. If her disappearing act has a cruel end, it's that she lived the bourgeois life she so mistrusted as a child.

"No more uptown, downtown," she pleaded, turning from the window that looked out on the reservoir in Central Park, holding her infant son, blaming her unholy confusion on the city.

Cyril set his daughter up in Connecticut, North Stamford, that's as far as she got from Fifth Avenue, a dream of a white house with shutters, stone chimney, shade trees, a garden with frogs in a swampy pool, all the comforts of home fit for married life. There she cared for her boy and fashioned pots, mugs, plates that hardly ever got sold. At times she drifted away, sang the old songs picked up on 12th Street—*The times they are a-changin'*. Strummed *Love, oh love, oh careless love* to the son she cared for, CARE the poison dart she'd flung at her parents. *Biscuit bakin' woman, don't you lie to me.*

Really cared for the boy, who was bookish, good at math. She sang to the men who came courting, men of no great interest to Fiona. And one day, *never, never enough stories,* one day when her very smart boy was eleven years old, she drove him into the city to stay with Cyril and Mae, good people, while she went off with, call him a lover, the man who took her to the Caribbean where one pleasure boat slammed into another, and down, she went down to her grave, red hair streaming in the luminous green sea.

Once upon a time there lived on upper Fifth Avenue a girl named Fiona. She was pretty, unruly, not pleased with her circumstances, which were not so bad as family stories go. She left home

MAUREEN HOWARD

and was loved. As far as we know she was not deeply unhappy. That is most of the story. We might have ended it there, but the rest needed telling, because

> *I long to talk with some old lover's ghost,*
> *Who died before the god of love was born.*

VI

Shadowbrook

'Tis an inevitable chance—All must die.
—Laurence Sterne, *Tristram Shandy*

How glad you'll be that I waked you.
—James Joyce, *Finnegans Wake*

He is on the defensive, black king cut off in the back rank. White threatens mate, at which point the Murph loses concentration. Flynn taps the board, calls him to attention. His opponent has wandered. It's been this way since they drove up in the van meant to transport soccer, football, debating teams—their kids at Loyola. They are in the vicinity of their old haunt in the Berkshires, seminary days. They share a room in a frilled and quilted B&B, Flynn's chessboard on a lace tablecloth.

Paul takes the game. "Sorry about that."

Joe's the one who should be sorry, drifting away. They have one day left of this jaunt before heading back to orientation spiels and opening classes. But, then, Father Murphy has already been away, alarming those who love him, his sister and Flynn fearing the old ticker giving out, his body awaiting identification at Bellevue. He left all certification of himself in the top drawer of his dresser, under the broken pieces of a teapot he meant to have mended, imagining Rita's cry of disbelief if the shards were discovered, the fate of their mother's teapot compounding the tragedy of his death. Or disappearance. One blistering morning, having recalled his matins with precision as though he said them each day, he takes the bus on Lexington Avenue. Just boards a bus, what's the crime? To be truthful, that's where he's at in the examination of conscience. To be truthful, he was in control, stealing away.

Not away: back, retracing his steps to the old schoolhouse downtown. The scarred oak door no longer bears the artistic sign with a rippling banner proclaiming Anima Mundi, the door open in the insecure city with guards at every turn, even at Loyola. The entrance hall much the same, in that urban poverty, when blessed, has a sameness in cement floors scrubbed, ammonia masking cabbage, in a dead quiet not to intrude on the city's hum of prosperity and well-being. Wandering the large schoolrooms, he recalls how cramped the shacks in Aguileres, their airless hush, chipped plates and battered implements. Very early, though his grandfather's watch is no longer accurate, he sits on the back steps leading to the rooms above where the inmates sleep. Inmates, joke of a word from back then. No one to listen, elegy of a sort, scars of love and war.

A clatter in the kitchen, morning smell of coffee. He remembers the back stairs with the broken fireboxes, the way to sneak behind the scenes, scenes of children tended to by the collection of mothers and fathers. Scenes of feeding the hungry, clothing the naked come in from the Bowery and Tompkins Square, of a collection of souls seated at long refectory tables, some residents, some travelers with their bedding and bundles. The back way to sneak upstairs, but he sits on the steps and they pass him by, the new people, some like social workers with clipboards and cell phones, one young woman in a sari, fair and plump, could be from back then. Her boy with knapsack wears a Catholic-school uni-

MAUREEN HOWARD

form. Oatmeal, the glutinous mess dealt out to welcome the day, a memory whiff from the few mornings he did not make it up to Fordham to teach his classes.

· · ·

"What the hell, Murph!" What the hell was he up to, going off without his meds. He looked a wreck upon his return, dumbstruck in the doorway of Flynn's room. When Flynn finished dressing him down: "Call your sister."

His sister has surfaced out of the murky protection of her marriage. At the end of a preposterous story, Flynn said, "The worst you can say, she set the dog up for the kill. You know it's the sort of thing they go for."

They were the television people with time to fill. Eager for any curiosity, they had blown Rita's cover. Then she was free to call, but Joe, Joey, had taken himself down to the old Mundi in the seersucker suit gone ragged at the cuffs, worn thin in the butt. A foolish game of hide-and-seek, rook to king's closing, hiding out on the back steps leading up to the iron cots of poverty, while his sister choked back her sobs. Sampling the preferential options for the poor, while Rita and Flynn feared for his life.

Flynn dialed the number, handed him the phone.

"This about the dog?" Rita's husband with the raspy voice of a crook, that's unfair, the phlegm of a man jolted from deep sleep.

"Joe Murphy."

"Sweetheart, it's the holy father."

Rita's weepy refrain, "Joey, where have you been?"

He's on the defensive. "Downtown, Rita, good works."

Listening to dog stories, to the confusion of a lost daughter found, not his sister. Oddly enough, they don't speak of their mother.

Where has he been? Another goose chase: fear of impending

death, *a case of angor animi*. How he does talk since he went off to the seminary. After many phone calls Thanksgiving is agreed on. Rita will come to New York. He learns that Rita is stretching and bending, connecting to the temple of her body.

"I get down on the mat, Joe, when my husband," a whisper here, "when *Manny* plays golf."

. . .

Two old priests in the Berkshire Hills with a purpose. Flynn's to accomplish another stretch of the Trail he's been piecing together for years, a dotted line slashing the Appalachians, his secular pilgrimage. Murph has suggested the climb to Assisi, a trek to holy sites in Ireland. Isn't Flynn Beantown Irish? All rejected for the final destination not yet accomplished, a mountain peak in Maine climbed in a state of Protestant ecstasy by Thoreau, who never made it to the top, got lost in the clouds. In Flynn's book, the wilderness holds off the fumes of life, clears the head for loss of self. Joe Murphy, ordering a cappuccino in a tourist café, thinks Paul's quest is the flip side of his sister's healing self-discovery of muscles and joints. Could be the same fix, who knows? Not Murphy, S.J., who fears life slipping away. Well, he did not find the cure at Mundi, waiting for the day to begin with the glob of oatmeal in his bowl, or for the flesh-and-blood apparition of the girl beside him in bed, or in some patient traveler listening to him come clean about back then. How kind they were to take him in, suspecting he was not a flophouse bum, letting him work on their newspaper, which was much the same, *caritas,* pacifist manifestos, blasting the present war taking place in the desert. Time not moving on for the poor: this was the miracle then, that it all worked, even the black and white television in the community room with the old rabbit ears, the evening count of missing and dead. They took him in for ten days without question, as they had the let's-pretend-poor girl—Fiona O'Connor. Joe Murphy—let him write the short, encouraging bits.

"Were you a teacher?"

"I was." Not revealing high school math at Loyola.

"Nice piece." A short take on Ignatius giving up his dagger and sword at Montserrat.

Not telling he'd written no more than pleasing letters home and graduate-student papers so long ago, studies celebrating the poets of contemplation, their lines now scattered in his head. *Love bade me welcome: yet my soul drew back.* He had asked too much of language. She put a finger to his lips. And there at this old Mundi, so out of this world, he was silenced again. No one to listen, busy with their worthy pursuits, in any case no survivor to look back to the first day he came to this schoolhouse in civvies. No authority sent him, all on his own, for some grail beyond belief in sonnets or the course set by Isabel Maher in a shingled house in Rhode Island, her boy would wear a black soutane. Back then, he had taken the Broadway Local downtown for clarity of conviction, found more than he bargained for. Rebellion of a sort, followed by the reward of Aguileres. The knowing eyes of the *campesinos* before the display of his gringo fear as he traded blessings with their women. Salvador was the hard place to go, too far, a world away from the girl's gift of a saffron T-shirt, from the purity of comforting manifestos. About love he was always certain. He'd simply gone missing, as always taking the easy path. *Sure it's your choice?* This time the Lexington line returns Murph, Padre, Prêtre uptown to his post. A blistering Summer day. Teetering on the curb, he waits for the light to change, makes it across Park Avenue to the far shore of Loyola.

• • •

Now Joe Murphy has this day with the shops in Lenox, little connection to their wares—silver jewelry, pottery, scarves of earthy colors, ski gear for the winter season. Glossy covers in the book-shop window promoting food, gardens, politics and the many paths to renewal hold no interest. He enters a store with expensive games and toys, buys a wooden chessboard for Flynn, the meticulous work of a craftsman inlaid with dark maple and pale ash, a purchase not in his plan for the day. He's free till the hour when he must pick up the hiker, top of Mount Greylock. In the van he heads out of town to find Shadowbrook, a rich man's extravagant *cottage*, where, as putty in his professor's hands, he was instructed in theology. When the order bought the mansion to house seminarians and their teachers, they did not change the name. It burnt to the ground in the Sixties, was rebuilt in industrial brick, the era of Jesuit grandiosity over. Loyola's followers dwindling, it was sold to a fraudulent guru. That act cleaned up, Shadowbrook is an upscale center for yoga, many in the community celibate. An amusing history to Murph, not to Flynn, who is after the transcendental experience, attempting this day an easy climb to the pinnacle of Mount Greylock. Flynn wants the panoramic view from the heights, the Civil War Monument lording it over the Housatonic River, not the backward view of personal history.

Women on the lawn of Shadowbrook sway and extend. Their bodies, hefty and slim, follow the supple movements of their leader. The priest waits by the van, looking out over the sloping expanse of green that leads to the tall pines and larches he remembers. Can that be? The same trees, chosen by a famous landscape artist whose name he once knew, arrested in their growth? And the glistening Lake Macinac, which he compared unfavorably to the bay in Rhode Island, every day finding it untroubled and dinky as he looked out from his cell in the mansion with marble floors, with ceilings embossed in white plaster, with a chapel where St. Ignatius, done up in mosaic, held aloft a golden cross. When the women end their session, their class—what to call it?—and trail into the puritanical pleasures of Kripalu, that is the true name of this spa, he discovers the path he once walked in contemplation, sees the spot where he made a pass at Loyola's exercises but never saw Christ conjuring wine at the wedding feast, multiplying loaves and fishes. Light plays through the dark cast by the branches above. He sits on a bench, heart having its protest at a small incline as it had at old Mundi when he climbed the back stairs.

If he were to walk down to the lake, then hike back up to the van, he might bring on his death, choose both time and place. He's been thinking about that, about a poet, one of his, who wrote a treatise claiming suicide not a sin, though noting the hands of a suicide are often cut off, buried separate from the body. Those severed hands may have been scare tactic, only a story—still?

He figures what Flynn will say, "It's against your religion, Joe. Play golf."

"Ride the little cart to redemption?"

The shadows of the trees stretch across the lawn, reaching toward September. An old maple early consumed in flames . . . *Summer ends now, now barbarous in beauty.* Shuffling, unsteady on his way back to the van. Hawthorne named this place while writing his first *Wonder-Book for Girls and Boys*: its play of light and shade enough this day to keep an old man among the living. Before driving on to the next lap of his planned excursion, sitting up high in the van, Joe Murphy closes his eyes against memorializing the view of his spiritual failure. Awkward with the key in the ignition, he feels the shade of his father's good hand, its swift moves with a clutch. The dead arm, swung with grace into position, holds the wheel steady, and they're off down the lane in the black Ford, property of Prudential. A supernatural event witnessed every day as a boy.

. . .

At Melville's house, he waits for the tour with a couple from Brooklyn. This day only the three of them will pass through the house where the great book was written. The wife, worn notebook in hand, asks if he is a Pequod Person.

"It's a Web site," the husband says, clearly proud. "They know it all, the binnacles, halyards."

"It's that you look like a scholar." The wife is girlish, excited as she grazes the gift shop items, whales on coffee mugs, T-shirts; prints of blubber being hauled on deck. "We've got that one." The one with the great splashing tail, little men cast into the consuming sea.

The husband is entertained by his wife's obsession, by her notebook packed with Melvillian knowledge. Joe thinks how very nice, the mild man in love with her love of a book. He tells Joe of the six thousand fans logged on as Pequod Persons, his wife a second mate, like Stubb. "She knows it all, the rigging, the mess, what Herman ate for breakfast." This is their third visit to Arrowhead, Melville's farm. They have been to the Seamen's Bethel, New Bedford, maybe ten times.

"I know it," Joe says. He pays up for the tour, buys a postcard to send to his sister.

And they're off to the Chimney Room of the farmhouse, trailing a chattering docent who's corrected at every dish, spoon, cradle, and daguerreotype by the second mate from Brooklyn. Here's what Joe wishes, to be alone, a boy's wish to be in his bed with a book, Ovid, the *Gallic Wars*, no—*Moby*. No teacher, no guide, just the neat story. He lingers behind in the parlor with the family portraits, the cupboard with fancy cups and saucers Bel might not have loved, never cherishing more than the Irish teapot. Loud and clear, the Pequod Person tells all, the year the writer, then famous, purchased this house, bossy mother-in-law moving in, social scene with well-to-do neighbors. In the Melvilles' bedroom, she identi-fies the child's cot as Malcolm's, the son who would shoot himself to death.

"On East 26th Street, not the Berkshires."

Finally, the upper room, the study with volumes (inauthentic, not the master's according to the second mate) of Milton and Shakespeare, Sterne, Montaigne, Chaucer, the writer coming on bookish, the desk, pewter inkwell, pen, tiny glasses, facsimile man-uscript pages of *Moby-Dick; or, The Whale*. Joe lingers, lets the tour retreat to embroidery and scrimshaw downstairs, stays on for the great hump of Mount Greylock swelling into the bright ocean of sky, Melville's view each day as he chased the thrashing enormity of his subject.

The book failed: Joe remembers from way back, the obligatory class in American Lit., duty for a doctorate never awarded. The writer failed, went mad for a bit, then lived out the time allotted. Joe sits in the forbidden chair where Melville put his bible to-gether, chapter and verse, his eye on the Leviathan fractured into six-over-six colonial panes. The constriction in his chest familiar, almost a friend. What was that fancy word he tossed at his sister, meaning fear of impending death? He is calm, piecing together Mount Greylock with his mother reading a book never finished, wonderfully calm. Why always day trips? Why had they not come to this upper room, the site of creation? Why home in time for supper? Bel lay *Moby* aside, a doorstop in an ugly library cover, though one day in the Spring . . . *never enough stories.* Dissolves to the Buick, sitting up front with his mother, girls in the back, Rita and tag-along Gemma.

Hair escaping the green cap, just a tendril, as though plotted by wardrobe or makeup, a cap military yet rakish, home-front fashion for the duration. Coat slung over her shoulders, epaulettes, brass buttons. Three children seated before her. A show, a game? A beam of light shines upon her through a dusty window. A dark, cold chapel. The girl with the chipmunk cheeks looks down at her magazine. Close-up of a housewife cutting an apple pie. Pages flip to chocolate pudding, 6¢ a serving: enjoy the Niblets, save the can; to a sweet woman embracing a soldier, From This Day Forward, *a complete novel in this issue*. The girl coughs, coughs again in this damp place, as though to forestall what's coming, her mother pressing open the book, reading to herself, then out loud. Too loud.

On one side of the chubby girl, who wears a navy Spring coat with velvet collar, childish hat with turn-up brim, the boy in long pants, older, takes baseball cards out of his pocket, eyes cast down on words he knows by heart. 1941, Ted Williams bats 400 until the last game. Takes the risk, goes six for nine. The boy looks up at the reader, then shuffles the cards till he comes up with the Yankee Clipper, fifty-six slams in a streak, reading stats, not flipping his cards for the picture.

The woman reading whips off the green hat, unclear if it shades her eyes or the page in her book, throws it toward the children, then shrugs off her coat. Now her voice rises, you must listen to this. You must listen. Alone in this performance, not a game. Her words, the words from the book, bounce about the empty chapel where men prayed before sailing off on the ships. Cut back to that scene in the Buick, attention of the children on the road, all three listening to her go on—whalers and fishermen, the sea with its dangers.

"Ask your father. Get him going on Lloyd's of London, marine insurance."

The billboards and towns flashing by. Lowlands by a river.

In the chapel, all three restless in the hard wooden pew, half listening to the writer's reflection on the dead; squirming kids, the boy turning to the girl in a coat too small, her big hands caressing a box camera, then cupping the lens. She smiles at the boy, the sly what-are-we-into grimace of adolescent superiority. The dead, Bel reads on, nose in the book, then chin tilted toward her audience, which might as well be the cranky *apparatus of silent movies. There is something terrible in her stumbling over an urgent sentence, then hitting her pace.*

"Yes, the dead, that they tell no tales, though containing more secrets . . . Why the Life Insurance Companies pay forfeitures upon immortals." *Skipping about, having lost her place on the page in the half-light of the chapel, beginning again,* "Methinks that in looking at things spiritual, we are too much like oysters." *Then, slamming the book closed, giving it up. Out in the sun, leaning against the fender for a photo, waving at the children, hers and the intense girl with the camera, waving, dusting it off, a bad show.*

Stubb, husband and guide block the view already blocked in Joe's reverie, alarmed that he is sitting in the master's chair, though kind to the faltering, the old. Sorry, Joe Murphy is ever so sorry, lost in admiration for the sacred room, though he doesn't think he has the necessary devotion to become a Pequod Person.

Flynn is waiting at Greylock, happy and hungry, piece by piece achieving his earthly goal. If not the world at his blistered feet, at least the Housatonic Valley. After prime ribs and a bottle of Merlot, they repair to the B&B, set up the craftsman's chessboard. We do not have to ask who wins or why they turn from each other to pray or not pray, each man to his quilted bed. Father Murphy sits upright in too much softness, too many pillows, breath coming heavy and slow. A porch light from below is switched off, giving the stars their chance. What had she wanted them to learn, a lesson to each excursion? The lesson that day in New Bedford, sixty years ago? Displaying the frail show of her immortality, she had failed to entertain them, closed the book. Failed, like Melville. The last day trip, Bel's final performance. And on, she went on, Isabel Maher outliving, as we all must, our myth.

. . .

Never enough stories. That semester, while Father Joe dwells on his death, he is given, depending how you look at it, a chore or reward. He is given Annie Pappas, a skin and bones girl with a strong mind. Preparing for SATs, she's far ahead of the pack, an irritant to her fellow students slogging through practice tests.

"I've got the math gene," she says upon their first meeting. "Can't help it."

"I won't ask you to help it, but I doubt I can help you. I only know what's in the books, the problems they explain."

"That's OK," Annie says, taking charge. "I'll just come and we'll talk, get me out of their way. I mean, I could sit at the back of the class and doodle."

"Come along. I've time on my hands." He thinks, a Greek nymph or naiad, she'd be pretty with flesh on those delicate bones, but maybe doesn't want to be pretty. They sit in his empty classroom with problems before them, problems she can solve, show him the theorem, display the proof. When Annie gets into fuzzy nominals, he knows she's overreaching. Finished with her instruction, they talk. How her father wants pre-med or business, even teaching, God help us, not risk her life tripping to Mars, as though that's where her smarts are heading.

"It's not the unfemme thing, math and girls. Nick Pappas was poor, really. Cut high school, bagged groceries. So—how to live?" Speaking of her father's grit and good fortune, Annie mimes nausea, quotes the *Times.* *"The café luxe . . . flawless cuisine.* Not to mention Papa's em-por-ium with globs of fab food." Apparently she will not be nourished by this abundance. On Fridays a car picks her up, drives her out to the Pappas farm in Connecticut, where she has horses, a mare and her filly.

"Your friends?" Father Joe has given up on algorithms and negative numbers.

"Draw a blank."

He thinks that his role must be pastoral, that the head of the department, a stiff young man given to regulations, has thrown Annie his way, unable to deal with her solitary ways, her extraordinary talent, then thinks, naturally, of his failure with Elizabeth Strumm, the model still starved for attention, Pet, this very week celeb, staring him down in the stationery store, cover of *Elle*. Annie wants no one, but comes to their sessions, knowing it's a joke.

Or not a joke. At their third meeting she gets him talking, Father José in Salvador, *a country where I spent some time*, dealing out beans to his pupils, fashioning an abacus of sticks and twigs, how he should have taught Spanish or English, how he once had a gift for math that backfired, so to speak, a twist of fate his job in this classroom, how he has finally mastered *Calculus for Dummies*, this said to get Annie's smile. What she wants, to be left alone with her head for numbers, lead her life. Annie wants early admission at Yale. New Haven, she'll be near her horses.

"My father," he says, "went to Yale for a bit." A fact of Tim Murphy's life he'd forgotten.

"Didn't finish?"

"There was a war."

The next week the old priest brings Annie his grandfather's watch, the watch Joe the Murph famously places on his desk during class, checking to see if it hits the hour same time as the schoolroom digital.

"I can't."

"Oh, you must, to please me." There's just time enough at the end of their hour to tell her the story of Patrick Maher, a man who fashioned every wheel and cog, who figured every half-second to the minute. "An old watch, old system, but you might enjoy it."

Tears mist the girl's eyes, not so tough after all, "Well, thanks."

"Now, then," says Father Murphy to lighten things up, "ever hear of the pancake problem?"

"Oh, that." Laughing, sniffling. "The knife bisecting the pancakes, that's dumb. It works with two, easy."

"Not with three? I never got hold of that one."

"You're not supposed to. A classroom game, unprovable theorem." And she's on to factoring polynomials while the Murph fights sleep.

. . .

That night, he begs off the evening news and chess. Father Joe at his desk correcting papers. When he has finished his work, he registers each grade in his grade book, to be transferred to his computer file next day. No student has flunked, no student has triumphed. He has no fear of impending death, though he seldom returns to the doctor who prescribes his medications, letting chance take its way. Watching his heart on the screen, its blip and wayward flap of aorta, the doctor pronounced: *Years of wear and tear.* To Father Murphy, a poetic diagnosis. He lives with his affliction, as he has learned to live without the higher calling.

He stands at the window to watch rain brighten the sidewalks, torrential rain transforming the city street. A man walking his dog against the wind gusting from Central Park is soaked, puddle jumping in the circle of lamplight, drenched, though he looks to be laughing. *What a set, Bel said, singin' and dancin' in the rain. What a movie!* The magic always got her, though she knew the spectacular effects of the business. Lights, camera, action—nothing to bother us with, to set curious children dreaming, leaving us in shadowland. Some lesson there. On one of his visits home, they'd watched Gene Kelly swing round a lamppost. After Salvador surely, just the two of them sitting through the credits. The gutters on 88th Street are flooded. The storm theatrical, foreboding, but tonight he has no fear of dying. He plans, or prays, to slip away without notice, in the family tradition. Forgetful, he feels for his workman's watch.

. . .

Rita begs to be left alone. Paul Flynn closes the door to Joe's room. She watches the cars make their way round the school buses waiting for the students of Loyola. It has been the longest day, not yet over. The funeral Mass, the lunch, so much talk from Joe's colleagues, all praise. *A saint*, one old fellow said, but Flynn laughed. She was glad of it, of her friend's closeness to her brother, his perspective. Rita wears the blue suit bought for her trial. She did not think Joe would want black. He was so cross about the black veil she wore to Bel's funeral. In a while she will call Manny. He'll be waiting by the phone. *You never met him,* she'd said. *I'll go alone. Nina and Ash will look in. . . .*

Manny not listening. *Babe? Babe?*

Perhaps she will have to pay for her slight, for wanting to be alone with her brother laid out in a black robe. Once Joe called her a cow, then took it back, but she never forgave him. She had gone moody and silent, not up for his kidding, some story he had been reading.

She sits on the bed, springs squealing under her weight. Can Joey have slept each night through this punishing music? His desk. His fat reading chair spilling its guts, books above in the closet. Paul has taken away the clothes. He has made a packet of photos and the remains of Joe's life: a tin skeleton, pieces of teapot, cigar box with Lieutenant Murphy's honorable discharge 1918, a letter from Bel begging forgiveness, a postcard of a rambling old house addressed to Rita Salgado, 63C La Cumbra Terrace, Tarzana. No stamp, no Zip Code, no message.

Rita sits on the bed with these things, all these things in her lap.

Daddy's Tontine, the prize goes to the last man standing. Fumbling, attempting through tears the printed words on the postcard, Rita's voice in the silence, soft as if for a *Chatterbox* story, *I have been building,* as if testing words in a dank seamen's chapel, testing—then strong and clear, reaching angels and clouds on the flaking ceiling of the Bijou—*I have been building some shanties of houses (connected with the old one) and likewise some shanties of chapters & essays. I have been ploughing & sowing & raising & printing & praying.*
> —Herman Melville to Nathaniel Hawthorne, 1851

A bit of a stretch, dear girl. Take it down.

> *The sun, whose rays*
> *Are all ablaze*
> *With every-living glory,*
> *Does not deny*
> *His majesty—*

Comfortable in this register. We do not play to an empty house.